THE
HIDDEN
PROMISE

LIAM O'NEILL

THE HIDDEN PROMISE

iUniverse books may be ordered through booksellers or by contacting:

iUniverse
1663 Liberty Drive
Bloomington, IN 47403
www.iuniverse.com
844-349-9409

ISBN: 978-1-6632-4359-1 (sc)
ISBN: 978-1-6632-4558-8 (hc)
ISBN: 978-1-6632-4364-5 (e)

Print information available on the last page.

iUniverse rev. date: 09/06/2022

I would like to thank my first-proof readers who have listened to and read my story for giving me courage, motivation to continue to write, do better with myself, Thank you to Tijen, Zak, and Missi. You guys have been not only some of my best friends I made, but been my second family to me

Much love, Leo

PROLOGUE

Our First Time Meeting Each Other

The sound of a school bell rang out as groups of elementary school kids exited the building. Most of them met with their parents to head home, while other kids made their way to the playground to wait for their parents to pick them up. As the last of the kids left the school yard, a lone boy walked out slowly looking around to see if everyone left. Once he saw that no one was left in the school yard, he let out a sigh of relief and made his own way to the playground. He knew that there was a risk of him getting caught, but his Dad had told him that they would pick him up at the park today.

As he made his way into the park, he went to the furthest tree that was away from the playground and the rest of the kids in his class. The boy sat down, took off his backpack to lean back against the tree to read his book. He opened his bag and pulled out the book that he had borrowed from the library. "I wonder if they actually did kill the whale or if the whale lives?"

The boy said to himself as he opened the book, to start reading it since he had been waiting all day to continue to read where he left off. While reading his book the boy listened to the sound of the tree branches rustling in the wind, the birds chirping, and the distant laughter of the other kids. On this warm and pleasant spring afternoon at the park. But then his peace and quiet was interrupted by two of his classmates running up to him and calling his name.

"Hey William! Kenny wants to see you under the playground set!" One of the boys yelled as he ran up to William, to tower over him, with his friend.

"Does it have to be right now? I wanted to finish this chapter of 'Moby Dick' before my parents picked me up…" William pleaded as he held his book close to his chest.

"Nope, you tried to avoid us after we were let out of class… So now Kenny is mad and you know better than anyone what happens when he's angry you're not there." The other boy said as the two boys moved closer and closer to William.

"You wouldn't want Kenny to choose one of our other classmates to take your place? Do you?"

"Ok… I'll go see Kenny… Just give me a sec-!" As William was standing up, one of the boys moved forward and snatched the book out of his hands.

"Hey! Give it back! I need to return that back to the library!" William shouted as the bully held William's book over his head, Out of reach for William to grab it.

"You'll get this back after your talk with Kenny! So don't make this difficult now!" The bully said as he tossed the book to his friend while the two of them laughed at William's attempt to retrieve his book. William stopped jumping after his book, and instead just accepted his fate. He walked with Kenny's friends to the play structure, where Kenny would usually hang out until his parents picked him up.

"You'll get your stupid whale book back after Kenny is done with you," The bully said as he pushed William into the under part of the play structure. William made his way through the structure to the center of it, he noticed some of the other kids looked at William then immediately turned away. Most of the kids in his class, and most of the students in the school, knew that Kenny always bullied William everyday. After wandering around in the playground, William finally arrived in the furthest part of the play structure, where Kenny and the rest of his gang hung out. Kenny was leaning against the wall with his father's leather jacket on, to make himself look more like a badass. His pals on the other hand, looked more nervous and kept glancing at Kenny once William arrived.

"Hey there Willy, You trying to run from me without giving me the lunch money that you owe me?" Kenny asked as he wiped the sweat off his forehead, as he was dripping from wearing the leather jacket in such warm weather. William instead of feeling fearful of Kenny was more worried for his health.

"But Kenny, my parents packed me lunch today... plus shouldn't you take that jacket off? Because we wouldn't want you to pass out due to heat exhaustion."

William said while keeping a straight face in front of the whole group. Kenny's sweaty face turned red with anger at what William just said, that he walked up to him and shoved William to the ground.

"Shut it you bookworm! All you ever do is read, draw and write all day! You even got in trouble with the teacher, because she caught you reading in class!" Kenny shouted out with anger, as he knelt down on William and started punching him in the stomach. William attempted to protect himself by raising his arms to block some of Kenny's punches.

"Hey Kenny.. Shouldn't you take it easy? You're hitting Willy pretty hard there... What if one of the parents hears us?" One of Kenny's friends asked nervously as the rest of the group all muttered in agreement. But Kenny looked even more pissed at the suggestion. "NO! Not before we destroy that book he has been reading...He probably cares more about that book's safety than the injuries that he receives everyday!" Kenny said as he gestured for one of his friends to go and get the book from the boys outside the structure. When WIlliam heard them mention his book, he instantly pushed Kenny off him and stood up with is fist balled up. "Well looks like we finally struck a nerve with the silent statue!" Kenny said with glee as he walked closer to William to fight him. William made the first move by shuffling forward to meet Kenny and punched him in the gut.

Kenny doubled over as he groaned in pain after being punched in the stomach. Before William could even make another move, Kenny's friends moved in to grab his arms and legs to stop William from moving. Kenny slowly picked himself back up while clutching his stomach, but had a smile on his face when he saw that William couldn't move. "You shouldn't have tried to fight back, when its a three on one you stupid loner!"

Kenny said as he punched William in the gut as pay back, over and over again to make William scream out in pain. William endured the repeated punches to his stomach and chest trying his best not to cry or shout.

"HEY! What the heck are you boys doing to my son!" A man's voice shouted from behind the group of boys.

All the boys froze in place as they turned to see that William's father had squeezed himself into the small play structure. Kenny's friends let go of William and ran off before they would get yelled at. "Kenny! I was just with your parents just now, so don't you dare run off after what I just saw!" William's father said with such an angry tone that his son had never heard from him before. Kenny stood frozen in place after being called out too.

"Go tell your parents that I want to talk to them before you leave, because what I just witnessed is something I can't forgive," William's father said as he walked past Kenny and approached his injured son.

Kenny just nodded his head without saying a word, and headed out the structure to find his parents. When he was leaving the room William noticed four boys watching from where his father entered from. They disappeared around the corner when William had noticed them, most likely to give him privacy.

"Are you alright? How badly did they hurt you?" William's father asked as he immediately checked his son's face, then his chest and his face went pale when he saw the fresh bruises on top of older ones. "After I finish talking with Kenny's parents, I will head straight home to your Mother... She should be back from her shift at the hospital." William's father said as he rolled his son's t-shirt back down to cover the bruises and slowly gave him a hug. After a minute they broke the hug, to make their way back out of the play structure and slowly walked over to where Kenny and his parents were waiting.

"Just wait for me here okay? I rather you don't hear what I will say to Kenny's parents."

William's Father said as he patted his son's head with a warm smile for him. But the smile soon turned into a frown when he faced Kenny's parents. "Martha, Jerry how have you been? Because I think we need to have a long talk about our sons!" William's Father said calmly and yet still sounding quite angry at the same time. William decided to wait by the tree that he sat at before all this happened, to pick up his school bag and realize that he didn't get his book back. Just then William felt a tap on his shoulder and turned around to see one of the four boys that were watching him, standing in front of William. "Hey are you doing alright? We hoped that we got there in time with your father, before you were too badly beaten..." The boy asked with a concerned look across his face as he looked William up and down to see any bruises.

"I'm alright, I was able to get a punch in before they ganged up on me... But thank you for bringing my dad when you did, because I think that Kenny wouldn't have stopped punching me if my Dad didn't show when he did."

William said as he noticed that the boy's other friends were standing further away, looked quite anxious and nervous about something.

"Don't worry about them, they are just shy when it comes to meeting new people. But when we saw how those boys were treating you and taking you into that playground we thought that something was wrong." The boy explained while reaching into his backpack and pulling out William's book that got taken.

With a surprised expression across his face, William couldn't believe that he got his book back. "Those bullies dropped the book when they saw your father coming, so I just wanted to give this back to you."

The boy said to William who in turn took the book and checked it to make sure there weren't any rips or missing pages. Once he could see that there wasn't any type of damage to the book, William wanted to thank this boy again for his help. But the boy had already left to join his three friends and left the park.

"Hey! Thank you for helping me and getting my book back! But what's your name so I don't forget it, if we ever meet again?" William called out to the boy, who turned around to answer him. "It's Berham, and hopefully we can meet again." Beraham said to William and continued to walk out of the park with his three other friends.

"Will talk more with the principal and teachers about how they can make sure that Kenny doesn't bully William or anyone else again." William's father said as he walked away from Kenny's parents, to pick up William to leave the park.

As they left the park the two of them were silent until William's father spoke up. "You won't have to worry about Kenny anymore, I will have a conversation with your principal about what happened… And Kenny's parents are already going to make sure that they have a long talk with him."

William just nodded his head to indicate he heard his father, but his mind was elsewhere as he thought that those four boys that helped him looked awfully familiar to him. And he hoped that he could meet them again so that they could be friends.

CHAPTER 1

Morning Routines, Morning Surprises

"Hey has anyone woken up William yet? He starts work today and he has to be there by nine-thirty," Berham called out to the household as he ran out of the laundry room, putting a small notebook into his back pocket.

"Not yet but I think that Joseph is finishing his shower so just yell at him to go wake him up." One of Beraham's Roommates said from the living room as he watched a cooking show about carrot cakes. "Thanks for the idea Lee, But why don't you go and wake him yourself?" Berham asked as he threw Lee's folded bed sheets at him to give some more motivation to head upstairs. "Because I don't want to miss how to make this carrot cake... That and I am too lazy to get up right now to do anything." Lee explained to Beraham who had already left to the kitchen, to see his fourth roommate. Who was making breakfast for all five of them to eat together.

"Hey make sure to call in late for work this morning, we have a meeting later alright?" Berham said to Heinkel who was wearing a kiss the cook apron, and gave Beraham a thumbs up as his response. Knowing that he wouldn't get any better response from him, Beraham left the kitchen and decided to head upstairs to the second floor to see if Joseph could wake William after his shower.

1

Beraham knocked on the bathroom door, and heard the sound of giggling and shushing could be heard behind the door. "Oh for the love of god… I wish I could just strangle this man…"

Beraham whispered to himself, while he recomposed himself to stay calm before he spoke up.

"Hey Joseph I was gonna ask you to do me a favour, but since you're occupied at the moment… I'll just do it myself. Also stop bringing overnight guests back home with you when you go out to bars!" Beraham swore under his breath as he left Joseph to climb the stairs to the third floor where Heinkel and William's rooms to and wake up William for breakfast and for him to get ready for work.

Beraham was just about to knock on his roommate's door, when he heard the sound of the floorboards creaking behind him. He turned around to see Lee, Heinkel, and Joseph who was just in a towel looking at Beraham.

"Really? Why is that when i ask you guys to wake up Will, you guys always say you're either too busy or lazy to do it… But when I have to go do it, you all are here to say good morning to him. Beraham said to his friends as all three of them looked hurt at such an accusation. Before Beraham could grill them further, the sounds of a thump and William shushing someone behind the door caught all of their attention.

"Joseph, you didn't take William with you to the bar last night… Did you?" Lee asked as he was curious to know who could be in William's room, as the four of them huddled into a circle to talk. "No, I left here by myself, but I definitely did not return home alone." Joseph said proudly, as he pushed back his hair and raised his hand for a high five. Everyone was silent as they all knew how corny and bad Joseph's jokes were, and how crigny he can be. "So how should we go about this? Wait until the person has left the house before we ask? Or wait and see who it could be?" Lee asked as he listed some ideas to the rest of the group, as to how they will handle this delicate situation. But Heinkel had a different idea, he broke from the huddle and walked up to William's door and kicked it open.

"Hey William, are you awake yet? I'm coming in so make sure you're covered." Heinkel said as he walked into his roommates room without even caring what he might see. Once everyone got over their initial shock of Heinkel's blunt action, they followed after him either to stop him, or to take a peel to see what William was trying to hide. As all four of them barged into William's bedroom, they were surprised to see William was fully dressed for today and was just closing his closet.

"Good Morning everyone? I see that you guys came to wake me up this morning for my first day back at the outdoor pool... William said as he had a confused look across his face when he saw Joseph was just in a towel.

"That is a questionable choice of clothing you're wearing to come wake me up Joseph…"

Joseph looked down at what he was wearing, and just shrugged without a shred of embarrassment. "Hey this should be a great way to wake up too, i mean have you seen these abs?" He asked as he flexed his muscles to everyone in the room, but everyone else was too busy trying to look around the room to see where William could be hiding his secret guest.

"So is breakfast ready yet Heinkel? Because it's gonna be a pretty long day at the pool today, so I'll need a pretty big breakfast to survive till lunch break." William asked as he continued to wait at his closet for his roommates to leave his room. Beraham noticed that William was trying his best to stay next to his closet, but decided not to bring it up.

"Yeah, I made some scrambled eggs with sausages and bacon for everyone, so let's get downstairs and eat it before it goes cold."

Heinkel said as he left the room with Lee to head down to the kitchen. "Well since Will's awake now, I will sadly have to put my actual clothes back on.. See you guys at the breakfast table," Joseph said with a sigh as he left the room leaving Beraham and William alone in the room together.

"You aren't seeing someone right now? Are you? Because last time I promised you to make sure that you wouldn't get heartbroken again so soon after you put yourself together again…"

Beraham asked as he moved back so that he could lean back against the doorway to show he wasn't gonna check the closet.

"No, I'm not Beraham… and even if I was don't you think that Heinkel would've told you that since he always has someone watching me from afar." William said, sounding a little pissed. But walked over to his desk to put his notebook and work uniform into his backpack.

"Heinkel only does that when you're going out at night just because he cares for your safety, especially when you drink a lot with Joseph and Lee… But that's besides the point, just remember that we're always gonna be here for you. And if you are gonna see someone in the future just let us know so we can support you."

Beraham said to William in a sadden and hurt voice, as they both stood in silence after this rather serious exchange.

"Hey if you guys don't hurry it up, then i'll eat all this food and leave nothing for you guys!" Lee shouted from the first floor making both Beraham and William forget about their exchange and headed downstairs to eat breakfast.

After putting away everyone's laundry in their rooms and the basket away, Beraham walked back downstairs. He headed to the kitchen to see Heinkel refilling Lee's plate full of scrambled eggs, William reading the news on his phone while eating his portion. "Jeez where the hell is Joseph? I left his clothes outside his room because I am not going into his room when he has an overnight guest."

Beraham asked as he went over to the cabinet to grab a plate for himself.

"He finished changing, he just is saying goodbye to his latest one night stand."

Heinkel said with just a bit of annoyance in his voice, when he answered Beraham's question while taking off his cooking apron.

"Keep in mind he is the one that brings in the most money in the household, plus pays most of the rent so we can't really complain too much..." William said as he finished his food and brought the plate to the sink for cleaning.

"If it's starting to affect any of you, we can always bring it up at our 'Roommate weekly meeting this evening."

Beraham said as his toast popped from the toaster and he started to butter his slightly burnt toast. As the four of them continued to talk about what their mornings were gonna be like, and finished eating breakfast. The sound of Joseph's screams erupted from the second floor, followed by the sound of a loud thump. Everyone rushed up the stairs to see what happened to Joseph. Beraham was the first person up the stairs, and he saw Joseph laying at the bottom of the third floor stairs. On his back with a small dog standing on his chest while licking his face.

"Okay so it wasn't a woman that William brought home with him, but a small dog as I just found out..."

Joseph explained while letting out a groan as he tried to stop the dog from licking his face. The rest of the group made their way up the stairs and were just as surprised to see the dog. Except for William who looked scared and embarrassed that his secret was out in the open, and licking his friends face. William quickly walked over and picked up the small dog, while Lee and Beraham tried to help Joseph back to his feet.

"Are you alright Joe? Sounded like you took quite the tumble down the steps?" Beraham asked as he patted Joseph's head and stared at it to make sure that there weren't any bleeds or bruises on his head.

"I'm fine, I just fell down a little hard on my ass when the dog came jumping at me, when I went to check to see what William could be hiding from us…"

Joseph explained as he brushed Beraham and Lee's hands away from him as he helped himself back up.

"Alright, there we go, Now that I'm back on my feet I will now go to work since I would rather not be late… But we will let William explain to himself why he brought a dog home, and what we will do about living arrangements for it."

Joseph said as he stretched his back, while everyone around him still had looks of concern across their faces.

"Joseph's right, I also have to meet with my next client for today, to chauffeur him to a lot of meetings today…"

Heinkel piped up as he checked the time on his watch, and then spoke up again. "Let me drive you to work Joseph, since it's on my way to where I have to go."

Joseph looked at Heinkel with a surprised look across his face, since he had never offered Joseph a ride or anything before. Heinkel turned around and headed downstairs with Joseph trailing behind him still shocked by Heinkel's offer to drive him.

"So i can expla-" William started to say but Beraham put his hand up to stop him from explaining himself.

"Like Joseph said we will talk about this once we all have today to think about if we want the dog in the house. And Will you start work in an hour so you better get going before you're late." Beraham said as he walked up to William, and ushered him to hand over the dog. As he was passing the dog over to Beraham, Lee was inching closer towards the dog, his eyes shining with curiosity.

"Before you go Will… What type of breed is the dog and did you give it a name?" Le asked as he scratched behind the dog's ears, and got happy howls from the dog after being petted.

William looked at his dog and turned away with his backpack on as he headed to work, but he turned around at the last moment to tell them.

"She is a Teacup Yorkie… And her name is Bianca,"

After that William headed downstairs, and Beraham and Lee waited till they could hear the front door open and close.

"So are you good with having a dog in the house?"

Lee asked while he continued to scratch behind Bianca's ears as she barked with glee.

Beraham was too busy lost in thought to have heard what Lee had asked him. Lee sighed with annoyance about being ignored, and so he lifted the dog up to lift Beraham's face. Bianca looked at Beraham and happily started to lick his face, making him fall back in surprise at being licked.

"So I just asked… Are you good with having a dog in our house?" Lee asked again as he put Bianca back on the ground.

"That is what I was thinking about before you decided to let the dog lick my face!"

Beraham said angrily as he wiped his face and tried to recompose himself.

"But if you want to hear my opinion Lee, then I think that it's good that William will have something to focus on… Especially since I think he is hiding something from me." Beraham said as he checked his phone, and noticed a text message from Heinkel.

"But anyways I doubt that Joseph and Heinkel really would be against having a dog in the house. Plus Heinkel loves dogs so he will definitely help with walking her."

Beraham said as he checked the message on his phone, then wrote a reply back to Heinkel.

"Did Heinkel actually bring Joseph to work? Because that would be a big surprise, since Heinkel only ever really offers to drive William to work and that's only if he is running late."

Lee asked as he walked over to peer over Beraham's shoulder to see what the text was.

"No… Heinkel was just using that as an excuse to make sure that William wouldn't suspect us of meeting up," Beraham said as he turned his phone off before Lee could see the text conversation.

"Before we meet up with them, we have to make a quick pit stop at the pet store."

Beraham said as he picked up Bianca to help her with going down the stairs.

"It seems we all have a weakness for dogs, just that some of us hide it better than others." Lee said to himself as he followed Beraham.

When Joseph and Heinkel left the house after finding out about the dog, they had headed straight to Heinkel's car that was parked in front of the house. Heinkel got into the driver's seat to start the engine, but when he turned to check if he could back out of the driveway he noticed that Joseph was still outside the car. Annoyed once again by Joseph's shenanigans, he reached across the car and opened the passenger door for him.

"Get in already before I grab you and force you into the car!" Heinkel said as his patience was starting to wear thin. Joseph quickly hopped into the car without a second thought.

Once Joseph put his seat belt on, Heinkel drove out of the driveway and into the neighborhood streets. After driving for a couple of minutes in silence, Joseph turned the radio on and then turned it off before he spoke up.

"Ok I can't take this anymore! Are you going to take me somewhere to punish me, after I brought an overnight guest back home again? Because I can find someone for you!" Joseph quickly asked, as he tried to bribe Heinkel and solve whatever issue he had with him.

Heinkel just continued to drive in silence, as he made Joseph feel more and more nervous and paranoid while he was in the car. Joseph was about to speak up again, but Heinkel made a sharp left into a parking lot of a Tim Hortons drive through.

"Oh no, you're giving me my final meal here??? You could've at least brought me something nice, but a Tim Hortons..." Joseph said as he overly reacted, to seem more dramatic and annoy Heinkel. As they pulled up to the order machine, Heinkel looked towards Joseph and gave him a death stare that silently said. 'If you scream at the machine I will kick your ass.' Joseph put his hands over his mouth to show that he wasn't gonna make a nuisance of himself. Heinkel turned back to his open window to place his order.

"Hi there, can I get two bagels with cream cheese on both of them… And can I also get them toasted as well?"

"Okay sir, and will that be all your ordering today?" A female voice asked over the speaker. Heinkel looked towards Joseph to see if he wanted anything.

"Just do the same order for me but add an espresso to the order, I want to at least have my caffeine fix for today."

Joseph said as he took out his phone to take a call.

"I'd also like to add two more bagels with cream cheese and a small cup of espresso," Heinkel said as he took his phone out of his pocket and placed it into the cupholder.

"Okay sir your order is now in the process of being made, if you could kindly drive to the pick up window and your order will be ready momentarily." the female worker explained to Heinkel, and then went silent. Heinkel continued to follow the drive through and stopped at the window where he could pick up their order.

"Here use my credit card because I don't want to wait five minutes for you to figure out how to use your debit card and remember your pin number." Joseph said as he took out his wallet and took out his credit card to hand to Heinkel. He went back to his phone while Heinkel didn't really care too much of who was paying for it, as long as he could get his two bagels.

After the employee handed over their order and they had paid, Heinkel drove out of the drive thru, and headed down the highway towards the lakeshore.

"Alright so i'll make sure to be there for the next meeting that's happening today, thank you for understanding… Goodbye."

Joseph said as he finished his phone call and placed his phone in the same cup holder as Heinkel's phone.

"So I have two hours before I have to head to work, so we will need to do our secret meeting soon."

Joseph told Heinkel as they quickly approached their destination.

"Alright, give me a second to message Beraham to start heading down someplace close by to William's workplace..."

Heinkel said as he pulled into one of the parking lots by Toronto's Lakeshore, he grabbed his phone to send a text message to Beraham. "You know that those two will probably bring Will's dog with them... What are your thoughts on if we keep the dog?"

Heinkel asked Joseph as he took off his seatbelt, to open the door and exit the car.

Joseph followed suit and exited the car before he answered Heinkel's question.

"Honestly I don't care as long as Will doesn't ask me to walk the dog, or pick up after it then he can bring a dozen of dogs home."

After they paid the parking meter, the two of them headed down the board walkway towards the pool that Wiliam worked at as a lifeguard. "Hopefully we get there before Will does... Or else he will be angry with us and accuse us of stalking him at his workplace."

Joseph said as a group of joggers passed by the two of them, and he followed their run. Until Heinkel smacked the back of his head when he saw where he was looking.

"We don't have to worry since Beraham just messaged me back as you were ogling at those joggers... Pay attention to this meeting or else it won't be your head I hit next."

Heinkel said as he pointed down with his head beneath Joseph's wasit. Joseph immediately put space between him and Heinkel, but didn't see the person passing by him causing the two of them to fall down.

"Oh sorry about that, I didn't see you there... Are you alright?" Joseph apologized to the man he knocked over, while offering him a hand to help him back up.

"Hey man it's alright just be more careful of the people around you, but anyways I can't stay very long now... I have to get to work." The young man said as he brushed the dust off himself, and continued to walk in the same direction as Heinkel and Joseph were heading to.

"That guy you just knocked over is heading in the same direction as where Willim's pool is… Right?" Heinkel asked with concern in his voice, as they watched the young man who looked like a Greek god with his shoulder length brown hair, and Hazel nut eyes.

"You better hope he isn't one of William's co-workers or else he will be able to recognize you and probably tell William if he ever sees you at the pool." Heinkel said as he face palmed at the luck they were having today.

"Probably will since I am quite memorable to everyone I meet. But will deal with any consequences after this encounter if it arises. For now let's go and find Beraham and Lee."

Joseph said as he continued to march forward with Heinkel trailing right behind him, with a scowl and annoyed look across his face as he followed after his friend.

CHAPTER 2

Who do we Like and Trust for You

Heinkel and Joseph finally arrived at Sunnyside Outdoor pool, where William worked as one of the lifeguards. The two roommates walked around the fence that surrounded the pool, to see if the staff were on deck.

"I don't see that guy I ran into... Did they postpone the opening of the pool to a different day?"

Joseph asked as he looked between the fence for any sign of the staff.

"They are probably just in the changeroom building, cleaning it or something like that... William would've messaged me if he didn't have work, or if he messed up his work starting dates."

Heinkel said as he pointed to the building that was by the shallow end of the pool, it was connected to the fences and outdoor pool.

"You guys look mighty suspicious looking into the pool like that," A voice said to Joseph and Heinkel from behind them, while a dog started barking at them. Heinkel turned around to see Lee and Beraham staring at them. While the teapot Yorkie waddled over to Heinkel and sniffed his work shoes. "Well Joseph and I wanted to do some quick reconnaissance of William's co-worker's before you got here,"

Heinkel said as he quickly came up with an excuse, but was too distracted by wanting to pet the small dog. Beraham looked at Joseph who was just looking everywhere else but his friends.

"Let's just head down to the beach shore and find a bench to start our meeting." Beraham said as he whistled for the dog to follow him since he held her leash.

The other three roommates followed after Beraham, since he was always the leader of their friend group. They headed down the beach shore to where there were less pedestrians to overhear them.

"There's a spot underneath that tree with a bench, we could use it for today's meeting!"

Lee said as he ran over to claim the bench before anyone else could take it. The rest of them went over to join Lee at the bench, and sat down to cool off under the shade.

"All right, so let us start our meeting of Protecting William... Today's topics will include, discussing his co-workers and who will need to keep an eye out. And whatever or not will be keeping his dog."

Beraham explained as he lifted the dog up onto his lap to keep her from running off on her own.

"Quick question before we really get into this meeting, what is the dog's name?"

Joseph asked while raising his hand as if he was back in class, waiting for the teacher to call upon him.

"Will named her Bianca though I'm not too sure why..." Beraham said as he braced himself for the numerous questions or theories that his roommates would have.

"It's not really a dog's name... She looks more like Bella to me," Heinkel said as he studied the dog who just barked with joy at being the center of attention.

"Could he have perhaps named her after one of his failed relationships? Perhaps after a woman named Bianca?"

Joseph said as he took out his phone and started to type away on his phone.

"Please tell me you're not actually searching through all of William's past relationships on social media for their names… We promised William that we would not look into his past relationships nor mess with any of them."

Beraham said as he reached over and took Joseph's phone away to stop him from searching for them.

"It ain't one of his ex's… He told me all of their name's once since he trusted me not to tell the rest of you," Lee said as he tried to get the dog to lick his hand from Beraham's lap.

"Okay so let's get back on topic gentlemen… So if we're all good with keeping the dog, say aye."

Beraham said as he waited a moment for everyone to decide. All four roommates looked at each other and all in, raised their hands and said. "Aye!"

"Alright, I will tell William the good news at our next Roommate meeting tonight, but for now let's move on to our second topic, William's co-workers."

Beraham said as everyone pulled out notebooks, pens and Lee pulled out a large folder for his roommates. He took out what looked like files of William's co-workers and started to hand them out to everyone at the table.

"So I was able to get a copy of the staff list from Will's email, and I see a lot of familiar names that William's worked with in the past."

Lee explained as pulled multiple papers out to hand out to everyone to look over.

"I see that some of the names are highlighted in different colors… Would you explain the color system we have for us?" Heinkel asked as he looked at the highlighted names that were colored either blue, green, or red.

"Well they are pretty self-explanatory but to put it simply… Blue is for those that William can easily talk to without any issue or cause any for him. Green means that we shouldn't fully trust them but shouldn't cause any problems for William but we should still keep an eye on them. And then finally Red means that they could make

William remember some painful memories or cause major social issues for him..."

Lee explained to the rest of the group as they all read through the names and different colors associated with.

"From what I can see so far, his managers are all blue so we won't have to worry about any of his bosses giving him a hard time. Plus I do recognize one of the names of his managers that Will worked with before."

Joseph said as he pointed out to one of the four names that were blue.

"Just a small side note, how did you figure out who deserved which names go where? And please tell me you didn't pretend to do a survey for all of his co-workers door to door?"

Beraham asked as he tried to keep Bianca from eating the papers that he was looking at.

"What? No of course not... I just asked Heinkel to spare some of his manpower to do a social media search on all of them..." Lee said quietly as everyone immediately looked at Heinkel who was very interested in the lake.

Heinkel continued to look embarrassed but it immediately turned serious when he spoke.

"If it's for William I don't mind bending some of the rules to keep him safe... If you all remember, it's my job to protect not only him but all of you from all types of danger."

Beraham stood up and handed the small dog over to Lee and walked over to Heinkel's side of the table. Beraham quickly grabbed him by the arm and stood him up. Beraham just stared at Heinkel for a moment, and then drew him into a hug.

"I understand that it's your job to protect us but don't forget that this place isn't ours to mess up." Beraham said as he broke off the hug, went back to Lee to take back Bianca and sat back down so that they could continue their meeting. Heinkiel stood there confused by the hug, but decided to just go with it, and sat down as well so that he wouldn't hold up the meeting.

"Anyways let's go through the red names before we move on to our last topic that I wanted to discuss with you all."

Beraham said, receiving a nod of agreement from everyone else around him.

"First one that I marked as a red flag is a woman named Annie Wallace. She is quite a social butterfly that gets along with everyone she meets. But she would definitely make William feel awkward or unsure of what topics to talk about with her... That or she might cause William to blurt out embarrassing topics without meaning too. Good news is that she is in a very stable relationship, so we don't have to worry about her taking advantage of Will's kindness and minimal experience with girls." Lee said as he finished explaining the first red name, to then move on to the second one.

"Next we have Matthew Daividson... He is a rather quiet gentleman that wouldn't necessarily make William uncomfortable to talk to, but more of William wanting to over share with him and tell him things you don't necessarily tell someone you only know for a short while.. He also is most likely someone that would notice us if we were watching William while he works and tell him..."

"Our final red name is Orion Neptune. Nice guy and really energetic guy from what his friends have said about him. From looking at this man's profile, he seems to be quite the hugger and is always the center of attention without even trying to. He is essentially the exact opposite of William, who is more reserved and away from the spotlight."

Lee said as he showed a photo of Orion, and Joseph's expression went grim and pale.

"What's the matter Joseph? Does this guy who looks like a Greek demigod look more handsome than you? Are you jealous?"

Beraham said with a chuckle, but then stopped laughing when he saw that Heinkel had the same look across his face.

"So me and Heinkel might have already bumped into this guy quite literally on our way over here... So he might be able to recognize me and Heinkel when we're at the pool..." Joseph explained as he got up to hide behind Heinkel to try and avoid Beraham's wrath. Beraham just sat there silently, staring daggers at the both of them as he opened and closed his mouth. Lose for words by what he was just told.

"Beraham... Buddy, why don't we keep that rage that I know you're about to release on us, but why don't you focus on staying calm and continue this meeting right?"

Joseph said nervously as Beraham slowly stood up while still staring daggers at Joseph as if he wanted to kill him. But just as Beraham was about to start yelling and run over to Joseph and Heinkel, a woman's voice interrupted them.

"Hi there! I was just wondering what type of breed is your dog?"

Beraham turned around and the first thing he noticed about her was the woman's eyes. Her hazel coloured eyes seem to just look right into Beraham's soul, that he started fumbling over his words.

"Oh it's a ummm... Teacup Yorkie though I'm not too sure how old she is... haha..." Beraham answered while he laughed nervously, as Bianca jumped from the bench and waddled over to sniff the women's shoe's.

"Well from the size of this little one, I would guess that she is at least a year or two old... Who is a good girl?"

The young woman said as she rubbed the little dog behind the ears.

"Sorry if this is too personal or random, but are you guys like quadruplets? Because you guys all look quite similar to each other."

The young woman asked as she looked between the four of them.

Beraham started to feel an emotion he hadn't felt in a while, panic. He raked his mind as he tried to figure out how to properly explain this to her. Just as Beraham was about to say something, Joseph piped up and said,

"Oh we are not related to each other, we all come from different countries, but people have had that same thought."

The young woman looked between the four of them with a suspicious look across her face, but shrugged her shoulders and looked at the time on her watch. Her eyes went wide when she realized the time.

"Shoot i'm late for work... My brother is gonna tear me a new one, if I miss my shift again, especially on the first day..."

The young woman said as she gave Bianca one last pat on the head and then stood up to run to work.

But before she ran off, she turned around and looked back at all four of them to say something.

"Hope you guys have a nice day, and see you guys next time!"

After she left Beraham sat back down confused by what just happened, while the other three stared at him with curious looks across their faces.

"Well this is a first... Someone has left the supposed 'emotionless one' not only lost for words but also seems to have quelled his anger and wrath he was about to rain down on us." Joseph said with a grin on his face as he sat back down across from Beraham. Lee and Heinkel exchanged nervous glances with each other by Joseph's big statement. Without saying a word Beraham kicked Joseph in the shins underneath the benches table. Joseph yelled out in pain as he held onto his shins.

"Thank you for reminding me Joseph... But before we get back on track, who was that? She looked like she was heading towards the pool."

Beraham asked as he checked his blundstones to see if they had any dust or dirt after kicking Joseph.

"Well from what I could gather from Heinkel's cyber team, is that she is Orion's twin sister, Margaret Neptune. She doesn't really get into any trouble besides being late to work... I highlighted her as just a green name since she wouldn't cause any issues for William and might be able to be good friends with."

Lee explained as he shuffled through the many papers till he found the list of green names and handed it over for Beraham to see. All the while Joseph was checking his leg to see if his leg was bleeding, since Beraham was known for hitting quite hard.

"Okay good to know, so before we let Heinkel and Joseph head off to their jobs, there is one more topic we should quickly discuss." Beraham saud as he took what looked like a journal, that was titled 'William's Journal.'

"I found this hidden behind the dryer while I was doing the morning laundry. I read through some of the beginning… William talks about how his guardian angels were tasked with helping him have a better life, and to better understand his emotions."

"I mean with the way he is describing us, he isn't that far off since we were essentially meant to do exact…"

Lee started to say while staring at the dog but was interrupted by Heinkel shushing him.

"We shouldn't be talking about our past like this somewhere so public, where anyone could overhear our conversation." Heinkel said as he scanned around the group to see who might have been listening.

"It doesn't really matter if anyone heard us, because who would really believe that we were—"

Lee began to say but was immediately stopped by Beraham, who smacked him in the back of his head to silence him from speaking anymore.

"Like Heinkel just said we shouldn't have those types of conversations in public alright?"

Beraham said as he ruffled Lee's hair, while everyone else just silently gathered all the papers that Lee brought for them.

"So this notebook is saying that William might be starting to remember us from when we were younger? Or at least has some suspicions of us being so concerned about his well-being?" Heinkel asked as he motioned for Lee to pass him the bag and folder that would store all the papers.

"Perhaps… He only just started writing in it recently, and most of it is just complaints about how we are disturbing his mornings, and that Joseph keeps on trying to hook him up with random girls he has met…"

Beraham said as he put the notebook back into his bag before anyone tried to read the contents of it.

"If there isn't anything else we need to discuss, then me and Heinkel need to leave for work."

Joseph said as he checked the time on his non-existent watch since Beraham still had it. Beraham took that cue to hand back Joseph's phone while Heinkel stood up, and nodded his head in agreement, but waited for Beraham to adjourn the meeting just in case he needed anything else from him.

"No worries we are done with today's meeting so you guys can go, Lee and I will observe Will's first day of work and then head home after that." Beraham said as he stood up from the bench to go and pick up Bianca so she wouldn't wander off.

"Ok, but make sure to keep out, not only Will's sight but also Margaret since she has seen all of our faces…" Heinkel said and then walked off in the direction of where he parked his car.

"Well then let us head over to the pool, will watch from the outside of the fence so that he doesn't see us too easily."

After the four roommates finished their meeting, Heinkel and Joseph split up from the other two so that they could head to their actual jobs. Meanwhile Beraham and Lee found a spot outside of the fence of the pool. It gave them a good view of the pool and kept them out of sight of the lifeguards, and their tall guard chairs.

"You know that if you just used 'that' we could easily stay incognito without needing to make sure we aren't found. Instead of just hiding behind a tree hoping no one will notice us."

Lee said as he kept trying to make sure that Bianca wouldn't run off towards the other dogs.

Beraham looked back at Lee with a pissed off expression across his face, after hearing what Lee suggested.

"You already know that it's impossible for me to use 'that' unless it's for an actual emergency."

Beraham said as he itched the back of his neck as he turned his attention back to the pool deck to see where William was.

"Oh come on Gan Chori! You literally have what it takes to…!" Lee was about to say but was interrupted by Berahman grabbing him by the throat, to shove him against the tree.

"Enough Lee! Keep pushing my buttons and I will send you back to where you came from!"

Beraham yelled quietly so that only him and Lee could hear it. The little dog quivered in fear at what was happening. Lee raised his hands up, and said to Beraham.

"Alright I understand now, Beraham… You don't usually get this easily angered by my jokes or remarks… Did that woman throw you off your game?"

Beraham loosened his grip around Lee's throat, and turned away as he let him breathe again.

"It's not that… I feel as though she is a lot more dangerous to me than I've ever felt before with anyone. She has this aura about her that screams for me to tell her the truth."

Beraham said as he tried to explain how he felt from encountering Maragret.

"Well if you let me I can do a deeper dive into her, all I would need is Heinkel's help with his cyber team to help me once more… With your permission of course."

Lee suggested as he stood back there massaging his neck where Beraham had held him. Beraham stared at Lee for a couple moments before he gave an answer.

"No… Let's not do that just yet, let us see how William continues to interact and how he is doing with his co-workers before we do that for one single person."

With a sigh of disappointment Lee brushed the dust off his pants to join Beraham in watching over the empty pool.

"There they are, took them long enough to get onto the pool deck… I honestly thought they might not come out." Lee said with excitement as the lifeguards came out of the building together, and were talking amongst themselves.

"Now Lee, you said that you can read lips correctly? I want you to figure out what William is talking about with his co-workers."

Beraham said as he noticed that William was walking and talking with Matthew Davidson, Orion Neptune, and one other person.

"Holy hell there are so many many female staff at this pool… But anyways from what I can tell, the women are just talking about how their summers are gonna go," Lee said as he went silent as he changed focus on William's conversation with his group.

"They seem to be talking about when they will be doing there staff socials and where they could be doing it at,"

Beraham peered at the group who was surrounding William, and felt concern about William attending these social events.

"Ok will need to make sure to find out when those staff socials are happening, but see if William's group is talking about anything else."

Beraham asked as the lifeguards started to split up to walk on either side of the pool deck to get into their positions for work.

"Umm… Shit they are saying, ugh they turned away before I could see what they were saying. All I got was just talking about their guard rotations, and meeting up after work to hangout."

Lee said as he rubbed his eyes, after straining his eyes for at least two minutes.

"So if what you're saying is that all they really are talking about is some very generic conversations that friends would have? Hmmmm, let's just leave for now since it's only the first day and William doesn't usually have any trouble on the first days."

Beraham said as he whistled for the dog to come back to him so that they could leave.

"Makes sense, and if nothing else we can always ask William if anything happened at work today as well."

Lee said as he checked his phone for the time. "It's already eleven thirty so they will probably be busy with many patrons today."

.

When Beraham and Lee walked away from the pool, Beraham looked at his phone to see that someone had sent him a text message. He opened the message on his phone. Beraham could feel his face go pale after reading who the text was from.

"Aghh, hey Lee can you do me a favor and look after the dog once we get back home? I can drop you off at the house but I have to leave right away."

Beraham asked as he picked up Bianca so that they could pick up the pace back to his motorcycle that he rode here on with Lee. But before he could make any further progress, Lee grabbed onto his shoulder to stop him.

"From how you're reacting, I'm guessing that you were just invited to have Brunch with William's parents? If so, let me take Bianca and I'll just walk back home with her so that you are not late."

Lee said as he took the leash and dog from Beraham, while having a gleeful expression across his face at Beraham's situation.

Beraham wanted to try and delay going there, but knew that William's parents were not one to wait on.

"I really hate leaving you to walk home, but make sure that you don't forget to feed the dog when you get home... I ordered some dog food to be delivered to the house for now. And if you don't feed Bianca I will make you get the most boring office desk job there is!"

Beraham shouted as he ran off to get quickly to his motorcycle.

"OooOo... I'm shivering in my shoe's at such a threat, Beraham!"

Lee shouted as he watched his friend run off.

"Well little doggo, looks like it's you and me… You've done enough walking for now so let's just head straight home and be complete couch potatoes. And best of all we can watch pet shows together to better train you!"

Lee said as he cheered with glee as he walked on the way back home with Bianca in his arms.

"The lazy sloth shall teach his way of laziness at a small cost of boops on the nose and snuggles from you!"

Lee shouted as the little dog tried to lick his face, while barking happily at all the excitement.

"Man, I haven't felt this excited or alive since I met with William again! When he first became my student, he taught me how to relax and be lazy." Lee said to the Teacup Yorkie as he ordered an uber for himself to be picked up. Since Lee didn't feel like taking public transit or walking all the way back home.

"Though if only William would've just invested in stocks and businesses, like I did… Then he could live his life as care-free and as lazy as could be. But sadly William is a hard worker, and plus him trying to stay as lazy as I am wouldn't make William who he is…"

Lee said to himself as he started to reminisce about when Beraham had first asked for his help.

"Beraham loves making contracts with anyone, but he wanted me specifically to do this as a favor… And it all happened three years ago, little pupper."

CHAPTER 3

Lee's Life Lessons As A Lazy Lad

It was three years ago when Beraham went to Dublin, Ireland to find Lee, to ask for his assistance. Beraham walked down the small stone village roads, until he saw a pub called "The Lazy Sloth.' He headed into the pub where folk songs could be heard throughout the busy pub. Beraham scanned through the crowded and loud pub of drunken irishmen and women, trying to find where Lee could be sitting.

After looking around the room with no sign of Lee, Beraham decided to try his luck with the barkeeper.

He slipped his way between many drunk patrons, who all were just singing along with the band, in rather off tuned voices. Beraham finally made it to where the bar was located in the back of the pub, and raised his hand to flag the barkeeper's attention.

A rather large and burly haired man in a dirty apron approached Beraham, to put a drink in front of him.

"Sorry not really that much into drinking alcohol, but thank you for the kind gesture sir."

Beraham said as he pushed the cup away from him, but the barkeeper stopped him and pushed it back.

"The owner asked that I deliver this drink, on the house to you personally… And remember to wipe your mouth with the napkin Gan Chori."

The Barkeeper whispered as he had a mixture of angry and serious expression across his face. Beraham looked at the drink with suspicion as he lifted the cup, to give it a quick sniff.

"It's just ginger ale sir... The owner told me that you have a rather small choice of drinks, so as to not make you worried."

He continued to say while cleaning some of the dirty cups that a waitress dropped off for him.

Beraham looked at the beverage one more time, he hoped that this man was telling the truth. He drank it all in one gulp so as to not waste anymore time.

"Aye! Look at that, the Gan Chori can down a glass of ginger ale, but how would he fare with alcohol i wonder?"

The Barkeeper said out loud as the rest of the bar either booed or roared with laughter. Beraham ignored the snarky comments, and looked at the napkin for instructions that Lee left him.

'Head upstairs and head to the room at the back of the hallway, then knock four times on the door if you want to enter.'

Beraham got up from his seat as soon as he finished reading the note, while tossing a couple pence for the drink. He headed upstairs to where the room was located.

As Beraham headed towards the door, he noticed two bodyguards that stood in front of where he had to go. Beraham let out a sigh of annoyance as he hoped that he wouldn't run into any complications with this visit. He already knew that he was spending way too much time being here already.

"Pardon me Lads, but would ya mind if I can shimmy my way through the two of ye to speak to da Owner?"

Beraham asked as he put on a fake Irish accent in front of the two bodyguards. At first the bodyguards laugh at him, as if they were just asked if the sky was blue.

"Aye let it all out of yer systems there lads."

Beraham said as he shifted his sleeves around as he slowly moved his hands around the knives he hid there. Just as he was about to give them hell, the door opened and a young woman appeared between the two men with a clipboard.

"Mr. O'Henry will see you now, Gan Chori... If you can just follow me inside I will wait outside for the remainder of your meeting with him."

The Woman said as she snapped her fingers so that the two bodyguards would make room for Beraham to enter. He quickly gave the two bodyguards a quick middle finger and then entered the office.

When Beraham entered the room he was expecting the office to look like an Irish Mob boss attire. With guns hanging on the wall, animal heads mounted as well either on the floor or walls. And a giant desk with Lee sitting in a big fancy chair, awaiting for Beraham's entrance.

But instead it was just a small office desk with an old computer. Instead of animal heads and guns hanging off the wall, there were either sticky notes with different numbers and names on them. That or cat posters with cheesy jokes on them.

Lee sat behind the computer tapping away at his keyboard, as he ate a dish of fish and chips.

"Ahhh Gan Chori you're finally here! Or do you go by a different name this time?" Lee asked as he leaned forward to offer Beraham his hand to greet him.

"Agghh... Right, that was my name when I was here, but now it's Beraham from now on. Anyways get up your lazy bones and explain to me why you didn't inform your bodyguards that I was coming?"

Beraham asked as he sat down on one of Lee's chairs with his arms crossed.

"Well I forgot to tell them to go on a smoke break when you would've arrived. But I was too busy looking over the stock market... These prices are outrageous to buy in!!!"

Lee said with anger as he slammed his fist on the desk in frustration.

"I'm guessing that it's been hard for you to make a decent living here, especially since you despise manual labor?"

Beraham asked as he had a smirk growing across his face by what he could tell from Lee's outburst.

"That's why I bought this Pub! So that I would have a steady flow of money for my investments... But I barely make anything to make a serious pay out."

Lee said as he angrily ate another couple of fries while groaning with annoyance of seeing his stocks drop again.

"Hmmm... So you're not living out that dream of yours? To be able to have a lazyful lifestyle with the power of investing and stock markets?"

Beraham asked as he unbuttoned his jacket, to pull out a folder from his jacket. He tossed it onto the desk in front of Lee.

Lee lifted his head up and rolled to the side of the desk, when he heard the folder hit the desk. He looked at the folder with distrust as he stared back up towards Beraham.

"What is that supposed to be? Is this supposed to be my pot of gold at the end of your bloody and painful rainbow?"

Lee asked sarcastically as he pushed the folder away from him and back towards Beraham.

"Lee my old friend, this isn't anything bad, nor does it involve anything illegal... It's a contract that enlist the help of you and a couple other individuals."

Beraham said as he picked up the folder and opened it to spill out the contents of paper.

"Others? What type of job requires you to make a contract and to ask for my help? I;m just a lazy Irish arse, who's only goal in life is to live a lazy life and stress free."

Lee asked as he picked up the papers just so that he could skim through the papers to satisfy his curiosity.

"There is someone that needs my help and I can't do this by myself anymore, so I already enlisted two others with almost the same contract that I'm offering to you. We can negotiate and change the contract to benefit you better than I put it there, but will you do this for me?"

Beraham asked as he showed two papers that were already signed by names that Lee recognized almost immediately when he read them. The names that were on there belonged to people that Lee hasn't seen in such a long time.

"Well now, you really do live up to your name's sake haven't you? You got both of them together, without them wanting to kill each other... Especially with one of them having a vendetta against the other."

Lee said as he laughed his head off in disbelief at what he saw on their papers what was required of them to work together.

Beraham just sat there silently as he slid a contract that said on the front, 'Lee's Personal Contract' and placed a pen on top of the papers.

"Now I just put down the basics of what you're expected to do for this job, I also put down the conditions to follow, but you also will be rewarded greatly if you complete the contract, and it can be negotiated."

Beraham said as he readjusted his jacket sleeves while making sure a certain sharp object up his sleeve doesn't come loose, and be seen by Lee.

"Well as long as I can change some of these conditions to suit my personal needs... Although I would like to sell my pub, I have a good amount of money to start with for your plan."

Lee said as he slowly grabbed the pen, but stopped himself before he signed it. He wrote out his demands and changes he would make to the conditions to his contract accordingly.

Once Lee finished writing out his conditions on the papers, Beraham grabbed the papers to read over. After he finished reading over Lee's changes, Beraham made an annoyed clicking sound with his tongue at the changes he saw.

"The first three shouldn't be too hard for me to handle... Since I have a good realtor that owes me a favor."

Beraham mumbled to himself but tapped on his final condition on the paper that he wrote out.

"Whatever do you mean? I feel like that one is pretty easy for someone of your skill set, and with the influence of so many powerful people… Of different types of lifestyles."

Lee said innocently, even though both men knew that it was a small test to see how far Beraham would go to get Lee's help. Lee could've sworn that he could feel the room temperature become a lot colder. When Beaham gave him a stare that screamed for Lee to run and hide away from him.

"Bi curamach sloth no elie beidh aifeala ort, do you understand ya Irish arse?"

Beraham asked as he stood up and slid the contract back to Lee, which felt like his final chance to sign the contract before things got ugly.

"Alright already, I understand what I have to do. There it's done so just give me a couple of days to sort out my finances, and properties. I'll meet you back here once all that is sorted out."

Lee said as he quickly signed the contract and put it back into the folder that it came from.

"That won't be necessary, I had good intentions that you would sign it. So I went ahead and got you a buyer already that is willing to pay for the price you would ask for."

Beraham replied as he collected the rest of the papers and put it back into his jacket. He then pulled out a different folder labeled 'The Lazy Sloth's Pub, ownership and deed.'

"Before I traveled to Ireland to meet you about my proposal. I knew that when you accepted my contract, that you would want to sell your businesses before you left… So I reached out to one of the best realtors I know, to find you a buyer that would buy it. Because I want to leave by tonight."

Beraham explained as he pulled out a photograph of the potential buyer, for Lee to see. And he recognized her immediately from the photo as his Assistant.

"Wow, my very own assistant, eh? She was always an ambitious lass… Very well, as long as she can pay for it I don't have any issues."

Lee said as he started to sign his signature on the papers without another fuss. After everything was all set and done, the two men stood there in silence not knowing what else today to each other.

"So since our business is all taken care of… What am I supposed to do now? Go home and start packing my stuff up?"

Lee asked as Beraham turned around to head towards the door. Beraham looked back at Lee when his hand was on the doorknob.

"Pack enough clothes for a week's worth and the basic essentials as well… Then meet me at this private air strip, where there is a private jet waiting on us."

Beraham said as he placed a piece of paper on a filing cabinet, and then walked out the room just as Lee's assistant opened the door for him.

But before he left, Beraham said one final comment to his friend.

"Also Lee… Did you really have to make your last name O'Henry? You ain't a bloody chocolate bar."

"So here's the deed to the bar, never thought that you would be the one to stay for this tiny bar."

Lee said with a smirk across his face as the assistant scanned the papers to make sure all the pages were in order.

"Well, I have so many ideas for this place, but you were too busy with making it big with your stock market or being lazy… So I bought it with the help of that friend of yours."

The assistant said as they both noticed that it had gotten very quiet outside to the office.

"Weird, it's peak drinking hours right now, but it's gotten so quiet down there…"

Lee said as he stood up from his chair to go and check if everything was okay downstairs. As he made his way downstairs he noticed that everyone was crowded around the entrance, whispering amongst each other.

"What's going on here? Did you all start another bar fight?"

Lee shouted as all the patrons turned around and made a pathway to show his two bodyguards groaning in pain on the ground. The two of them were beaten to a pulp and had several cuts across their whole bodies.

"B-boss... That friend of yours... He wanted to fight not only us but also the barkeeper... I think Connor might be unconscious behind the bar... But never had I seen someone move so quickly and without hesitation with his punches."

One of the bodyguards said as he spat out some blood, while the other one was having trouble catching his breath.

With a sign of disbelief, Lee told the bodyguards to go visit the clinic with his co-worker to get checked-out. After speaking with the barkeeper who only really had a black eye from Beraham, Lee told everyone to leave the bar after the last call. Once they all left his bar, Lee said his goodbyes with his assistant and made himself one final drink from his bar. After he finished his drink he left the bar and locked up the doors one final time.

"Goodbye my investment, you may not have been the most successful business venture... But definitely my most peaceful and fun venture I have done.

"And that my small, cute friend is how I started to help Beraham with his contract."

Lee said as he laid on the sofa with the little dog sleeping on his chest. In a high-pitched voice, Lee pretended to be the dog's voice.

"But Mr. Lee sir, how does that have anything to do with meeting with William?"

"Well I'm glad you asked little Bianca! You see that meeting is what set me on the pathway to helping William!"

Lee answered with high energy even though he was only talking with a dog, all by himself at home.

"The reason that Beraham required my services is because he needed someone that could teach William how to find his inner peace and be lazy. Teach him different techniques or strategies to calm down his panic attacks and to de-stress."

Lee lifted the little dog from the sofa into his arms, then carried her over to the bookshelf to grab a book from there. The cover showed a sloth laying down on a couch, and the title was called 'Live a great life by being lazy.'

"Wrote this book myself, and it's about how you can make a fortune with the power of the stock market, investments into businesses, and to live a stress-free life."

Lee said proudly as he showed off his book to Bianca, who just stared at Lee then licked his hand.

"Once I finished the first draft, William offered to edit it for me, so it gave him some practice to edit a story since he wants to be an author himself. But there is also another reason why Beraham needed me specifically, but I can't talk about it or else it would breach my contract if I talked about it…"

Lee said as he looked the dog in the eyes to show how serious he was trying to be. But Bianca instead licked his face with love.

"Sweet hell… I really need to go out and make some actual friends, I'm literally talking to a bloody dog."

Lee muttered to himself as he put the dog back down to let it run around the living room. While Lee contemplated his life choices and sanity, his phone buzzed to tell him he had a phone call. It showed the caller id was Beraham trying to call him. Lee answered the phone and was about to say hello to his friend, but Beraham cut him off before Lee could say anything.

"Hey I need you to come and bail me out of this brunch with William's parents… They are overwhelming me with questions and I'm this close to escaping from their bathroom on the second floor."

Lee considered hanging up on Beraham after being smacked in the head and getting shoved against a tree, but he decided to take the high road and help his friend.

"Very well, give me fifteen minutes to get there and I'll get you out of there, after I feed Bianca her lunch."

Lee said as he read the recommended amount of food the little dog was allowed to eat.

"Thank you Lee, I'll see you in fifteen minutes to bail me out of here."

Beraham said as he hung up on Lee without saying goodbye.

"Well ain't that just being rude hanging up like that… Don't worry little doggo I made sure to leave you some food for you to eat while I go out."

Lee said as he put the food bowl and water bowl on the floor so that Bianca could eat and drink while he left the house. Lee quickly grabbed his running shoes instead of his flip-flops just so he wouldn't take too long. But Lee could feel that something had gone wrong, he could feel it in his bones, he needed to get there quickly.

Two Hours Before…

After Beraham had arrived in front of Wiliiam's childhood home, He parked his motorcycle in their driveway and walked up the steps towards the front door. He knocked on the door three times and waited for it to be answered.

The door flew open and William's father stood inside with a big smile across his face, that Beraham had arrived for Brunch.

"Beraham! It's been too long since you last visited us, you should get William and the rest of the gang to come over for dinner."

Joshua said as he held onto Beraham for a rather long time, to the point that Beraham had to pat William's father on the back. To indicate that he should wrap this hug up.

"Sorry about that, I forgot that you aren't really much for hugs… But anyways please come inside. Eve has the day off so she will be happy to see you again."

Joshua said with excitement as he ushered Beraham into the house, towards the backyard towards the deck to sit at. As the two men exited outside the house, to find Joshua's wife Eve. Who was already seated with a cup of tea and reading Lee's book. 'Live a great life by being lazy.'

"Ahhh if it isn't Beraham, you finally arrived for our brunch… Though I don't understand how my son could edit such a book, for so little money that Lee gave him for doing it."

Eve said in a disgusted tone as she placed the book on the deck, before she grabbed a plate to start eating the food that was put out beforehand.

"Sweetheart… Let's not insult our son's roommates like that please…:

Joshua pleaded as he placed his hand on his wife's shoulder as he sat down beside her.

"Of course you are right, They have helped him though some tough times over the years. Especially Beraham who helped him longer than the rest of them for years."

Eve said as her expression softened by the touch of her husband. Beraham took the opportunity to take a seat across from William's parents.

"Well besides that little comment… How has everything been for the group of you and your roommates? You've been keeping yourselves busy?"

Joshua asked as the three of them started to dig into the sausages and eggs that were prepared to be eaten.

"Work has been rather slow these days, not too many people need a private eye for finding out if their spouse is cheating on them. But I still get some clientele at least once a week."

Beraham answered as he grabbed a piece of toast for himself and started to butter it up with cream cheese.

"Of course, though it does sound like you have a lot more free time now… What about Heinkel and Joseph? How are their jobs going?"

Joshua asked, trying to keep the conversation going since Beraham wasn't really talking that much about his job. And giving short answers to Joshua and Eve.

"Well Heinkel is still doing security escorts while his company continues to grow, he even has started a cyber division as part of his company's services that they can offer."

Beraham started to explain and then moved on to talk about Joseph's job life so far.

"Joseph is still in that construction firm... He was going to a meeting today to talk to investors about backing him for a new project, though he still is quite a man of the night when he is not working."

Eve studied Beraham as he was explaining how his roommates' lives were going at the moment. She was watching him like a news anchor, presenting the news for today.

"So from what I'm hearing from you is that Joseph's sex life is much beter then all your's combined together? And that includes our son as well?"

Eve asked casually, causing both Beraham and Joshua to choke on their water or spit it out with a look of surprise.

"Eve! We agreed to only ask about their relationships... Not about their sex life!"

Joshua said while Beraham was in the middle of a coughing fit, after swallowing the water the wrong way. Once he finished clearing his throat he addressed what Eve had asked him.

"Joseph likes to make sure that he and his partner have a good time together, but most of the time he sleeps with them so that he can show them that they could do better than him. And the rest of us... We have had our hearts broken so many times that we were looking for someone that we can have a future with."

Eve and Joshua looked embarrassed and guilty that they brought up a rather sore topic for Beraham to answer for them.

"Beraham, we're sorry to hear that has happened not only to you but to everyone else… But does that mean our son has the same mindset as you guys?"

Joshua asked as he slowly moved his hand to hold onto his wife's hand. Beraham took a moment to think about how he wanted to answer their question.

"William isn't seeing anyone at the moment, but he is still keeping an open mind of trying to find someone to date… Unlike the rest of us."

Beraham said as he made sure that he didn't mention the dog that William had gotten. Or at least until William decided to inform his parents about it.

"Well that's good to hear… William never really talks about his love life, nor asks for advice from us." Eve said as she continued to hold onto her husband's hand, while trying her best not to look guilty.

"Well he is quite a reserved and quiet person when it comes to his emotions. But he has started to rely on other people to help him."

Beraham said as he finished eating his toast, and could feel his stomach churn. He stood up from the table and raised his hand to stop William's parents from getting up as well.

"I just have to use the bathroom, I'll be right back in just a moment." Beraham said as he excused himself from the table, headed back into the house and into their washroom.

As he entered the bathroom, Beraham took out his phone to immediately call Lee to get him out of this awkward situation. On the fourth ring, Lee picked up the call.

"Hey, I need you to come pick me up from William's parents house… They are overwhelming me with questions and I'm this close to breaking."

Beraham said quickly before Lee could even say a greeting. The sound of Lee's breathing was all that Beraham could hear but wasn't saying anything yet. Beraham was about to repeat the same question again, but Lee spoke before he could ask.

"Fine… Give me fifteen minutes to get there and I'll bail you out,"

Beraham felt relief knowing that Lee was on his way to bail him out, from having to continue to answer these hard questions.

"Thank you… I'll see you soon at the front door of Will's parents house."

Beraham said as he hung up the phone call and went to the sink to splash some water across his face. After finishing his business in the washroom, Beraham opened the door and walked out to head back to the backyard.

Just as he was passing by the kitchen, Beraham suddenly felt a sharp pain in his chest. The pain in his chest was a pain that Beraham has not felt in a very long time.

"Fuck sake! What the heck is this? What is happening to make me feel such a severe amount of pain?!?"

Beraham said to himself as he hissed in pain, while trying not to let out his screams. He collapsed to the ground as he could feel himself lose consciousness from the amount of pain he was in. The last thing that Beraham felt before going dark was a sense of happiness.

CHAPTER 4

A Problem has Arised and A Doctor can't Help Him

Beraham never liked to sleep, it always ended up with him having nightmares. He didn't need to have the rest of his roommates worrying about the emotionless one in their group having nightmares. But just like when he slept at night, when he had lost consciousness from this mysterious pain in his chest, he started to have another nightmare.

Beraham found himself lying down in a bed of dead leaves and snow, staring up at a cloudy sky while it snowed. He sat himself up to look around to see where he was.

From what Beraham could recognize, he was by a river under a large bridge and everywhere else was covered in snow. Beraham stood up to start walking through the snow, he noticed that he wasn't wearing his regular street clothes. But rather he was in a black and red suit, with a red tie and black dressing shoes.

"Oh you gotta be kidding me... At least I could've at least worn my blundstone boots, and a winter coat, rather than this bloody outfit that is gonna freeze my arse off.."

Beraham said out loud as the very thought of getting these clothes dirty or stained, was a nightmare in itself. But he took a deep breath in and out, to prepare himself for whatever night terrors he was about to encounter. Beraham walked to the side of the bridge to have a better view of his surroundings. Snowflakes started to fall down onto him.

"For a nightmare that is supposed to be of my own creation, it's rather peaceful in this place."

Beraham said to himself as he held out his hand to catch a couple of snowflakes. As Beraham studied the snowflakes that fell, he turned around to see a figure walking across the bridge with purpose. Beraham felt a sense of dread when it dawned on him what was going to happen.

"No… Not this memory, I already know how this one ends!"

Beraham said as his voice trembled as he tried not to let his fear take hold of him. Beraham broke out into a sprint as he made his way up the hill that would allow him to get to the person quickly on the bridge.

"Please… Mujhe samay se vahaan pahunchane do!"

Beraham shouted in Hindi as he spoke in a different language as he wished that he wasn't in this dumb suit and dress shoes to get there as qucikly as he could. He jumped over the barricade that stood between the hill and bridge, and made his way across the deserted bridge to where the figure stopped and waited by the edge. Beraham slowly got closer to the figure to approach this mysterious person to not spook them.

"Hey… What are you hoping to achieve with this?" Beraham asked as he started to take small steps towards the person, so as to not make any sudden moves.

"I'm not going to understand your reasoning for wanting to do this, but I can try to listen to you or at least hear you out."

Beraham continued to say as he slowly put his hand on the railing, as he was a few feet away from the person.

The mystery person spoke, but for some reason Beraham couldn't hear the words as if someone muted this person like a television.

"Wait … Please wait! I can't hear you… I want to help you just give me a second to figure out why I can't hear you!"

Beraham said in a panic as the mystery figure started to climb over the railing where there was a long drop into the rushing cold river and ice. Beraham tried to intervene but could feel an invisible force holding him back, to let it happen.

That's when he realized that he had forgotten that this was a nightmare and that he had already experienced this before. But it still hurt Beraham to see this person fall off the bridge towards the cold iced river.

Just as he was about to see the person hit the river, Beraham woke up from his nightmare with tears streaming down his face.

"Wow, it's been a long time since I last woke up crying from my nightmare." Beraham whispered to himself as he looked around to see where he was. From what he could tell from the book shelves and drawings on the wall, that he was in William's old room. Beraham sat himself back up, he noticed that someone had taken his shirt off to reveal all his scars from past fights and incidents.

"Aghhh... Where the hell is my shirt? Aghh nevermind that, the pain in my chest seems to have subsided." Beraham said to himself as he looked around to find his shirt, while checking his body for any bruises from when he fell.

"We can't just let Beraham die here! He needs a bloody hospital!"

Eve shouted at someone from outside William's room, as multiple footsteps approached the door. The door slammed open to reveal Eve and Joshua entering the room, with Lee, Heinkel and Joseph coming in behind them. William's parents were surprised to see that Beraham was awake and moving around.

"Beraham, lay back down! You shouldn't be moving around so suddenly after experiencing a cardiac episode!"

Eve said as she forced Beraham to lay back down on the bed while checking for his pulse. While she was checking Beraham's pulse, he looked towards his roommates who were giving him a 'what happened to you?' Look. Beraham mouthed back to them 'I'll tell you guys later,' and turned his attention back to Eve who was still counting Beraham's pulse.

"Eve, I'm fine now, I don't feel any sort of pain. I believe that I was having a simple fainting episode… I've had them in the past so this isn't a random occurrence."

Beraham explained as he looked to his roommates to back him up.

"That is true, Beraham has fainted in our house before, and for the most part it only really happens like once or twice a month."

Joseph said to Eve, while the other two nodded their heads in agreement. Eve stopped checking on Beraham's pulse, and looked up at his face. He could tell that Eve was not believing anything that Beraham or the rest of his roommates were saying.

"Beraham, when Joshua found you on the floor of the kitchen unconscious, he said that you were not responding to his attempts to wake you. He also couldn't find your heartbeat or pulse."

Eve explained as she continued to stare into his eyes to check for any other symptoms.

"Even now I am having trouble trying to find your pulse… I can still find it but it's rather weak and almost non-existent."

Eve finished explaining while feeling his forehead to check Beraham's temperature. While Beraham sighed with a defeated tone in his voice.

"If you're still adamant about my health, Eve, then I'll visit a hospital or a clinic to get a check up with Heinkel to put your mind at ease."

Beraham said as he sat up, while Heinkel moved forward to toss Beraham his shirt to put back on.

Eve still had a suspicious look across her face, but when she turned to face her husband for guidance. He just nodded his head and mouthed to her 'trust them.'

Eve turned back to Beraham and continued to stare at him before she spoke.

"Very well… Since I know that Heinkel is a man of his word and will always do everything in his best interest. But I want you to tell us what your doctor thinks happened to you from their results."

She gave the rest of the roommates a stink eye to them, and then left the room without another word. Joshua walked up to Beraham and sat him down on the bed next to him.

"I know it doesn't seem like it, but Eve was genuinely worried for you when she saw you on the floor. She wanted to call an ambulance for you, but ..."

Joshua started to explain but stopped mid sentence, when he noticed Joseph going through William's desk, Heinkel and Lee stare at Beraham.

"Do you think you three could wait outside while I speak to Beraham alone?"

Joshua asked nicely as he moved his head to subtly tell them to leave. The three of them looked to Beraham for whether or not they should leave him alone with William's father. But Beraham nodded his head and rolled his eyes to the door. Once they all left William's room, Joshua turned back to him with a tired smile.

"We were really bafulled by Lee showing up at our front door at the same time you fell unconscious. He said that he needed your help with an issue with your landlord... And when he saw you lying on the ground he immediately asked for us to move you to William's room and not call the paramedics."

Joshua told Beraham who was listening closely to understand what had happened around him when he went unconscious.

"So then Eve being the doctor she is, started to argue with Lee that a hospital was what you needed, but Lee kept saying that this was normal and that this has happened to you before. And that you usually wake up after an hour or so."

Beraham interrupted Joshua's explanation with a question of his own.

"So how did Heinkel and Joseph get involved in this? Did Lee call them?"

Joshua shook his head to continue his story.

"No, Lee was too busy arguing with Eve that he didn't even have any chance to pull out his phone to call them, much less any time to take out his phone… They were just at the front door waiting to be let in."

Beraham knew how Heinkel would've known that he was in danger, but Joseph wouldn't have known unless either Heinkel went and picked him up or texted him.

"Beraham are you alright? You have been silent for a while now…"

Joshua asked as Beraham looked up at him to see a serious expression over the usually happy man.

"But sir, why didn't you or Eve call for an ambulance? Did you just trust what Lee told you about my condition? Or did it feel like something was stopping you?"

Beraham asked as he got off the bed and stood in front of Joshua looking down at him.

"Well ummm… I've been asking myself that very question. It felt like whenever I left the room to grab a phone, I would hear Eve calling for my help… But when I came back she was still arguing with Lee."

Joshua said robotically, as if he was under a spell. His eyes looked tired as he was talking about that experience.

"And then when Joseph and Heinkel showed up Eve seemed to listen more easily to Joseph's reasoning, but still was quite skeptical so they said we could call an ambulance in thirty minute…"

"It felt like someone was watching my every move at one point… Like someone was whispering to me to 'stay where I was and wait with your wife.' It felt like I was being watched by a predator and I was the prey."

Joshua said as he shivered with fright, even though it was the middle of summer.

"Don't worry about all of that sir, I can't thank you and your wife for helping me and for being so worried about my health. But after such an event today, you're probably pretty stressed out from all that just happened, so why don't you take a nap?"

Beraham suggested as Joshua layed down onto the bed as he let out a loud yawn.

"Your right, Beraham... Oh and can you tell William that we can't wait to see him for dinner next time."

Joshua asked as he closed his eyes and fell asleep before Beraham could give an answer. Beraham took this opportunity to leave the room while Joshua was asleep and tried to sneak out of the house to get out of this situation. On his way to the front door he ran into Eve who was talking to his roommates. Eve noticed that Beraham was walking towards them and raised an eyebrow when she didn't see Joshua.

"Where is my husband?"

Eve asked as she crossed her arms and tapped her foot impatiently.

"Joshua said that he needed to take a nap after such a stressful event, so he is taking a nap in William's old room."

Beraham answered as he moved around Eve, and quickly put his blundstones on his feet.

"That is understandable, Joshua would probably need a nap after witnessing such a sight from you. Though I don't understand how you and Heinkel can wear blundstones all day, or Joseph wearing such fancy dressing shoes, and especially Lee who is only wearing socks and flip-flops."

Eve said as she looked at each of the young men's choice of footwear.

"Well we all like to wear what is most comfortable for us, ms. Eve."

Lee said proudly as he stood there in his sandals and socks.

"I see that very well... It was nice seeing you all here despite the circumstances. Oh and Beraham I will be hearing from you about what the hospital says about your results or else you'll have to answer to William."

Eve said, causing all the guys to freeze in place when they heard William's name being brought into this conversation.

"Interesting, you all seemed to have a weakness for William finding out Beraham's Injury with how you're reacting. I thought it was only ever really Heinkel that was the sensitive of William, but all of you?"

Eve said as she noticed that all of them had started to lose their smiles and looked more like grim expressions.

"Madam, we all care about William's well being. So telling him about what happened to Beraham would only add unnecessary stress and worry for him."

Joseph explained nervously as he looked at Heinkel who fell silent at the mention of William's name, and his expression was obvious that he was angry.

"That is true Joseph, but William hasn't visited us for dinner in quite awhile. So I think it would be nice for him to have dinner with us next week."

Eve said innocently as Heinkel took a step forward. But was stopped by Lee who grabbed him by the shoulder and guided him outside.

"Don't worry about that Eve, I'll tell you the results when I get them… But even you know that hospitals take a couple days or weeks to get any results."

Beraham explained while gesturing for Joseph to wait outside with Lee and Heinkel.

"Of course you're right, but it's still a bad idea to keep this a secret from my son… Especially when it involves one of his closest best friends passing out without a pulse in his parents home."

Eve said as he raised an eyebrow when everyone else left her house except for Beraham.

"Well then, that seems to be the type of conversation that should be explained by me. And not by his own mother who was sticking her nose into someone else's business." Beraham replied and then left through the door to end this conversation, before it got too out of hand. Because he knew that if he tried to talk with Eve anymore then this, he might say something he would regret.

After Beraham left the house, he met back up with his roommates and had Heinkel drive his motorcycle back home while they took

Heinkel's car. Once they arrived back at their house, they all got out and headed to the front door to have a discussion.

"Okay so should we have greek food or indian for dinner tonight?"

Joseph asked to break the silence that the group had been doing for the whole ride over.

"Really Joe? You know that we need to talk about what the hell happened with Beraham!" Heinkel shouted with a lot of anger in his voice. Heinkel stomped up the stairs without another word. While the rest of them all looked at each other with worried expressions.

"Man it's been a while since someone has gotten under Heinkel's skin like that, I'll go and try to calm him down before we try and discuss anything."

Lee said as he followed after Heinkel to try and help him. Joseph was about to follow after them, but Beraham grabbed his shoulder to get his attention.

"Hey, do you have a second to talk?"

Beraham asked as he held onto Joseph's shoulder with an iron grip. Joseph looked down at the hand on his shoulder then back up to Beraham's face.

"Sure, no problem boss man... but let's keep it short since we shouldn't leave Lee on his own to deal with an angry Heinkel."

Joseph said nervously as he slowly took Beraham's hand off his shoulder. They both leaned on the front of Heinkel's car to talk.

"Joseph, I need you to be completely honest with me, alright?"

Beraham asked with a serious look across his face while Joseph had a curious one across his.

"Did you use your persuasive charms on William's parents when they were trying to call an ambulance?"

Beraham asked as he studied Joseph's blue eyes, and noticed that they widened for a split second. But he quickly answered Beraham's question.

Ahh Blyat, of course you wouldn't miss that or fail to notice... How is your russian?"

Joseph knew better than to try and lie straight to Beraham's face.
"Good enough to hold a conversation."

Beraham spoke in Russian to answer Joseph's question, but was curious as to why they had to speak in Russian.

"The reason that I want us to speak in a different language is so that Heinkel and Lee can't listen in on our conversation."

Joseph explained himself, as he pointed with his head to the kitchen window where Lee was handing a glass of water to Heinkel.

"But anyways to answer your question, yes I did use my power of deceit and persuasion on Will's parents… But in all honesty you gave off quite an aura that even I could feel from across town."

Joseph said as he took out a pack of cigarettes and a lighter.

"I thought that you were getting off cigarettes? Or do you only smoke them after stressful situations?"

Beraham asked as Joseph lit the cigarette and watched it burn away without taking a puff.

"Heh no… I just like the feeling of burning these away. Because that's one less cigarette for someone else to use."

Joseph answered as he pulled out a plastic bag where he kept all his remnants of the cigarettes, he put it out and placed it back into the bag.

"But you must know that it wasn't just me who used their talents… But you probably already knew that from your expression."

Beraham looked at Joseph with a grin across his face, to confirm what Joseph had just said.

Beraham got off the front of Heinkel's car, and waved his hand to indicate to Joseph that they were done with this conversation.

"Let's head inside now that you confirmed what I already knew, and help Lee before Heinkel turns all John Wick on us."

Beraham said in english while he headed off towards the house.

"Blya radi, Besserdechnyy nichego ne mozhet s soboy podelat."

Joseph said under his breath in Russian as he followed Beraham up the steps into their home. They walked through the house to the kitchen where Lee was talking to Heinkel about what went on at William's workplace.

"Will probably know more when he gets back from his shift... But he seems to be quite happy with his co-workers."

Lee was explaining but grew silent when Beraham walked into the kitchen.

"So Heinkel, have you started to calm yourself? Because trust me, no one can push someone's buttons like William's mother."

Beraham said as he got a dry smile from both Lee and Heinkel. All the while Joseph walked into the kitchen with Bianca in his arms.

"So Bianca was what William named the dog, right?"

Joseph asked while the rest of the men all nodded their heads in unison to confirm Joseph's question.

"WELL, Bianca here was rolling around in my bed and clothing, so now it all smells like a dog!"

After hearing this complaint, Heinkel walked over to Joseph and ushered him to pass over the little dog. Once he held the dog, he raised her into the air above his head and said.

"You can finally stop Joseph from bringing over midnight guests, and having them stay the night!"

Everyone but Joseph burst out laughing at this statement. They continued to laugh together until Beraham spoke up.

"Just to let you guys know that I know you all used your talents while I was unconscious at William's house."

All of them stopped laughing and had pale looks across their faces. Heinkel spoke up first, but still had a nervous look across his face as he tried to talk to Beraham.

"Well we all knew that you would know that we used them... But the situation called for us to use them or else it could've gone wrong if we didn't intervene!"

"I know this was a rather unexpected incident... And in no way am I scolding you for using them, but to have all three of you use them on William's parents could arouse a lot of suspicion from them or neighbors."

Beraham said as he stepped forward, making all three of them step back in fear.

"Keep in mind that this time around I'll look the other way because it was a complicated situation. But next time you guys try to use your talents again without my permission, I'll see that as a breaking of your contracts and punish you accordingly."

Beraham said coldly to everyone, who in turn nodded their heads to show they understood what he said.

Great, now that we all have come to an understanding I will be taking a nap up in my room. While I'm asleep, if you guys can find me a doctor that can give me a private exam and isn't one for asking too many questions, then we can keep Eve off my back about what happened today."

Beraham said to the three of them while leaving the kitchen and towards the staircase. He climbed the stairs leaving his three roommates alone in the kitchen with the little dog. Once He left the kitchen, everyone else let out a sigh of relief that Beraham let them off the hook so easily.

"Jesus bloody christ! I honestly thought that we were about to die… Almost bloody pissed myself from just looking at his expression."

Lee said as his Irish accent came out whenever he was scared or lost his composure.

"Blyat… I haven't seen him look so cold hearted in awhile, the last time I saw him like that was when he found out how much debt I accumulated when he was recruiting me back in Russia."

Joseph said as he swore under his breath and made his way over to the fridge to grab a beer for himself.

"Joseph it's literally two in the afternoon, I don't want William coming back home to your drunk ass and having him worried that something bad happened to you."

Heinkel said as he regained his confidence after Beraham left, and from petting the dog in his arms to calm his fast beating heart.

"But that is besides the point right now, did you guys also feel that presence before we all dropped what we did to help Beraham? Like a voice was telling you that he was in danger?"

Heinkel asked as he saw that everyone else had a surprised look on their faces when they heard his question.

"So as far as we know, Lee can make people forget what they are doing or can make everyone forget their anxiety and troubles. While I can persuade some to a certain degree and can show someone who they truly love."

Joseph said as he went through each of their 'special talents.'

"Right and Heinkel is about instilling fear in those around him or the fact that is almost unstoppable in any fight with anyone or tracking them down like a bloodhound."

Lee piped in as Joseph gave him an annoyed look for interrupting his explanation. But just glossed over that interruption, to continue talking but was once again interrupted by Heinkel this time.

"But the one person that we don't really know his talent is Beraham. I have my own suspicions of what they might be, but he made part of my contract include not telling anyone what they possibly can be."

Heinkel said as Lee and Joseph exchanged glances between each other, knowing that they had a similar condition on theirs as well.

"Beraham had also given Joseph and I a similar condition as a part of our contracts. But still when I first arrived and saw Eve perform CPR on Beraham, I could've sworn that he had a smile on his face and what looked like a tear streaming down his face."

Lee said while he shuddered at the memory of seeing it happen right in front of him. Heinkel walked over to Lee to offer the little dog to comfort him, and Lee graciously accepted Bianca and cuddled with her in his arms.

"Will figure that out later, for now I'm gonna talk with someone from work since I know a few people there that were field medics and doctors without borders that can examine Beraham without the need of a hospital. Since if any hospital examined Beraham they wouldn't ever let him leave again…"

Heinkel said as he pulled out his phone to make some calls to his employee's, to try and set up an appointment for Beraham per his request.

"Well I guess that leaves you and me to take this little dog on a walk around the block. Since she probably hasn't had another chance to use the washroom when you left to handle Beraham's situation."

Joseph said as he booped Bianca on her snout. Lee had an annoyed look across his face, when he realized that he would have to go back outside again to exercise.

"Come on Lee, don't give me such a disapproval look like that. This poor little dog needs to go outside and do her business."

Joseph said as went over to his briefcase and pulled out a collar and a blue leash while he continued to speak.

"Now then, let's go around the block and have her get more familiar with the neighborhood."

After heading to his room, Beraham took out his phone and quickly messaged William to see how he was doing at work. Once he finished his text message and sent it, Beraham went into his room to lay down and rest his eyes for a little while. As he laid there in his bed, Beraham thought about what could've caused him to experience just pain in his chest that he went unconscious. His first thought was that maybe he accidentally broke one of his contract's rules, or was close to breaking one and it was warning him harshly. Another was that perhaps William had been under extreme wave of emotions or pain and it was being transferred to Beraham to lessen it for William.

There were too many unknown variables for Beraham to come up with a definitive answer yet. As he continued to try and figure out different ideas or theories, His phone rang to notify him that he received a text message. Beraham quickly checked to see who it was, but sadly it was just Heinkel messaging him to see how he was doing and that he found someone that could give him a private check up, and get it into the system of a hospital without too much issue.

With a sigh of disappointment escaping from Beraham's mouth, he responded with a thumbs up emoji and told Heinkel to message him when they can schedule an appointment two days from now.

After going through some last few details that Heinkel needed to give to his contact that would perform the exam. Once he was done with his conversation with Heinkel, Beraham closed his phone and went back to his nap. After closing his eyes for what felt like just a couple seconds, he actually slept longer then he would've liked to sleep. He woke up and looked at his alarm clock to check for the time, and was surprised to see that it was almost eight in the evening.

Beraham grabbed his phone and noticed that William had messaged him while he was asleep. The texts he read were just simple answers like, 'Work was going pretty good,' or 'Everyone was quite friendly and helpful.' Beraham finished reading the text messages that were sent about two hours ago. When the sound of his door being knocked on by one of his roommates.

"Hey we're just about to start our meeting, everyone is just waiting for you to come down so… Hurry up!" Lee yelled from the other side of the door, since he was probably too lazy to even check and see if Beraham was actually awake and heard him.

"Alright… Time to put on your business mask on Beraham… You got this and everything will be alright."

Beraham said to himself as he got out of bed to exit his room to head downstairs.

CHAPTER 5

We Need to Talk about Our Issues in this Household

When William had gotten home from his first shift at the pool, he opened the door to find Lee and Joseph having an argument. When William walked closer to try and hear what they were arguing about, Joseph noticed him approaching them and stopped arguing with Lee.

"Will! God to see your back from work, How was it today?"

Joseph said as he walked past Lee to greet William at the door.

"It was alright, though it was quite a slow day since I don't think many people knew we reopened today. So there weren't too many patrons to watch over in the pool."

William answered as he was quite curious about what Joseph was talking about with Lee, As Lee walked over as well to greet William.

"Don't say that now or else it's gonna be busy as hell tomorrow, because you jinxed it."

Joseph said as he turned around and headed towards the living room, while Lee was looking at William with a curious look across his face.

"Did anything bad happen at work today? Or did you feel overwhelmed, anxious about anything in particular?"

Lee asked William as he was hanging his bike on the hooks that held William's bike in place. William looked at Lee and was quite suspicious by the line of questions that he had asked. William tried to read his face for any hint as to why Lee would ask such questions, but his face always remained quite the same tired and resting expression. But he couldn't figure it out so William just decided to answer his question.

"No, like I was saying before to Joseph, we weren't that busy today. Besides a couple swimmers doing some rough housing and some small arguments, there wasn't anything too hard to deal with."

Lee looked like he wanted to ask more questions, but was interrupted by the sound of a dog barking. Bianca came barreling from the kitchen to William's feet, barking happily to see him. William picked her up from the ground to say hello to her, to give some pats on the head, and scratches behind the ears. Whatever that Lee was gonna ask, he decided to hold off from asking it for now.

"Hey Lee, could you go upstairs to tell Beraham that we will be starting our weekly Roommate meeting soon?"

Heinkel yelled from the living room as Lee looked annoyed that he was tasked to go upstairs.

"Right... I'm on it..."

Lee said half-heartedly as he walked at a snail's pace towards the stairs to go wake up Beraham. William decided to just head to the living room since he didn't really need to do anything before the meeting started. As he entered William noticed that Heinkel and Joseph were sitting on the couch watching the news on the television.

"Hey William, good to see you back home. Do you already eat? Because we ordered some Greek food if you're hungry."

Heinkel asked William, who in response shook his head. And then took a seat in one of the arm chairs with Bianca in his arms.

"No, I already ate with a couple of co-workers after we finished our shift at the pool. But enough about me, how was your job today?"

William asked his two roommates. Who both looked at each other, having a silent conversation between the two of them. Before they turned their attention back to William.

"Well after I dropped off Joseph at work, I went to my main office building that will house my cyber security branch. After that I was watching over some new recruits on their first job outing with some new clients for the rest of my shift."

Heinkel explained to William just as Lee walked in and sat down on the sofa between Heinkel and Joseph.

Everyone looked towards the entrance to the living room expecting to see Beraham coming in right behind Lee. But he didn't show up at that moment.

"Lee… You did make sure that Beraham was awake before you came back down right?"

Heinkel asked Lee as one of his eyebrows started to twitch whenever he got annoyed by one of his roommates.

"Yea, I knocked on his door and heard him move. So he probably is just taking his time to come down the stairs."

Lee answered as he took out his phone and started to scroll through something.

Heinkel was about to yell at Lee, but before he could even utter a noise Beraham walked in looking tired.

"Apologies everyone, didn't know that I was quite as tired as I first thought. But I'm here and ready to get our roommate meeting started."

Beraham explained as he made his way over to the other arm chair across from the rest of the group to sit down.

"Alright, so let's get this meeting started with our first decision on whether or not we keep the dog that William wishes to adopt. So let's put it to a vote, and make sure that everyone agrees to keep it."

Beraham said as he looked around the room to see if anyone had any objections or had anything important to say. Everyone looked at each other then to the dog in William's lap and all raised their hands in sync to say.

"Let's keep the dog!"

"But I am not in charge of doing any early morning walks nor will I allow it into my room, especially when I have guests overnight."

Joseph stated to the group as he gave the little Teacup Yorkie the stink eye.

"Don't worry, we will just make a schedule for us to take turns walking the dog or taking care of her when the rest of us are at work. But on the topic of overnight guests…"

Beraham said as he turned his gaze to Joseph, who realized what Beraham was about to bring up.

"Ni Khrena… Are we still on my case about the women I bring home when I go out?"

Joseph asked, while William let out a sigh of relief that he can keep Bianca.

"Joseph, you bring a new woman every week, and most of the time you are either really tired and depressed for a day after you break up, or just move on to the next girl saying you need to find someone else…"

Heinkel started to explain as the rest of the roommates fell silent to see how this would play out between the yin and yang of the group.

"I can be quite the sociable kind of guy… But keep in mind that I won't do anything that they aren't okay with… Sometimes we just talk all night about ourselves, so that they can realize that they can do better than me."

Joseph said as he tried to keep calm and not lose his temper in front of his friends.

"Joseph, we're not telling you to stop with your dating life… But rather you should take a break to emotionally heal yourself."

Beraham piped in before Heinkel could respond back to Joseph.

"I know why you're doing all these one week relationships Joseph, but please know that we're worried about your emotional and mental health when going through all these break ups."

Beraham explained himself, as he looked to everyone else for support. And they all agreed with what Beraham was saying.

Joseph's expression changed for a split moment, but no one other than William noticed how it went to a happy and thankful expression by his friend's words. Though instead of letting everyone else see how touched he was, Joseph went back into his cheerful and sociable mask he wore whenever he wanted to hide his emotions.

"Fine... For you guys I'll take a break from dating or relationships for a couple months, Plus I'll use this time to research how to flirt better and help play matchmaker for all of you to find that special someone!"

Joseph said with a sigh of defeat, he went onto his phone and made a couple quick messages by the sound of all the tapping.

Heinkel looked like he was about to ask what Joseph was doing, but Beraham blocked his path with his arm and shook his head.

"There we go, now that all my issues are out of the way, I think we're good to continue on with our meeting right?"

Joseph asked as he looked around to the rest of the roommates.

They continued to just discuss just how they should continue with who pays for which bills, who will be in charge of this month's grocery shopping, and other minor details for their living conditions. William did have something that he wanted to ask, but felt uneasy about whatever or not Beraham would want to discuss it in front of everyone else. Everyone sat there in silence, waiting for anyone else to speak up or had something to discuss. But no one piped in. And just as everyone was about to get up and leave for the night, William spoke up quickly before he lost his confidence.

"I was wondering if I should tell my parents to stop calling you guys over to their house just so that they can find out how i'm doing behind my back!"

All of his roommates stopped where they were sitting back down, and turned their attention to William.

"What do you mean by that Will?"

Heinkel asked as he looked towards Beraham with a worried expression across his face. But to William that was just reconfirming what he already thought was going on with his parents and roommates.

"My mother called me after I finished my shift today... She said that Beraham had gone over to have Brunch with them. But they felt like they made you quite uncomfortable with their questions about your love life and saying rude comments about everyone else."

William explained as he stared at Beraham to see how he would react to what William just said. But from what William could tell from Beraham's expression, He looked quite fine, even relieved by what William asked. As if he had expected him to ask something else entirely. William wanted to ask a follow up question for Beraham, but he spoke before William could've asked.

"It's true that I went over to your parents house for Brunch, it's also true that your mother was asking some uncomfortable questions to me. But I hope you know that I would never reveal any of your secrets to them..."

"Even though they are quite nice people, and can sometimes be a little too forthcoming and opinionated about our lifestyles. I know that they are only just curious about whether or not you're doing okay or causing any trouble for you."

Beraham said as he continued to talk the entire time locking eyes with William's dark brown eyes, to show he wasn't lying. Heinkel also chimed in to make a comment on the situation.

"If you find it's too uncomfortable or getting too worried about us William, we can decline the next time your parents ask us over for dinner or anything of the sorts."

Heinkel suggested as he and three other roommates continued to look towards William to see how he wanted to handle this.

William was thinking over this suggestion in his head, looking at the pros and cons of it.

"No, it's not about putting me in an uncomfortable situation... But rather more for you guys having to deal with my overly curious parents. Since they can be quite intrusive, and you guys are like a second family to me, and I don't want you guys to have to go through that..."

William said as his voice got more and more quiet as he looked down at his feet in embarrassment.

William continued to stare down at the ground, Bianca whimpered at the sudden mood that her owner was going through. He could hear footsteps approaching him, and William prepared himself to be yelled at or hear the disappointment his friends were about to say to him.

"Will... Stand up for me and look me in the eyes."

Beraham said calmly as put his hand on William's shoulder. He followed what was asked of him, William stood up from the chair to put Bianca on the ground. He then looked up to see that Beraham looked worried rather than angry or annoyed. Beraham pulled William into his arms and gave him a hug.

"I wouldn't care if I had to sit twenty four hours answering your parents questions Will, if you were this worried about the rest of us having to go through such trouble with your parents."

William could feel the tears streaming down his face, as he felt relieved that his friends were supportive and understanding of his small outburst. William could hear the rest of the group walking from where they sat and joined the hug.

"You know, since I feel like this has been a rather successful meeting... Why don't we have a drink to celebrate?"

Joseph suggested to everyone as they broke off the hug, to give Joseph a look of confusion.

"You do realize that it's a Wednesday and we all have work the next day except for Lee?"

Heinkel pointed out to Joseph who had already started to walk towards the kitchen. But stopped where he was, when he heard what Heinkel had said.

"Bu- but guys, it's been so long since we've had a night of drinking all together in quite a while… Can't we just do one or two shots before we go back to our boring jobs tomorrow?"

Joseph asked as he tried to appeal to his friends, who were all on the fence about whatever or not they wanted to drink in the middle of the weekday. William could tell that Joseph wanted to just lighten up the mood, since they all just talked about a lot of heavy topics in the past hour.

"Sure I'll do a couple of shots with you Joseph as long as we don't do more than double digits,"

William said while receiving multiple surprised looks on everyone's face, even Joseph looked surprised that William was the one to agree to this.

"Will… You were the last person that I thought would want to do shots,"

Heinkel said as he was the first person to recover from the initial shock from what William agreed to do shots.

"Well like I said, I'll only do a couple of shots as long as I don't do more than nine of them."

William repeated himself to his roommates all the while Joseph had already left for the kitchen when William had said yes.

"I know but I'm just worried about your intolerance, since who knows whatever drinks that crazy Russian playboy has in store."

Heinkel said as he had a look of worry across his face when Joseph returned with a creation that had a Russian sticker on top.

"My fellow comrades, we will drink something good that a friend of mine sent back home to me!"

Joseph said with glee as he opened the lid and removed the bubble wrap to reveal the drink.

"Now it's not vodka since I rather not get William full on f*cked up, so will have the brother of vodka horilka!"

Joseph shouted as he pulled the first bottle and placed it on top of the coffee table. Beraham silently walked over and checked the drinks ingredients and alcohol percentage.

"You do realize that this drink only has a slight difference in alcohol percentage, right?"

Beraham stated as he placed the Horilka back down on the table, looking towards Joseph to see what his answer would be.

William quickly glanced at the bottle and was taken aback by the alcohol percentage that was in it. But William knew that he still would try to drink it, because he knew that Joseph was just trying to bring everyone's spirit up with this plan.

"Well, it doesn't matter to me, because I think we all deserve a boys night of drinking!"

William said as he picked up the bottle of Horilka, opened it and took a gulp of it. At first William could immediately feel the drink give him a slight buzz. But quickly went away once he let out a loud burp.

William looked around and saw that all his friends had different reactions across their faces when he drank the Horilka straight out of the bottle. Heinkel looked like he just watched William swallow poison, while Lee looked surprised and yet fascinated by what William did. And Beraham just let out a long sign and then said,

"I am not going to be drinking that, but I will go and whip up some whisky type drinks... Anyone else want one?"

Lee's hand shot right up after hearing that Beraham was gonna make himself a drink. Especially since Lee loved the way that Beraham would make his drinks, that it became a favorite of his.

"And bring more cups for all of us to drink since I'm gonna be getting drunk tonight!"

Lee shouted as he walked over to William and took the bottle out of William's hand and drank down a good quarter of the bottle.

"Pace yourself Lee, because I will not clean up your vomit if we're all gonna drink tonight."

Heinkel said as he quickly took the bottle away from Lee, before he went and tried to drink the whole bottle on his own.

"Oh come on Heinkel, let's not get too worried over Lee. I've seen him out drink plenty of my friends back in Russia… Must be because of that Irish tolerance they have."

Joseph said after downing his first cup, and afterwards pouring two more cups to offer to Heinkel and one for himself. Heinkel looked down at the cup that was offered to him. William could tell that he was gonna decline the drink, but then Heinkel looked towards William and then back at the drink. He quickly grabbed the cup out of Joseph's hand, to quickly drink it all in one gulp.

William didn't know what made him decide to drink it, but he decided to chalk it up to just going with the flow of the group. William heard the sound of glasses clinking together behind him, so he turned around to see Beraham coming back from the kitchen with a tray of drinks that he had made for everyone.

"Ahhh… There's the drink to get rid of the after taste from Joseph's drink. So what have you made tonight for all of us, Beraham?"

Lee asked as they sat down around the coffee table so that Beraham could place the drinks in front of Lee and himself. He picked up his drink and gave it a quick sniff, then proceeded to remove a slice of apple from his drink.

Beraham smiled as he raised his glass to explain his creation, since he loved to tell his guest how he made the drinks he served.

"Well you see, I used crown royale whisky, added some apple juice, a pinch of cinnamon, and to top it off I added a slice of apple to it. The apple slice is too soak up some of the alcohol to make it like a mini snack."

Lee studied the drink while the rest of the group quickly gave a small round of applause for his explanation.

"Alright, I think that is enough explaining about drinks, so let's get this night started everyone!"

Joseph said impatiently as he raised his glass of whiskey, to raise a toast.

"Cheers all around lads!"

Lee said as they all clinched their cups together, then they all took a sip of Beraham's drink that he made for them, or in Joseph, William, and Heinkel's case another shot of Horilka.

"Not gonna lie here Beraham, but it is not too bad… I think if you added a tad too much whisky to apple juice. But it still tastes pretty good."

Lee said as he took another sip from his drink and gave Beraham a thumbs up.

Beraham looked quite happy by the feedback he was getting about his drink. And yet William could see that he was trying to hide the smug look of accomplishment in front of everyone else.

"Hmmm you've piqued my curiosity about this drink now, Hey Beraham do you think that you could make one for the rest of us?"

Joseph asked as Beraham while refilling Heinkel and William's cups back up, for the next round of shots.

"Sure that isn't a problem… Though I think you can snack on the apple slice, it should've been long enough for it to soak in the drink."

Beraham said as took out his apple slice and snacked on it while he stood up and walked back to the kitchen. As he walked away Heinkel called out to him.

"Oh hey Beraham! Can you get some chips while you're in the kitchen? I bought some the other day."

"Well this is just like you Heinkel, to worry about us drinking on an empty stomach even when you're also drinking."

Joseph said as he passed back the refilled cups to everyone, except for Beraham who went to the kitchen.

Heinkel's eyes narrowed at Joseph's comment and decided to speak up about it.

"Are you trying to say that I shouldn't try to make sure you guys don't end up keeling over the toilet retching your empty stomachs?"

Heinkel asked as he downed his drink quickly in anger.

"Oi! These shots are supposed to be done together as a group! Not for whenever you're feeling thirsty!"

Joseph shouted as he grabbed the empty cup from his friend's hands, to refill it but left it next to him so that Heinkel couldn't drink it again.

"Now ignore that little outburst of yours, and I will keep your cup until Beraham returns with the rest of the drinks."

Joseph said to Heinkel who in turn responded back with the middle finger. Everyone else started to laugh at the interaction between Heinkel and Joseph. The four of them continued to crack jokes amongst each other; Beraham came back from the kitchen with the whisky concoctions and a bowl of chips to eat.

"Nice, now we have our secondary drinks and some snacks to munch on."

Joseph said as he grabbed a handful of chips from the bowel and started to eat it up.

"Will you be joining in our shots, Beraham? Or are you sticking with just your whisky?"

Lee asked him as he sat back down in his armchair with his drink in his hand again.

"No, I will not be mixing two different types of alcohol tonight…. But I'll still stay up for a little bit longer before I head to bed. Just so then I can stop you guys before you give yourselves alcohol poisoning."

Beraham answered with his usual blank expression or neutral face.

"Well with that happy thought from Beraham, let's move on to round two of our shots for tonight!"

Joseph said as he passed back Heinkel's cup back to him so that they could drink it all together. And he quietly added under his breath.

"Even though someone is on their third round and decides to flash the middle finger to someone who is looking out for them."

Everyone glanced towards Heinkel who didn't look the least bit guilty nor sorry about his actions.

"Well I guess to make up for my rude actions, I'll be leading the cheer for this round of shots... So is everyone ready for this?"

Heinkel asked in a dull tone. Making it quite obvious that he didn't like being the leader in these types of social events. But nonetheless everyone raised their cups and were ready to cheer.

"Alright, on the count of three... Eins, Zwei, Drei, Prost alle zusammen!"

Heinkel said as they clicked their cups and downed the cups of Horilka, excluding Beraham who was just sipping his whisky concoction.

"Ahhh... That hits the spot! Nothing makes me feel better than alcohol!"

Joseph said as he took one of the glasses Beraham had brought out for them, and took a quick sip of it. After they all finished their second round of shots, the five of them continued to eat the chips, while talking about all sorts of random topics. William felt that these types of moments were the ones that he would remember and hold onto whenever he was feeling sad or alone.

"And William, I believe that your dog likes the stories that I tell, since she kept barking so happily when I told her the stories of how we first met... Well at least how Beraham introduced me to you. But small details right?"

Lee said, making everyone give him a concerned look on their faces, that Lee has been talking to the dog all day.

"Oh come on guys, don't give me that look. If we're gonna keep the dog she needs to get to know how this family got together."

Lee said as he chugged down Beraham's whisky concoction, with a happy expression on his face.

"You really need to get out and socialize with other people Lee, you're so lonely being here all by yourself that you're talking to dogs more than you talk to our neighbors..."

Joseph said as he also took away Lee's cup to stop him from draining his cup before the next round of cheers.

"I mean it might be good practice for Lee, since he doesn't really talk about himself too much with anyone besides us."

William suggested as he remembered seeing Lee some time ago practicing small talk in front of the bathroom mirror.

"Well as long as Lee doesn't teach the dog any bad habits or tricks that affect me, then she should definitely tell her the stories of my accomplishments with the ladies."

Joseph said as he finished pouring round three of Horilka, and then passed the cups back around to his friends since he couldn't trust them not to drink them beforehand.

"Alright gents, it's time for round three so get ready. And this time Beraham will be the one to lead our cheer, so take it away my friend!"

Joseph announced to his friends while pointing his drink towards Beraham, to let him know that he had been chosen. Beraham looked down at the cup, then looked at his friends who were all waiting patiently for him.

"Sure it would be my pleasure to lead the next cheer, but let me just say for you guys to take it slow with those drinks, or else you will be regretting it in the morning."

Beraham answered as he checked his glass to see that only a quarter of his drink remained.

"Though for this cheer it will have a theme to it, on the count of three shout out who you think will have the biggest hangover tomorrow."

Beraham explained as everyone got their cups ready to be drained once again. Everyone nodded their heads to indicate that they all had a name ready to shout, Beraham started to count.

"Okay guys, here we go! One, two, three!"

"Lee!" "Joseph!" "Lee!" "Joseph!" They all shouted their choices except for Beraham who stayed silent as to not show who he would've chosen. And then they all drank their drinks till they were empty.

"Well ain't that just plain rude of da both yee!"

Lee said even though he was starting to slur his words as he talked.

"Ha! You're already slurring your sentences Lee! Guess that legendary alcohol tolerance you kept bragging about has become weaker."

Joseph replied as he started to laugh, while Lee's face was turning red with anger.

"Oh ho Just you wait you Womanizer! The night is still young and I ain't even the least bit tired yet!"

Lee shouted as he reached for the bottle to drink the rest of it, but William smacked his hand away from the bottle. William knew that when Lee drinks angrily he won't stop until he passes out.

"Lee… We're taking our time with our drinks so that we can enjoy and remember this night. So let's hold off on trying to go super hard on the drinking right now."

William explained to Lee, who just looked very confused by what he was being told. Lee's anger subsided once William stopped him, he just muttered under his breath that he would just snack on some chips while he waited for the next round.

William let out a sigh of relief that Lee had decided to listen to him instead of going onto a rant or worse.

William heard someone let out a small chuckle, he looked around and noticed everyone else was talking amongst each other except for Beraham who had a grin across his face.

William was going to ask him why he chuckled, but before he could, Beraham grabbed everyone's attention by tapping his glass.

"Well guys, it's been a rather long day for me and I'm still feeling quite tired so I'll be heading to bed now. Don't stay up too late drinking till the crack of dawn, remember that we all still have work to do."

Beraham reminded everyone as he stood up to leave.

"Understood Boss! Will probably be staying up for a couple more hours, so don't worry about it and have a goodnight."

Joseph said nervously as he seemed to notice something that the others didn't see. Once he left the living room, William's dog Bianca quickly followed after Beraham barking to get his attention.

"I think your dog has figured out that Beraham is the alpha dog in our group,"

Joseph whispered to everyone just in case Beraham was listening in on them.

"So does that make you the beta of the group Joseph? That would make the most sense since the dog doesn't seem to like you that much."

Heinkel said with a smug look across his face, making Joseph pretend to look hurt by that remark.

"How dare you insinuate such a term to me Heinkel! I might not be a giant CEO of a company like you are, but in this household we are all treated as equal Beta's."

Joseph said sarcastically as he over dramatized what he was saying to make everyone else laugh at his little performance. Heinkel started to argue with Joseph, while Lee tried to stop them from getting physical. Meanwhile William was lost in thought at the fact that Bianca seemed to have warmed up to Beraham quite quickly. He knew it wasn't uncommon for a dog to follow after someone they favored over others, but Bianca only knew Beraham for around half a day. And from what he remembered Bianca's previous owner telling him, she tended to take some time to warm up to new people or to strangers.

William continued to make different theories on this dog conundrum, all the while his three friends had run off to the kitchen to grab more alcohol. Once they returned back from the kitchen they had packs of beer they put onto the coffee table.

"Alright you guys keep saying that the beer brands that my country makes are not the best, you have another thing coming."

Joseph declared as he took out a pack of Wellington Imperial Russian Stgut, and took out a can to place in front of him for everyone to see. Lee let out a loud laugh at Joseph's declaration, as he took out a six pack of Guinness.

"That is utter bullshit if I've ever heard in ma bloody life! Back home we know what beer you always can look to get when you go out to a pub with your mates!"

Lee said as his accent started to become thicker as the night continued.

Heinkel joined this contest by silently placing his choice of beer, which was Okocim Pilsner. Lee and Joseph both looked at Heinkel with his beer and in sync said, "No!"

"So we're gonna need a judge who isn't gonna be biased, since we're all friends... Someone who can be brutally honest with us and know will always tell the truth."

Heinkel said as he already knew who to ask to be their judge for this contest.

"But Beraham already went to bed Heinkel... He doesn't like to mix his drinks, nor does he like to be disturbed when he goes to sleep."

Joseph said as he put away his almost empty bottle of Horilka away, so that he could drink his beers and so that no one else could drink it.

Heinkel smacked his forehead in amazement at how dumb Joseph can get when he gets drunk. As Joseph couldn't even figure out such an easy answer to who can be their judge for their beer contest.

"No you stupid drunk idiot... William was who I meant to be our judge for this beer contest, to see who has the best beer."

Heinkel explained to his very drunk roommate who was just petting his drink like a dog. That's when William snapped back to reality, when Heinkel had mentioned his name.

"Wait, what is it you want me to do?"

William asked as he noticed all of the beers on the table and all his friends looking at him.

"So we need you to taste and judge to see which country has the best crafted beer."

Joseph explained as all three of them picked one of their beers, to place in front of William to drink.

"So will ya do us a solid mate, and tell these assholes that Guinesses is the best one here,"

Lee asked as he inched his beer closer to William.

"Oi! Don't be trying to convince him like that you asshole!"

Heinkel yelled as he slapped Lee's hand away, who in turn just rolled his eyes in annoyance.

"Okay I'll do it, but after this contest is done I'm gonna head to bed so that I can get some sleep."

William said as he massaged his temple as a way to indicate to everyone that the alcohol was starting to have an affect on him.

"Great! This will be the first time in a while that we competed against each other. The last time we did something like this, it was when Heinkel wanted to see who was the best fighter and make a hierarchy or something like that."

Joseph said and quickly dodge out of the way of Heinkel's fist. Heinkel had a pissed off look across his face, as if Joseph had said something he wasn't supposed to say.

"Jezz Joseph, you're lucky that Heinkel has been drinking a decent amount tonight. Or else he would've knocked the fuck out of you if that fist of his hit you."

Lee said while he started to drink one of his Guinesses and put his whole body across the sofa.

"He has every right to hit me right now, since I just said something that a certain someone shouldn't know about."

Joseph whispered to Lee and looked towards William, who was looking confused at what just happened.

William was gonna start questioning why his friends were fighting each other, until Heinkel spoke up before anyone else could say anything.

"Before you start asking a million questions William, I have a proposition for you, I'll answer three questions in complete honesty. In exchange you need to drink each beer if you want me to answer, and you're limited to just three questions from me and only me."

William wanted to ask more than just three questions, but he knew that the offer that Heinkel gave him was the best outcome he could get. Since he knew that they would just either avoid or change topics if he tried to get the real answers.

Plus William knew that Heinkel would be honest for all three questions.

Once he decided on what he was going to do, William quickly grabbed Lee's can of Guinness and drank it all down in two gulps. Then placed the empty can back on the table with a satisfied burp.

"Well? What do you think of the taste William? Best bloody beer ya ever had right?"

Lee asked eagerly as he awaited for the final verdict from William.

"It's not bad… If I wasn't in a hurry I would definitely like to drink this once a week with my dinner… I would give this beer a seven out of ten."

William explained to Lee, then turned his attention to Heinkel and asked his first question.

"Why did you want to fight everyone?"

Heinkel took a moment to think about his answer, while Lee muttered under his breath about how his beer deserved a higher score than what was given.

"Where I grew up there was always a hierarchy of sorts or a pecking order. Who was the strongest of the group, to be the leader to make the decisions that would best suit the group. So I wanted to see who out of the four of us could be the leader of the group and fighting was an easy way to figure it out."

Heinkel explained his reasoning to William, while Joseph moved his choice of beer in front of him. William looked down at the beer and could feel his stomach churning over at the thought of having to drink another beer in such a short period of time.

"Just give me a minute to let this beer settle in my stomach, before I drink the next one."

William said as he let out a loud burp, as the rest of his friends cheered him on. Though after a couple of minutes of talking with each about how he had judged the previous drink. After some time had passed; and a couple more chips… William was ready to judge the drink that Joseph had brought.

"Now this is called Wellington Imperial Russian Stgut, I don't usually drink beers when I go out for my nightly encounters… But when I'm drinking with my buddies or old friends, this is what I usually get."

Joseph said as he poured half of the beer into a new cup for William to drink out of.

"Thanks for pouring only half of it for me to drink, I don't think I can finish the whole thing after all I've drunk so far."

William said as he slowly sipped this beer, instead of downing it all in a couple gulps like the first one. William finished the beer and tried his best not to vomit the drink back up, since to him it tasted awful, and he just barely held it down.

"Nope, Nope, and nope! I do not like it, and I don't think I'll drink this brand ever again! Three out of ten!"

William shouted as he got up and ran to the kitchen sink, to wash the taste out of his mouth. Once he got the taste out of his mouth, William returned to the living room to ask his next question.

"So you fought everyone that lives here, except for me… Why did you not include me in the fights?"

It took a while for Heinkel to answer William's question, he probably was being careful with his choice of words. Heinkel was always careful with his word when he talked with anyone, except for Joseph who he was brutally honest with.

"When I moved in here four years ago, after I had started my security company with Beraham and Joseph's help. I was told by

Beraham that you were coming out of a bad relationship and you were in a fragile state… You looked like you had a lot going on and a lot of stress on your shoulders. So making you do something as trivial as fighting us seemed rude and not something you needed to add on to your stress."

Heinkel explained to William, but seemed to be slightly happy about something, perhaps when he heard the score that Joseph's beer had scored.

William could tell that Heinkel was speaking the truth, but it felt like he might have left out some details so as to keep his word about not lying.

Though now William was down to one final question, one more beer to drink and judge as well. Heinkel moved forward and placed a can of Okocim Pilsner for William to drink. Heinkel had a serious look across his face as he watched to see if William would like his choice or not. William drank half of the beer, to notice that he didn't feel like he wanted to vomit like the last one. And he actually liked the way it tasted.

"So, how was the beer? And know that I still will answer your question without any bias towards your final judgment."

Heinkel said as he awaited his answer. William took his time to gather his thoughts, not only for the score of the beer, but also for what his final question would be. After long consideration William knew what he wanted to ask.

"So for me I enjoyed Heinkel's drink the best out of the three, the score he got was nine out of ten."

William said, getting mixed reactions of either Heinkel getting up to do a little winners dance, while Lee and Joseph sat down and started to drink their beers silently in defeat.

"Well gentlemen, I do believe that I came out on top again!"

Heinkel said with glee as he opened another of his beers to celebrate his small win. When William mentioned being the top dog of the group, he took his chance to ask the question while he was too busy celebrating his win.

"With the way your flauting that title Heinkel, does that mean that you are the strongest fighter of the group? That you are ranked first in the group?"

Heinkel's expression changed instantly by William's question, and seemed slightly nervous of how to answer that question.

"Ahhh... So the way we ranked ourselves was whoever lost the least amount of fights against each other would be the winner. Joseph lost all of his fights since he would rather talk his way out of a conflict than fight someone."

Heinkel was explaining but took a moment to take a sip of his beer, to then continue the rankings.

"Then it was Lee because he would simply use tricks and distractions, to taze people into submission. I placed myself in second because Lee can't trick me and Joseph is a pushover, and I have years of experience in combat when I was a bodyguard in Germany."

William could understand Lee beating Joseph in a fight, but he was more surprised that Heinkel had lost to Beraham. Did that mean that Beraham is also skilled in combat as well?

"So then how did Beraham beat you? Was Beraham also a skilled bodyguard?"

William asked Heinkel with great interest to know how the fight went down. But Heinkel turned away to hide his expression from William to say,

"Sorry but I only said that I would answer three of your questions, plus Beraham asked that our fight stay between us. Anyway it's getting late so I think we should all head to bed, that way we can sleep off the alcohol by tomorrow."

William wanted to press Heinkel for more information on what happened, but then William realized that it was almost two o'clock in the morning and he had only a couple of hours left before he had to go to work.

"Yeah Heinkel has a point, I need to head to bed or else I'll be so tired when I go to work... But can you make sure that you leave a blanket for Joseph and Lee? They will probably keep drinking till dawn and sleep down here."

William asked as he stumbled over to the staircase so he could go to bed.

"Sure William, and don't worry about getting to work on time. Either Beraham or I will drive you to work."

Heinkel said as he started to clean up the empty beer cans. William gave him a thumbs up and slowly made his way up the stairs. Once William had disappeared up the stairs, Joseph stood up from the arm chair, leaving Lee to just mutter to his beers on the sofa.

Why did you lie about promising Beraham about keeping the fight a secret? Beraham wouldn't really care as long as you didn't say certain details involving the fight."

Joseph asked Heinkel while trying to help him clean up as well.

"When Beraham went to Germany four years ago to recruit me to help him again, I refused and didn't want to take a bodyguard job ever again at the time. Weren't you there to help him when he decided to ask me in person?"

Heinkel asked Joseph who for some reason had an annoyed look on his face. As if he had just remembered something important.

"Wait, yes I was there, and I just remembered that when we arrived you knocked me out!"

Joseph said angrily as he unconsciously rubbed the back of his neck.

"Heh, Oh ya I almost forgot about that part... My bad I was more of a man of action then of words back then. And even then I was not in a very good place, when you guys found me."

Heinkel said with a sadden smile on his face, as he remembered that day very well. And remembered how Beraham was able to save Heinkel from himself.

CHAPTER 6

To Catch and Convince
A Hunter to Join Us

Frankfurt, Germany
Four Years Ago...

"Beraham! Do we really need to enlist this man's help? He already told you no once, so what makes you think you can convince him now?"

Joseph asked as both Beraham and himself made their way through the fall-like forest.

"Because he can help protect William better than anyone I know, He could figure out if William is in trouble before even we would. Plus with the different training he's gone through and his years of experience in the field he is a perfect candidate."

Beraham explained his reasoning to Joseph, while he tried to read the map a local gave to him that would lead to Heinkel's cabin.

"So do you know why Heinkel said no to your offer? And why did he isolate himself out here in the woods like a hermit?"

Joseph inquired as he was stopped suddenly by Beraham's arm, as they stopped in front of a stream that had a small makeshift bridge to cross.

"From what I heard from rumors at his workplace and the town folks, something went wrong with his last client and he took a leave of absence. From what I've been told after escortes died on his watch, he left behind numerous bodies to avenge them."

Beraham said to Joseph as the both of them crossed the makeshift bridge, and continued to follow the directions on the map.

"Still... Why the hell would anyone want to take a vacation all the way out here in the middle of a forest? This makes me feel like we're in a horror movie, and we're about to stumble upon a serial killer."

Joseph complained as he kept looking around the late afternoon, and fall-like forest. Beraham looked back at Joseph with a very annoyed looking expression across his face, at all of Joseph's complaining.

When Joseph saw the expression across his friend's face, he pretended to zip his lips and tossed the key away.

After displaying his silent action, Joseph quickly grabbed the map out of Beraham's hands and walked in the direction that was shown on the map.

"I don't really understand why we're taking such a long trip–!"

Joseph was starting to say but was interrupted when the sound of a rope snapped, and suddenly Joseph was pulled upside down. He hung upside down by the rope around his legs, and swung around aimlessly. Beraham carefully walked over to where Joseph hung, picking up a stick and threw it beside where Joseph would've walked into next. The stick landed on the ground, and not a moment passed before the bear trap snapped shut, breaking the stick into pieces.

When Joseph saw what had happened, he went into a fit of screaming out in distress and frantically swinged around. Beraham sat down on the ground, as he waited for Joseph to calm down and stop swearing like a sailor. After five minutes of endless screaming, swearing, and yelling, Joseph finally quieted himself down and waited silently to swing himself around to face Beraham.

"So the reason why we're taking our time was because you were checking for traps that 'he' setted up?"

Joseph asked Beraham who just responded with a nod of his head.

"Makes sense… Make sense… So are you gonna cut me down now? Because I will pass out after hanging upside down for so long!"

Joseph yelled to Beraham who stood up from where he sat, brushed the leaves and dirt from his clothes. He carefully tip-toed around Joseph so as to not trigger any other traps. And walked over to the tree that was holding Joseph upside down, to slowly undid the knots and lowered him to the ground. Once he was able to get the rope off his legs, he calmly walked over to Beraham to give him back the map.

"Honestly I thought you were gonna just cut the rope and let me drop like a sack of potatoes, Especially with the way I was acting out like that."

Joseph said while Beraham opened the map and was about to start walking but turned back to his friend.

"I did want to drop you down as hard as possible to teach you a lesson, but if you got hurt or knocked unconscious then I would have to drag your idiotic ass to either cabin or back to the village."

Beraham explained in a cold tone to Joseph who just smiled nervously as he followed after him.

After hiking through the forest for almost two hours. Both Beraham and Joseph decided to take a break to rest, before they continued their search for the cabin.

"Fuckin hell, this is such a pain to find his cabin… How can he think that it would be relaxing to walk this far for a cabin?!?"

Joseph vented as he took his hiking boots off to massage his aching feet.

"Why don't you ask him that question when we get there? But it shouldn't take much longer to reach the cabin, perhaps another twenty minutes and we should arrive."

Beraham said as he opened his bag and passed a bottle of water for Joseph to drink. As they bantered amongst the two of them, another man watched them from afar behind a tree. The mystery man undid the strap that held his crossbow on his shoulder, and aimed it carefully towards Joseph's head.

As the mystery man was about to pull the trigger, he felt the glare of a predator's eyes on him. He turned around quickly with his crossbow ready, but when he turned around there was no one around him. When he realized that there wasn't anyone behind him, the man turned back around to find his targets had finished resting and continued on their hike.

The man punched the tree he was hiding behind out of frustration that he missed his targets. Back with Beraham and Joseph, they continued to try and find their way to the cabin without running into any more traps. After twenty minutes of hiking; as Beraham predicted, they arrived at the spot on the map where the cabin would be. The two of them looked around and couldn't find any obvious signs of a cabin in the immediate area.

"Doesn't the map say that the cabin would be right here? Or did we take a wrong turn?"

Joseph asked as he peered over Beraham's shoulder to have a look at the map.

"Yes, it's supposed to be here... But unless we went the wrong way when we took a break at those rocks, I was following the map to a T."

Beraham said as he studied the map and its instructions to see if they followed the correct pathway.

"Hey Besserdechnyy, I think there's a sign or remnants of a broken sign behind that bush."

Joseph said as he walked over to the bush and dragged out a sign that had carved letters on it. They examined the sign, and noticed that it was written in German except for the last two words which were in english.

'Sorry Traveler.'

"Es tut mir leid dass sie ausgetrickst wurden, um in den tod zu sterben… You wouldn't happen to be fluent in German, Besserdechnyy?"

Joseph asked while Beraham put the map away, and took out a German to English dictionary and started to flip through the pages to translate the sign.

"You know, I'm starting to dislike the nickname you gave me… I rather you call me by the name I told you to call me. But from what I can translate from this dictionary the sign says 'We're sorry that you were tricked into coming out here to die'… It seems that the villagers have used us as sacrifices."

Beraham said in a nonchalant tone while Joseph looked around in a panic to see if there was anyone around them.

"Stay calm Joseph, the more we panic and lose our cool the easier it will be for the assailant to kill us."

Beraham said calmly as he scanned through the forest to try and spot anyone. Just as Joseph was about to say another witty remark about their situation, the sound of the wind whistled past Beraham and the sound of a thump moments later.

Beraham quickly turned his head to see that Joseph had a bolt sticking out of his left shoulder. They both looked at each other with a shocked expression across their faces, at seeing the arrow in Joseph's shoulder.

Joseph stumbled forward and fell to his knees, while holding his shoulder trying not to scream from the rush of pain he was in. Breaham quickly grabbed his injured friend by his good shoulder and dragged him behind a tree to act as cover.

"Okay so from what I could gather at the moment, is that the bolt came from behind us since the tip is facing out of your front side instead of the back. And with the lack of follow up to the first shot, it might be just one person."

Beraham quickly explained to Joseph while he rummaged through his bag, and brought out a pack of gauzes.

"Aggghh... Of course you packed bandages, did you predict that we would need bandages for such an occasion?"

Joseph asked as he grit his teeth when Beraham wrapped the bandages around the bolt to slow the bleeding.

"I always need some bandages just in case if someone gets injured or I hurt myself on the job, now keep pressure on the wound and if it bleeds through then just apply another bandage over it."

Beraham instructed Joseph who in turn nodded his head weakly, as he held on to his injured shoulder. After making sure that Joseph was moderately treated and hidden from sight, Beraham stood up and tried to peek from behind the tree to see where the assailant was shooting. He slowly peeked out from behind the tree, when another bolt flew and pierced the tree inches away from Beraham's head.

Beraham took the opportunity to pull the bolt out from the tree and ran to a different tree, while the assailant was presumingly reloading their crossbow.

Once Beraham hid himself as best as he could, he took a moment to study the bolt to confirm the suspicions he had were correct.

The arrow itself was a thin black bolt with a sharp point, and the feathers were a pattern of black, red, and yellow.

"Hmmm... Not enough to confirm it's him just cause the feathers are the same color concept as Germany's flag... It's time I actually started to get serious,"

Breaham said to himself as he pulled out his hunting knife from his back belt, and held the bolt in his other hand as a second weapon.

Beraham took a deep breath in and out, then he turned to the left side of the tree and doubled back to run from the right side of the tree. And just as he hoped the assailant had shot the bolt towards the left side of the tree, missing Beraham completely and giving him an idea of where he was taking shots from.

Beraham saw that the assailant was at least fifteen feet away from him, and was having trouble reloading his crossbow.

Beraham took the opportunity to sprint as fast as he could towards the assailant before he had the time to reload his weapon.

Once Beraham was close enough to see the assailant, he noticed that they were dressed up in a ghillie suit head to toe and were wearing an Oni mask. Beraham decided to make the first move by swinging his hunting knife down towards their shoulder. The assailant quickly sacrificed his crossbow by intercepting the knife with the crossbow, to push Breaham away and took out his own knife from underneath their ghillie suit.

"Good reflexes but I would give you a five out of ten for losing your weapon and falling for my feint before."

Beraham said to his opponent as they circled each other like lions, ready to pounce at a moment's notice. Breaham took the initiative to attack first, by lunging forward to slash at his opponent's arm. But they saw where he was aiming for and sidestepped out of the way, and countered by punching Beraham in the face to then jump back and waited for Beraham's move.

Beraham felt his cheek, running his fingers across where he was punched and burst out laughing. The assailant was momentarily confused by how Beraham was just laughing after being punched.

"Hmmm... Still need a bit more practice, I think I'm still quite rusty since I am actually fighting someone that I can actually lose too. Bear with me since I haven't fought someone seriously in a while so this will hurt... A Lot..."

Beraham said as his smile faded and his expression turned cold and distant. Beraham once again lunged forward to slash at his opponents arm, he was just gonna side step out of the way again. But Beraham was prepared for that and used his other hand that held the bolt, to stab the assailant's upper right arm.

The man screamed out in pain, while swinging his uninjured arm with the knife wildly. Beraham retreated backwards so that he didn't get caught in the wild swinging.

"Not bad but if you're gonna be my bodyguard candidate, you have to rein in that anger of yours, for you're not reaching all of my expectations for you right now."

Beraham said as he paced back and forth while the assailant examined his arm once he calmed down. Once he finished assessing his arm, he pulled the bolt straight out of his arm without hesitation and threw it behind him.

Beraham raised an eyebrow at how aggressive the assailant just pulled the bolt out of his arm, without a single worry or thought for his wounded arm.

"Strange… Usually he isn't this aggressive and restless in any type of situation, especially when he sustains injuries…"

Beraham whispered to himself as the assailant charged towards Beraham, his knife aimed towards Beraham's leg. Beraham let out a sigh of disappointment at the barbaric tactics the assailant was now showing.

Beraham decided to charge at the assailant as well but quickly grabbed some pebbles and leaves, to throw at the assailant's face.

He wasn't expecting the underhanded tactic and by instinct raised his arms to block the pebbles and leaves. Beraham took the opportunity to rush forward while swinging his knife down and stabbed it into the assailant's leg. Then after that, Beraham pulled the knife out and body checked the assailant to the ground. Beraham grabbed his opponent's arm and began slamming his fist into the assailant's wrist over and over again, Beraham could feel a light smack on his back as his opponent tried to defend himself by punching Beraham with his already injured arm.

"You've lost already, so let's stop resisting or else I will have to hurt you into submission if I have too."

Beraham yelled as he was finally able to get him to let go of the knife and flipped the assailant onto his stomach, and held his uninjured arm in arm lock.

"I will not surrender, so just kill me and be done with it quickly!"

The assailant shouted back as he continued to try to break out Beraham's grip, but to no avail with an injured arm and leg.

Beraham let out a sigh, disappointed and saddened by what he knew had to be done.

"How did you lose yourself in this forest? The friend I know would never have made it this easy of a fight, nor fought like a wild beast…"

Beraham said as he raised his knife to the sky, while the man just layed on the ground already accepting his death.

"Sadly I won't be granting your wish today, I need your services so please forgive me Heinkel."

Beraham whispered to Heinkel as he brought the knife hilt first and slammed it against Heinkel's head, knocking him unconscious.

While Beraham was busy fighting with Heinkel, Joseph was trying his best to wrap the bandages around his shoulder with little success.

"Ughh… Why couldn't I have been hit somewhere else? Somewhere that is easier to bandage around it."

Joseph muttered to himself as he grabbed Beraham's backpack that he left behind, to see if there was anything useful to Joseph.

While rummaging through the bag, Joseph found a couple of fruits, granola bars, a first aid kit and three more bottles of water.

"Did you seriously not pack a gun, Beraham??? This is more like you packed for a hiking trip!"

Joseph muttered to himself as he started to feel woozy and quite thirsty.

"Shit, I'm starting to lose it… Probably should drink some more water…"

Joseph said as he grabbed one of the bottles that had a different label on it then the others, but ignored it and downed the water to quench his thirst. After Joseph drank the water he suddenly felt light headed and sluggish.

"What the hell did I just drink?"

Joseph slurred as he struggled to lift the bottle he drank out of, and tried to read the label.

'Don't drink this unless it is used on Heinkel if he is being uncooperative.'

'Oh you gotta be kidd….ing me…"

Joseph barely muttered as he fell unconscious against the tree, while seeing Beraham walking towards him with a man with a ghillie suit on his back. Joseph's last thought before closing his eyes, was wondering if he should've just stayed up home, instead of following Beraham here.

Heinkel slowly opened his eyes after his fight with Beraham, and was surprised that he was able to open his eyes after thinking he had finally died. But he could still feel the pain in his shoulder and leg, so he wasn't dreaming or in some type of limbo. Heinkel looked around to see that he was in his cabin, he also noticed that someone had bandaged and treated his arm and leg injuries. He sat himself up from where he laid on the floor and tried to sort out his thoughts. Just then the front door banged open, to Beraham carrying the person that was with him inside and settled them on the couch.

Heinkel quickly looked around the room to find one of his weapons he kept hidden all around his cabin just in case.

"Just so you know, I moved all your guns and other weapons to the kitchen… And I mean **All** of them so don't try anything funny."

Beraham said with his back turned to Heinkel as he attended to his friend. Heinkel knew that Beraham was telling the truth, since if the roles were reversed he would've done the same thing. Except for treating his opponents wounds like Beraham had done for him.

"Though this is a very nice and secluded cabin you have here Heinkel… It's a pain inthe ass to get here, especially when you have to carry two heavy men that are both injured."

Beraham commented as he turned around holding the oni mask that Heinkel had worn during his fight with his friend.

"This is a rather interesting mask you wore Heinkel, didn't think you were the type to wear such a fancy mask while trying to kill someone."

Beraham said as he tossed the mask back to Heinkel, who just sat there in silence as he caught the mask. Beraham kneeled down in front of Heinkel with a look of sadness in his eyes.

"What happened to you Heinkel? Last I heard from one of my contacts, you were bodyguarding a small CEO for a year and that it was going quite well. Then all of a sudden I get a call from your boss asking if I can cover up a mess you made, where you killed ten people and left the scene without telling anyone where you went."

Beraham said as Heinkel turned away from Beraham to hide the shame across his face. Heinkel stayed quiet for a while as he was unsure how he was going to explain what happened to Beraham.

"Just remember that I am not one to judge your actions Heinkel until I have both sides of the story... Both the report I got from your boss, and the one I want to hear from you."

Beraham said as sat down in front of Heinkel with a neutral expression.

Heinkel took a deep breath in and then out, and then started telling Beraham his story.

"The man I was charged with watching over, was a fairly small business manager who was getting numerous threats, so he asked our company to protect him and his family. At first it was a good, easy and simple job that there were times we reduced our security staff on smaller outings like for restaurants or grocery shopping."

"But then one afternoon the family wanted to eat dinner out at this new restaurant his wife had found. We wanted to push it to another day so that we could have a better idea of the location and hadn't swapped our details that day either as we were all pretty tired."

"But I guess your client didn't want to follow your advice?"

Beraham asked and in turn Heinkel nodded his head to answer his question.

"He thought that since they weren't getting too many threatening messages of any kind, so he said that just a quick dinner wouldn't really be too bad for us to get done quickly... We had arrived at the restaurant with two of my colleagues and myself. I sent my colleagues to quickly conduct a sweep of the restaurant, they went inside and I waited with the client and his family in the car."

Heinkel continued to explain but he paused for a moment, as his expression softened for a moment. As if he had recalled something good or remembered someone.

"While I worked under this client he had a son named Jakob who was such a nice kid who had dreams of playing in the league for Germany when he got older… Anyways once my colleagues gave the all clear we got out and headed towards the restaurant."

Heinkel quivered as he became nervous and nauseous about what he would have to tell next. He looked up at Beraham who still was intently listening to him, with absolute focus.

"Jakob stopped us because we had been talking about his soccer player cards, and he had recently obtained a rather rare card so he asked if he could go and grab it from the car. I was gonna tell him we can look at it after we had left the restaurant, but his father said that he could go get it as long as I went with him… I truly regret that I agreed to leave with them…"

Heinkel said as he remembered the screaming, the gunshots and the actions he did that afternoon.

"Jeez Jakob you know that we have plenty of time to once were done eating to look at these,"

Heinkel said to Jakob while the little boy was too fascinated by the sports card in his hand to hear Heinkel talking to him.

"Kids these days, they're always glued to their phones… But you Jakob are glued to that soccer card."

"Well you said that when you were younger you collected a lot of rocks with your friends so what's so different about my obsession?"

Jakob asked innocently, making Heinkel not know how to respond to that type of question. The young boy gave Heinkel a smug smile at rendering his father's bodyguard speechless.

As the two of them approached the restaurant the sound of gunfire rang out and people ran out of the restaurant. Heinkel's instincts instantly took over and he immediately picked up Jakob and ran back to the car to place him inside since the windows were bullet proof.

"Mom! Dad! Where are they!?!?"

Jakob shouted as he was thrust into the car and was locked inside.

Heinkel looked around to make sure no one was heading towards the car, before he sprinted towards the restaurant with great urgency to see what had happened. When Heinkel entered the store he was in utter shock of what he saw.

Two of his co-workers were shot dead on the ground, while one of the new recruits stood in front of their clients with a gun in his hand and nine men wearing ski masks surrounded them.

"Shit, your boss is here, what do we do about him? He had the kid with him..."

One of the masked men said as he tapped Heinkel's co-workers shoulder.

Heinkel went pale as he realized what was about to happen in that next moment, he was about to react when the sound of the gun rang out two times.

"I guess we will have to kill him and the kid outside as well since the client doesn't want the kid to grow up and wants vengeance."

His co-worker said with a sadistic grin across his face as Jakob's parents both flopped to the floor without another sound. Heinkel looked down at the clients he was in charge of protecting, to his colleagues who looked like they were also shot in the back. And when he heard them mention Jakob's name Heinkel felt something inside of him break, and he felt something that he hadn't felt since he was a child. As soon as the first masked man walked up to him and grabbed his shoulder, Heinkel's vision went dark and the next he was standing over nine dead bodies and little Jakob was staring at him from the front door with a scared expression on his face.

"So from what I gather from you, is that your colleague was paid off to follow and kill the whole family as soon as you were rotated off his shift, or when an opportunity presented itself?"

Beraham asked for clarification from Heinkel as he finished his story.

"Yes, one of the client's upper bosses wanted him gone since he was going to get promoted before he was, so they decided to just kill him off... When they were gonna go after Jakob I went and went into a trance and killed them all with minimum injuries. But Somehow little Jakob had found a way to open the door and wandered over to see the astroasidies I had committed to all his parents murderers."

Heinkel said as tears started to run down his face when he mentioned Jakob's name.

"You had probably used your powers back then, or else how else were you able to kill all those men with minimum injuries?"

Beraham said as he moved himself in front of Heinkel and offered him a tissue.

"Remember all those years ago when you had first offered me these powers, Herzlos? To track anyone down as easily as a bloodhound, or to be able to reveal and materialize someone's deepest fears so that I could be a better protector? You said that this power would be both a blessing but also a curse to reveal to someone?"

Heinkel asked as he accepted the tissue from Beraham, who in turn nodded his head to answer his friend's question.

"Jakob... He must have seen moments of my powers since, normally, anyone that witnesses them in action is instilled with fear so that I can easily deal with them... But after that incident, Jakob couldn't speak or respond to others. He has been treated at a hospital since then, and all because of me... A boy that has always been talking about playing in the pro leagues of football, stopped talking to anyone and is too scared to talk to them..."

"The worst thing is that he keeps on having these nightmares of that day, and he draws what he sees and it's mostly a monstrous version of me and the litter of bodies surrounding me."

Heinkel said as his voice faltered when he described Jakob's condition.

Beraham reached over and grabbed the whole box of tissues to sit down in front of Heinkel on his left side so that he could easily grab them. And Beraham scooted over to his friend to pull him into a hug. Heinkel silently cried into his friend's shoulder, and let out all the emotions he had hidden for the past year.

"So I'm guessing with that sign that we found before you started to shoot all those bolts at us, you set yourself up to be some type of mythical legend for the villagers?"

Beraham whispered to Heinkel as they were still hugging.

"Yes, I brought the people that had hired the hit on Jakob's parents, and made up some rumors that they were mauled by bears or wolves when they had decided to have a company trip to the village. The villagers were quite cooperative with helping me with the narrative, that they would send any criminals to this forest to be killed by me. When justice couldn't be served the legal way."

Heinkel said as his expression darkened, and got out of the hug to try and stand himself back up again.

"Woah! Now let's not do anything hastily, even though I avoided cutting your arteries that doesn't mean that should put weight on your injured leg."

Beraham warned as he made Heinkel sit back down before he attempted to stand up.

"Aghh... Fine but can you grab that brown notebook from the coffee table over by your friend?"

Heinkel asked as he pointed to where the was located.

"Is this a list of all the people you had to kill during your time here in the forest? Because it took a lot of convincing to get a map drawn out to find your cabin from the villagers, so I guessed they were worried that we were here to arrest you."

Breaham said as he walked to the table and picked up the notebook. When Beraham walked back to give the notebook to his friend, Heinkel shook his head and motioned for him to read it. Beraham opened the book, and noticed that there were many pages filled with names of criminals and the crimes they had committed.

"I count at least twenty names in this book alone, how did you manage to keep yourself hidden and under the radar?"

Beraham asked while closing the book and tapping the front of the book.

"This forest has many rumors about it being a place that many hikers get lost for weeks in, and sadly some run into wild animals or have been buried somewhere around here."

Heinkel said with a small smile that felt forced.

"This is really the only way I can atone and forgive myself for not only failing my employers but for what I did to Jakob."

Beraham studied Heinkel looking him up then down as if trying to answer a question he had for himself.

Beraham went over to his bag and produced a folder with multiple papers inside it, and a pen as well while he said.

"I believe that I can help you Heinkel, that's why I came all the way out here with Joseph to hire you for your services."

Heinkel slowly grabbed the folder to open it and read through the contents of the contract, he raised an eyebrow while reading what was required of him and what his roles were.

"So from what I am reading here is that I need to protect, socialize with the client and be ready to track him down at a moment's notice?"

Heinkel asked Beraham in disbelief by what was seemingly an easy job.

"Yes, that and you will not mention that you are under a contract to protect the client William. Nor will you treat him like you would any client, but more like a roommate or friend. Oh and also you will be living with him like the rest of us that are a part of this team."

Breaham answered as he motioned his head towards the sofa, where his friend was still lying unconscious and snoring away in his sleep.

"I don't know how ethical it is to liv— Wait, that isn't Joseph on my couch is it? That damn Russian womanizer who always ends up getting in trouble with the Russian mob a while ago... Is it?"

Heinkel asked as Joseph turned in his sleep to let out a loud fart, making both Heinkel and Beraham groan in disgust by the smell.

"Don't worry about his past, I already sorted that out, plus he is now under a contract that is similar to yours so he won't be getting into any illegal trouble for that matter."

Beraham said to Heinkel while walking over to Joseph to lightly tap on Joseph's foot to wake him up. Joseph barely stirred in his sleep from the tap on his foot.

"Did he lose too much blood from when I shot him? Or is he just that delicate when he gets hurt?"

Heinkel asked in a more insulting tone then out of concern after finding out who that was, lying on his couch.

"Actually no... Joseph knows how to take a bullet, or I guess a bolt for this situation. But it seems like he drank my plan B for you if my first plan didn't work."

"Wait a second, you were going to drug me??? Then why the heck didn't you just do that instead of fighting me?"

Heinkel asked his friend in disbelief what his plans were.

"Well in all honesty you did fire the first shot, plus it seemed like you were in a daze or a shadow of yourself when we fought... But that's besides the point."

Beraham quickly said then switched the topic back to the contract,

There will be a set of rules that you will have to abide by in the contract, You'll also get to run your own security firm as both a cover and as a means of making money. You will of course have full control of how to design and run the firm under your discretion."

While Beraham was discussing with Heinkel, he brought out a couple of photographs of the building where the firm would be located and the blueprints and deeds of ownerships. Heinkel studied the photos and blueprints, and he could already imagine how he would run the firm to be the best of the best worldwide.

Heinkel looked up to see the look of victory written across Beraham's face. Heinkel tried to hide his excitement from Beraham, just so that he wouldn't assume that he was gonna accept the contract so easily.

"This is a very good job offer you set up for me Herzlos... save the fact that I have to work with Joseph, it's practically a perfect gig. But what are you willing to do if I had special conditions that needed to be done before I sign the contract?"

Heinkel asked as he kept his business face on, to see if Beraham how far Beraham was willing to go to hire him.

Though Beraham's expression lit up at the mention of special conditions, or the fact that He was close to having Heinkel sign the contract. Heinkel let out a chuckle, making Beraham give him a confused look and questioned why Heinkel was laughing.

"You always have this look in your eye when you close a deal, like a look of excitement when a child gets to buy his favorite food."

Heinkel explained making Beraham hide his face at this rare moment of embarrassment that rarely ever occurred.

"Moving on to those special conditions you were talking about, is one of them for me to make little Jakob forget that he ever witnessed your powers?"

Beraham asked as turned back to face Heinkel with a neutral expression. He was spot on with his guessing, Heinkel knew that Beraham's powers and influence could instantly solve Jakob's problems.

"Yes you are spot on with my first condition, which is non-negotiable for me. I will also be in charge of the hiring progress of who can join my security force and who won't be joining. And lastly whoever you hire onto your team must fight me just so that I can assess their fighting capabilities."

Heinkel explained his three conditions to Beraham.

"The first two conditions I can accept and get them done in the next little while, But the last one that involves little Jakob. For me to cure him I would need to erase all memories of him witnessing your powers as well as meeting you Heinkel.

But other than that Heinkel, do we have a deal?"

Beraham asked while putting out his hand to see if Heinkel would accept the deal. Heinkel sat there mulling over the contract to make sure he didn't forget anything to add to his contract. Then Heinkel gave Beraham his answer,

"Alright it's a deal, I'll help you to the best of my abilities with this Wiliam kid."

"Huh, interesting that you don't recognize him…"

Beraham whispered under his breath as he shook Heinkel's hand.

"So do you have a pen I can use to sign the contract? Or did you also hide those as well in the kitchen?"

Heinkel asked as he went through the papers that he had to sign his signature.

Beraham let out a cough as he carefully took out a pen from his jacket, to give to Heinkel.

"Honestly I did move them to the kitchen as well since I watched that movie Jon Wick. I would rather not have you stab me in the eye if you were still in that killer mode state."

Heinkel was confused that Beraham had hidden the pens that he didn't even know he had in his cabin, but dismissed it since he didn't want to get into that conversation with Beraham. Just as he was about to sign the contract, he noticed there was a small snag that was needed before he signed.

"You do realize that we need a witness to sign this contract. Joseph is still knocked unconscious, so maybe you should go and wake him up."

Heinkel suggested to Beraham who nodded and got himself up to go and wake up his loud snoring friend. Beraham kneeled down right beside Joseph's ear to whisper something to him. As soon as he finished whispering, Joseph's eyes shot open and sat himself up looking around frantically.

"W-where the fuck am I? And why the hell did you spike one of the bottles with my sleeping pills that I take???"

Joseph quickly asked in a frantic state, then groaning in pain since the drug's effects faded away and the shoulder pains returned with a vengeance.

""Okay one, calm yourself Joseph, you're in a safe place. And two I need you to sign and witness Heinkel sign his contract."

Beraham quickly explained as he motioned to Heinkel to start signing the documents.

"Wait a second, weren't the two of you fighting each other last time I saw you? Also I feel like I was body slammed by a football player."

Joseph complained out loud as Heinkel finished signing all the required documents, to hand over to Beraham who in turn also started to sign them as well.

"There we go… Now all we need is for Joseph to sign his signature, and we can leave here and head back to Canada."

Beraham said as he assisted Joseph with the pen and papers to make it easier on him to sign it. Joseph slowly signed the documents to make sure that all was in order, and once they were, Beraham stored them back into the folder for safe keepings.

"You better keep your end of the agreement Herzlos, or else I won't follow your orders,"

Heinkel stated as he slowly stood himself up with the help of an armchair, to give Beraham a death stare.

"It's disappointing that you have such little confidence and faith in me to not keep my word. After all the years we grew up together and worked with each, you would trust me Heinkel."

Beraham said with a sad expression across his face, but changed to a serious one when he spoke again to Heinkel.

"I give you my word that I will do whatever it takes to complete the conditions you gave to me."

"Well then, if we're all done with all the deadly staring contests, and subtle threats.

I would love for us to leave this forest so that I can get proper medical attention to not let this scar."

Joseph piped in to break the tension between the both of them. Beraham broke off the stare first to check his watch for the time.

"Sadly by the time we leave now it's gonna be midnight soon, and if I have to carry two injured men as well it's going to take forever to get there in the dark."

Beraham explained as he made his way into Heinkel's kitchen while taking his jacket off.

"Will sleep here for the night, then will leave in the morning since you guys don't have life threatening injuries. For now let's see what we can do for dinner shall we?"

Breaham shouted from the kitchen as the sound of shelves opening, the fridge rattling open, pots and pans clacking together.

"I caught an elk just yesterday so the meat should be in the fridge, plus there should be some pasta and mushrooms you can use."

Heinkel yelled back as he sat himself down in the arm chair he was leaning on. Since he couldn't stand for much longer, after making himself look assertive in front of Beraham. Heinkel quickly checked to see what Joseph was doing, who was starting to fall back asleep. Heinkel quickly grabbed Beraham's bag and searched through it to find his folder that had his contract and two other folders.

He noticed that one was labeled 'Joseph's contract,' while another was labeled 'William's profile.' Heinkel took out William's profile, to read up on his soon to be client as to better prepare for his protection.

As he read through the multiple pages on William, he didn't notice anything out of the ordinary about his family or education background.

But when Heinkel turned to William's psychological evaluation, he noticed that it was Beraham who had conducted the evaluation. From what he read in Breaham's notes was that William had developed numerous different types of phobias, due to constant bullying, having trouble with socializing with other people. When he read the list of Phobias that William had developed, Heinkel let out a gasp of surprise by what he read. Joseph heard his gasp and turned around to see what Heinkel was doing, to immediately signal to Heinkel to put the file back in Beraham's bag.

"Don't mention anything you just read in front of Beraham or else he will immediately null and void your contract!"

Joseph whispered quickly to Heinkel, who put the folder back into Beraham's backpack.

"Was what I just read in there true?"

Heinkel asked quietly, and Joseph nodded his head to confirm his question.

"It is true, Beraham thinks that we shouldn't know everything about what happened to William after we all went our separate ways back then. That and the fact that William is a part of his own contract."

Joseph whispered but stopped when he saw Beraham walking back into the living room with a large ladle in his hand.

"Well I just put the meat on and the pasta is going to be another twenty minutes, so dinner will be served soon."

Breaham said as he watched Heinkel and Joseph like a hawk, noticing how they both looked uncomfortable.

"I hope that we are all able to get along gentlemen, if not for the job... Do it for William."

Beraham said as he turned around and headed back to the kitchen to continue to cook their dinner. Once he left the room Joseph turned back to Heinkel to whisper to him.

"Please forget what you just read for now, I'll explain all of it once we find Lee and get him on board with all this."

Heinkel was going to demand that Joseph explain it to him now, but he saw the desperation in his friend's eyes.

"Fine, but you better do a good job in explaining or else how can I protect this kid if there are secrets being hidden from me."

Heinkel whispered back to Joseph who looked quite relieved by his answer. But in the back of Heinkel's brain he wondered what sort of job he signed himself into with Beraham. And he would need to protect his new client.

CHAPTER 7

A Hard day's work, Especially after a Night of Drinking is Hard

William woke up in his bed with a killer headache, Bianca jumped up onto the bed to greet William as soon as he woke up.

"Aghh… Morning Bianca, Just be careful since I don't feel too good right now,"

William grumbled as he lifted his dog into the air so that she wouldn't give him any more kisses. Just then there was a knock at the door, and Beraham walked in with a glass of water.

"Good morning William, I thought you might want a glass of water and aspirin to get you through the morning headaches."

Breaham said as he walked over to leave the pill and glass of water on William's night stand.

"William grumbled as he placed Bianca beside him and took the aspirin and water.

"What time do you need to be at work today Will? Because I will give you a lift to the pool so that you don't have to rush out the door on your bike. Especially after last night's drinking."

Beraham asked as he looked at the time on his watch.

"I have an afternoon shift so it will give me some time to deal with my hangover, and I'll definitely take you up on that ride."

William said as he slowly got out of his bed while Bianca happily jumped from the bed to waddle over to Beraham's feet to get some belly rubs from him.

"I wouldn't worry too much Will, you're not the only one having a rough morning… And honestly you are handling it alot better than the rest of the guys."

Beraham said to William before leaving his room with Bianca so that he could get changed and ready for the day. After he finished getting changed William slowly made his way down the steps to the second floor, where he could hear someone yelling.

"Agghhh… The bloody alcohol betrayed me!"

The voice yelled out from the bathroom as William went over to check on whoever it was inside. When he got to the door he found Lee hugging the toilet, vomiting everything he had eaten or drank last night.

William approached Lee and waited for him to finish vomiting before he spoke.

"Are you doing alright Lee? Because it seems like you continued to drink more after I left, since you're hugging this toilet like your life depends on it."

"Aghhh… Yeah me and Joseph had a drinking contest to see who could tolerate the alcohol the longest before they passed out."

"So who won?"

William asked as he filled up his cup of water with the bathroom sink, and handed it over to Lee to drink.

"Thank you for that, but that's the thing Will, we don't know who won since I can't remember who won and Joseph is still asleep in his bed, oh god!"

Lee was telling William, but was interrupted by his body needing to throw up again. William decided to leave the washroom since Lee was probably going to be there for most of the day. As he was passing by Joseph's room, William noticed that Joseph had buried himself under blankets and pillows to keep the sunlight from hitting his face. William could hear Joseph's snoring from within the numerous blankets and pillows that he was covered with.

William closed Joseph's door to try and dampen the echoing sounds of Lee's vomiting. Once the door was closed William turned around to see that Heinkel was walking by him wearing a pair of sunglasses, and nodded to William.

"Are you doing alright Heinkel? Maybe you shouldn't go into work today since you kinda look like shit."

William asked as the both of them headed downstairs, passing by the living room where Beraham was watching the news while petting Bianca in his lap. They headed into the kitchen where Heinkel grabbed the coffee maker.

"Mach dir keine sorgen, mir geht es gut. I have had worse hangovers than last night William so don't worry."

Heinkel said as he saw the time and grabbed his briefcase that he used for work.

"Sounds good Heinkel, I'll be giving William a lift to work, plus I'll also pick him up after work. So can you do me a favor and start making dinner when you get home?"

Beraham asked as he walked into the kitchen to say goodbye to Heinkel. Heinkel in turn answered with a grunt then walked to the front door to leave for work.

William started his search for something that he could easily eat in the kitchen, since he had to be careful with whatever ate. Since he wasn't too sure if his stomach could handle it at the moment.

As if he read William's mind, Beraham walked over to the fridge to grab a cantaloupe.

"Go lay on the couch, while I cut up some cantaloupe for you to munch on. Since it always helps me when I have a hangover to eat some cantaloupe."

Beraham said as he placed the fruit on the kitchen island so that he could cut it up. William decided not to make a fuss since he didn't have the energy to decline Breaham's offer.

When William sat himself down on the couch, Bianca immediately moved to her owner and the little dog made itself at home in his lap.

"Can I ask why your hangover food is a cantaloupe Beraham?" William asked as he showered his dog with belly rubs, while Beraham started cutting up the fruits into cubes to eat.

"Well, the reason is because when I had my first hangover at a staff social hosted by one of my co-workers. That night I had drunk too much whisky causing me to vomit all along his outdoor balcony."

Beraham started to explain to his friend as he continued to cut up the fruit, as he continued his story.

"I was overwhelmed by what I did to his deck, that in my drunken state I went all the way down to the kitchen on the first floor to fill up my glass with water. Then took that cup back upstairs to the balcony to try and clean it."

Beraham let out a chuckle as he reminisced in the memory he was remembering.

"That's kinda hard for me to imagine you being drunk Beraham… Especially since the only times I've seen you drink alcohol I could count them on one hand."

William said as he played peek-a-boo with his dog's paws. The sound of Beraham placing the knife down, to bring the fruit on a plate for William to eat in the living room.

"Here, eat it while it's still cold. It's quite juicy so you'll be able to have some liquid in your body in the meantime."

Beraham said as he put the plate down and passed William a fork to eat it. William was a bit skeptical about eating it, and he was prepared to run to the washroom if he was feeling sick. He slowly nibbled on a small piece, to his surprise he quite enjoyed the taste.

"Now that's the same expression I had when I ate cantaloupe after my biggest hangover. Though eat it slowly Will, just so then you don't upset your stomach."

Beraham suggested as he munched on a couple of pieces as well.

"Hey Beraham, why did you drink so much that night in your story? Because even last night you barely drank anything except the two drinks you made for yourself?"

William asked him since the story piqued his interest in hearing about Beraham's past. But when William looked towards his friend, he noticed that Beraham's expression had pain and sadness written across his face.

"Sadly Will, I would rather not tell you the rest of that story right now… But maybe one day when I'm more comfortable about talking about it, I'll tell you the rest of it."

Beraham said as he got up from the sofa, to leave the room without another word to William.

———————— ❖ ————————

After taking a short nap, plus being able to eat the lunch that Beraham had made for him without throwing up. William got his work bag together so that he was prepared to head to work once Beraham was ready to take him.

William double checked his bag to make sure everything he needed was in there, and once he made sure that everything was in there he headed over to Beraham's room on the second floor to see if he was ready to take William to work.

As William was about to knock on the door, he could hear Beraham on the phone with someone. William decided to listen in on the conversation since Beraham was a man who kept a lot of secrets from both his friends and everyone around him.

"Hey are you the person that Heinkel suggested calling to make an appointment with no questions asked?"

Beraham asked from inside his room while he was on the phone. William was even more keen on listening to this conversation since it now involved Beraham's health.

"I know we were scheduled to meet the day after tomorrow, but I'm pressed for time and was wondering if you're able to do it today?"

Beraham asked the caller while the sound of footsteps could be heard approaching the door. William quickly knocked on the door so as to not get himself caught.

"Great, so I'll meet you at the place that you just suggested after I drop off a friend at his workplace, see you soon."

Beraham said as he opened the door and ended his phone call as he left his room to see William waiting for him.

"Hey are you good to go? Or do you need to do something else? Because I can take the bus if you do."

William asked quickly as he knew that he was being quite obvious that we might have heard Beraham on the phone. Breaham's eyes narrowed at the question that he was asked, but soon it softened after a few moments.

"Will, If I had any issues or problems, I would tell you that I need something from you."

Beraham said with a grin while he passed William a helmet to wear, urging him to follow Breaham to get going to work.

As they were leaving, they noticed that Joseph and Lee had made their way to the couch with coffee in their hands.

"I'll be gone for a couple of hours, so remember to feed Bianca and take her out for walks every so often once you get over your hangover."

Beraham reminded the two of them, making them both flinch at Beraham's voice.

"We... Will do that, once we stop seeing double Berahams..."

Joseph whispered as he weakly put his hand up to get Lee to give him a high five. But Lee just flipped Joseph off and went back to slowly slurping down his coffee.

"Alright... So let's hit the road William,"

Beraham said as he opened the front door and grabbed his keys to his motorcycle. Before he followed after Beraham, William realized that he almost forgot to say goodbye to his dog.

"I'll be right there, I just need to say goodbye to Bianca and at least leave some food for her before I go."

William said to Beraham, who just shrugged his shoulders, then left through the front door to get his motorcycle ready.

After William had refilled Bianca's water bowel and half filled her food bowl. Beaham drove William towards Toronto's lakeshore on his motorcycle in as few as twenty minutes. Beraham turned into the parking lot that was close to William's workplace to make it easier for him to walk there. William got off his friend's bike and wanted to thank Beraham for the ride to work.

"Thanks for the ride Breaham, I'll take the subway back home once my shift is finished tonight."

William said as he held up his fist for Beraham to fist pump. Breaham obliged the fist pump as he stored the helmet that he lent to William.

"Sounds good… I also packed another aspirin into your bag, just in case you have another bad headache. And remember to drink plenty of water as well!"

Breaham said to William once he finished putting the helmet away.

"I'll keep that in mind, have a good day Beraham and remember to take care of yourself."

William said to Beraham and walked towards the pool for his shift. William looked back once more to see Breaham speeding off, out of the parking lot and onto the highway that was heading downtown.

"Hopefully you're not trying to carry the world on your shoulders all by yourself."

William whispered to himself as he climbed the steps to enter the pool through the emergency exit gate the staff used. William walked across the deck to the building that had the staff's lockers and pool incharges office. He noticed that one of his bosses was pouring the chlorine, and the rest of the chemicals required into the pool to meet the city standards.

"Hey William, how are you feeling for this evening's shift?"

The pool-incharge asked him as she put the pool's cleaning shark back in the storage closet.

"I'm good, I might have a small headache from an evening of drinking with my roommates."

William explained as he noticed some of his co workers leaving the staff room, talking amongst themselves. William watched them head down the deck towards the building that housed the pool's change room, to clean it up before the patrons arrived.

"Don't worry about rushing over to help clean the change room William, Orion and the rest of them will get it cleaned up. So take your time and get yourself ready for guarding."

William's boss said as she went back into the pool in-chrages office to finish up her checklist.

William nodded his head, heading into the staff locker room to get changed into his lifeguard uniform and swim trucks.

William decided to head down to the pool deck toward change rooms to see if he could help his co-workers clean up. William entered and could hear his co workers talking and laughing amongst themselves. William took a deep breath and hyped himself up for the amount of socializing he will need to get through the day.

"Hey guys! How was this morning? Was it very busy?"

William asked with enthusiasm, as he saw that it was Matthew, Orion and his sister Margret, Sonya, Warren and Annie.

"It was alright… Nothing much happened besides a minor nosebleed, while the lane swims were going on."

Warren explained to William as he finished scrubbing the shower room floors.

"Yeah, Juliana and Soya took care of it pretty quickly so we didn't even need to stop the lane swim to take care of it."

Margret added as she headed into the staff lounge to grab a snack, before her afternoon shift started.

"Enough about our day, how was your day William? Because you look quite tired."

Orion asked as he removed his disposable gloves to throw into the garbage can.

"I'm just tired from last night, I was drinking a couple of beers with my roommates. So this morning I was just getting over a mild hangover."

William replied to Orion's question, while also getting a couple gasps from his other co-workers.

"William, how much did you drink in one night? You told me that at best you like to drink a maximum of two beers on a work night."

Warren said as he headed out of the shower room and went to go and store the mop back in the storage room at the front.

William let out a small chuckle at Warren's good memory, and was going to explain his night with his roommates. But was interrupted by the last three lifeguards walking into the lounge with their dinner containers to be put into the fridge.

"Hey guys, just to let you guys know Mary Jane and Julianna told us that we have ten minutes before we open the pool. So just make sure to refill your water bottles or finish eating, and be ready to guard."

One of William's other co-workers said as the three of them walked past everyone to store their food in the fridge.

"Then I'm gonna see if I can leave early since I've been feeling quite tired so far during this shift."

Annie said excitedly as she quickly rushed out of the room and back up the pool deck. After she left everyone else started getting ready to leave as well, except for Margret who was still eating her salad.

"Margret, don't take too long with your salad, we don't want to wait on you when Mary Jane and Julianna ask where you are for a huddle."

Orion reminded his sister as everyone started to file walk out onto the pool deck with the rest of the staff. William decided to wait outside the room for Margret, just so then if she was late that she wouldn't be the only one in trouble. Two minutes later, Margret walked out of the staff lounge and was surprised to see that William was waiting for her.

"Hey Will, why were you waiting for me?"

Margret asked him as the both of them started to walk out of the change room building, to walk onto the pool deck where everyone else was waiting at the deep end of the pool.

"I thought that you might want someone to chat to while we head back to the office and get ready to guard the pool."

William answered as he noticed that everyone was waiting for the two of them to get there.

"But still, you don't have to wait for me William, or else then will both be late to our assigned positions."

Margret replied back to him just as they were about to make it to where everyone else was.

"Well you're right, but I wanted to get to know you better as colleagues. Since we will be working together for the whole summer."

William explained to the best of his abilities since he didn't want to give the wrong impression to her.

"Sure I wouldn't mind, but let's wait till the water polo team comes to their practice in the evening, since we will have a half hour dinner break before they start. So let's talk then."

Margret suggested as the two of them joined the rest of the group and went on their own separate ways, to join the different group of friends.

The group of lifeguards waited till the gatekeepers at the front called to say that the patrons had arrived and would be on the deck in a couple minutes.

William checked the schedule board to see where he was positioned. And he saw that he would be guarding for forty five minutes across three different stations, then be on the first aid bench for fifteen minutes after that.

"Hey William, we were wondering where you went when you weren't behind us, but then we see that you're walking back with my twin sister."

Orion said, as Warren and Orion patted William on the shoulder.

"Yeah I waited for her so that she wouldn't get into trouble by herself if she was late, and I wanted to get to know her better like you guys."

William said as he felt like Orion and Warren would misunderstand the situation.

"Well then you can count on us to help you get to know her, so if you need advice just ask us."

Orion said with a warm smile across his face, while Warren nodded in agreement.

"Thanks guys, I—"

William began to say but was interrupted by Mary Jane shouting to everyone to get their attention.

""Patrons on deck guys! Let's get to our chairs quickly before any of the kids try to jump in!"

Everyone rushed to grab their rescue tubes and speed walked to their positions, to allow the patrons to hop into the water. William climbed up his chair to sit down in the tall guard chair. He noticed once he was sitting, that Margret was right across from him sitting in another guard chair.

She waved to him and gave a smile when there were only ten patrons in the water so far. William responded by putting his hand up to give her a thumbs up, before focusing back on the pool and its occupants in his area of sight.

William thought to himself that he should practice talking with Joseph or Beraham about how to be more confident with talking to people. Then another thought came into his head, how is everyone at home dealing with their hangover's either at work or at home.

After Beraham dropped off William at the pool, he drove downtown to meet with Heinkel's employee to get a private check up. That way Beraham can get Eve off his back about his fainting spell at her home, and also oversee whatever information gets recorded and make sure that his secrets won't be discovered. When he arrived at the building he was meeting the person Heinkel had tasked with helping Beraham. He parked his motorcycle in the front of the building on the street, and then made his way into the building.

As Beraham entered the building, he noticed a woman that was sitting on a bench near the entrance getting up when he walked in.

The woman looked Beraham up and down, then stuck her hand out for a handshake.

"Huh, Heinkel said that you guys aren't brothers… and yet you both have such similar faces, like you might be very distant cousins."

The woman said as Beraham shook her hand.

"Yes we have been mistaken for each other, but really we just happened to have one of those common looking faces."

Beraham answered as she escorted him to the elevator to get to the place where the check up was to happen. They silently waited in the elevator to reach the floor, Beraham noticed that the elevator never stopped once as they headed up.

"Did Heinkel send everyone home early or not to come into work today?"

Beraham asked as more of a joke but the woman wasn't laughing.

"Heinkel didn't ask us to, but I thought that since Heinkel asked me for such a rather private and need to know favor. I thought it was best to have everyone in this building to have the day off or work from home."

The women explained as the elevator pinged to notify them that they had reached the correct floor. The two of them walked out into one of Heinkel's cyber security teams office floors, towards the back of the room where a bigger office was located.

"I forgot to ask but what might your name be? I know you're one of Heinkel's workers but what do you do for him?"

Beraham asked as they stopped in front of the door that led to a bigger office from the rest of the cubicles.

"My name is Grace Monroe, Vice president of Heinkel's security firm and former army medic."

Grace said as she tilted her head to the plaque on the office door. Beraham hid his surprise in front of her, since it had been quite awhile since he was caught off guard by someone.

"It's great to meet you Ms. Monroe, and I am in your very capable hands for today."

Beraham said as he walked into her office, he could hear her say something under breath as she walked in behind Beraham.

"I'll tell you this right now Beraham, what I am doing here today is a one time favor to Heinkel since he helped me years ago. So you better not think I'm like your underground doctor you go to every time you get hurt, do you understand?"

Grace stated as she remained serious and stern about what she told him.

"I understand Ms. Monroe so don't worry I won't be calling you unless it's to ask where Heinkel is, also most of the stuff you will be performing today is all normal tests you would do at a doctors office.

You will just be plugging all the information and test results into the hospital data place to make it look like I went to a hospital to be checked out."

Beraham said as he was trying to assure Grace that he only had good intentions.

"As long as you understand that this is a one time favor, we can get started by checking your heart rate."

Grace said as she reached out to check Beraham's pulse by his wrist.

Before she even touched Beraham's wrist, he pulled back as if her hands were snakes trying to bite him.

"That is a rather simple task for you to do, why don't you do a different task that takes a longer time to complete?"

Beraham suggested as he tinkered and fiddled with his sleeves.

Grace studied him while standing in front of him, trying to figure out how to proceed from here.

"It might seem like a trivial test to do since you're still young but, this is both a basic and necessary test to rule out certain aspects of your health."

Grace explained to Beraham the importance of it, and he let out a sigh of anguish before he spoke again.

"You're right, you're the doctor here so you'll know what's best for me."

Beraham took off his long sleeve to make it easier for Grace to perform her examinations. She approached Beraham's arm once more to check his pulse with his wrist then with the testscope on his back and chest. She listened closely to his breathing, but noticed that his heart beat was quite faint to hear. As if it wasn't even there, or was even beating in his chest.

"Does any of your family members have a history of heart problems?"

Grace asked with concern in her voice as she continued to listen to his heart.

"No, as far as I know my family hasn't had any trouble with any cardiac issues or any diseases related to the heart."

"Have you experienced any dizzy spells or lost consciousness recently? Or had an increased heart rate after something stressful at work, home, anything of the sort?"

Grace continued to ask him questions, which Beraham always hated to answer personal questions about himself.

"I have had headaches every now and again, but it's nothing that some medication can fix."

Beraham answered with half truths to Grace's questions, since he didn't want to talk about his fainting yesterday or the many nightmares he recently had about his past either.

Grace finished her assessment of Beraham's pulse, and decided to move on to the next assessment.

"Alright, can you stick your tongue out for me? Or is that also too much for you to do?"

Grace asked as she put away her testscope to pull out a popsicle stick.

"Oh aren't you funny one Ms... I can already see that this is going to be a great day for the both of us."

Beraham said sarcastically to Grace, as he remembered another reason why he hated check ups.

"Trust me, I will try to be as quick and efficient as medically ethical as I'm allowed to be."

Grace said as she approached Beraham once again to continue with her various tests.

After starting his guard shift at Sunnyside's outdoor pool, William repeated the same pattern of guarding for forty five minutes at three different guard rotations. Then fifteen minutes stationed at the first aid station on stand by, just in case of an emergency. Some of William's coworkers would say that it can be quite a tedious work, especially since it can be a quiet day of just people swimming and playing for hours without incident. But to William, he didn't mind the peace and quiet of guarding and watching over the swimmers.

As long as they didn't stir up trouble or cause problems for the rest of the staff. William's train of thought was broken when he heard his coworkers that were up on their chairs blowing her whistle, to indicate that the afternoon leisure swim was over.

"Hey William, Can you and Matthew make sure that all the patrons leave the pool deck and head into the changerooms?"

Julianna asked as the three of them monitored the deck from the first aid table, as the patrons hopped out of the pool and made their way to the changeroom building.

"Sure it shouldn't take us too long to get everyone off the deck."

Matthew said as William walked down the north side of the deck, while Matthew walked down the south side of the deck. As they were halfway down the pool deck, William could hear Julianna on the microphone calling out to the staff.

"To the lifeguards on the pool deck, please gather up at the swallow end steps after all the patrons are off the deck for our pow-wow."

The lifeguards made short work of making sure that all the patrons were off the pool deck, they gathered themselves at the shallow steps to wait for Julianna to make her way to them from the pool incharge's office. Once she got there she immediately addressed the group.

"Alright guys, so today was a pretty quiet day which is always a plus... William, Margret, Matthew, and Mel. You guys can go for your dinner break while the rest of you clean up the changerooms before the water polo teams get here for their practice."

Julianna quickly looked down at the sticky note she was holding to see if there was anything else left to discuss.

"And that's all I have to say, so once you guys finish cleaning and make sure that all of the patrons have left the building, you guys can go home except for the four that will be guarding the water polo team."

Julianna said, then turned around to head back to the pool in the charge office to have her own dinner. Meanwhile the rest of the lifeguards headed down to the changeroom buildings to follow Julianna's instructions. As the group entered the building they splitted up into the one's on their dinner break, and the other getting ready to clean up the changerooms.

William was the last one to enter the staff lounge, to see that Margret and Mel had already grabbed their dinners and started chatting with each other.

While Matthew quietly ate his dinner while listening to music on his phone. William quickly went to the fridge to grab his sandwich, while brainstorming topics he could try to use to talk to Matthew.

Matthew noticed Beraham staring at him, he took out one of his earbuds to talk to him.

"So what type of sandwich are you eating there William?"

"Huh? Oh it just has an assortment of different meats, some brie cheese and some mayo."

William answered as he figured out a topic he could talk about.

"Just was wondering Matthew, but are you listening to a guitar instrumental cover? Just cause I noticed that you were practicing the hand motions just before."

William asked, getting a look of surprise across Matthew's face at noticing such a small detail.

"Yea I am, I'm in a band so I like to practice the song's in my spare time."

Matthew answered as he turned his phone around to show William what he was currently listening to. As they continued to discuss their favorite type of music genre, Margret and Mel joined in on their conversation as well.

So William, what are your roommates like? Because they seem like quite the rowdy and party type of guys."

Mel asked as she moved her seat closer to William so she could hear more about his roommates.

"Well I have four roommates that live with me, but I wouldn't really say they are party animals. Maybe one of them is, the other three all have different personalities that make people wonder how the heck we are roommates. But at the end of the day we all support each other, because we're good friends."

William explained to his coworkers as he relished in the good memories he has had with his roommates.

"So would you know if any of them are seeing someone?"

Margret asked William, receiving a look of disapproval from Matthew. But Margret just gave a playful expression and didn't seem fazed by him, as she was only joking.

"As far as I know one of them is taking a break from the dating scene, another said he thinks relationships take a lot of work and effort. And the last two are both workaholics saved by the fact that one of them might be seeing someone in secret... But who knows, you might have a chance with one of them."

William said, making everyone turn to face him with surprised looks, after what he said to them.

"What? If she tries to date one of them at least I give her a warning about how they are when it comes to dating. For all I know she might become my sister in-law if she can get one of them."

William said with a grin as everyone burst out laughing, as they realized that he was just joking around.

"Well then future brother-in-law, I will need all the help and advice you can give me."

Margret said as everyone settled down, as the rest of their coworkers shuffled into the staff lounge after they finished cleaning the change rooms after the patrons had left.

"Hate to break up what's going on here guys, Julianna called the front desk to tell you guys to finish eating and to get ready for the water polo practice."

Orion said as the four people who were on their dinner break packed up their lunch packs, and threw out their garbage to get themselves ready to guard for the next hour.

"Thanks for telling us Orion, will head out since I need to go grab my sweater for the evening winds when we're up on those chairs."

Mel said as she left with Margaret to go get her sweater from the staff locker room. Just as Matthew and William were finishing cleaning up after themselves, then followed after Mel and Margret.

"Time for me to finish my shift for today... probably should take that extra aspirin that Beraham packed for me."

William said to himself as he walked out of the building and noticed a red and orange evening sky, the cool summer air felt nice after another hot day of work.

CHAPTER 8

My Secret will not be Revealed to Anyone Not Even You

After many hours of different tests, Grace finished her final assessment for Beraham by storing the vial of blood she took from him in a secured container.

"And with that we are finally done... It's gonna take some time for the results from the test to be runned and for me to log all the information into the hospital records at the clinic I help on the weekends."

Grace explained as she put away her medical equipment, as Beraham put his shirt back on.

"Well once again Grace, thank you for doing this favor for me,"

Beraham said as he put his hand out to her, as a way of showing his thanks. Grace looked down at the hand that was offered to her, then back up at Beraham's face.

"Like I previously told you that I am only doing this as a favor to Heinkel, and as a one time favor nothing more after this."

Grace said, as she ignored Beraham's handshake and walked over to her office door to open it and pointed for Beraham to leave.

"Understood, you will not hear from me unless it's to find out about my results,"

Beraham said with a grin as he walked over to the elevator with Grace following close behind him. Once Beraham pushed the down button on the elevator, he could feel the sharp pain in his chest resurfacing.

"Have a good evening Grace... I'll find my own way out of here, since you probably have a lot of work to get done."

He quickly walked into the elevator and pressed the ground floor before Grace could say anything to him, or notice his reaction to the pain he was experiencing. Once the doors closed Beraham let out a quiet scream as the elevator descended downwards.

"Fuck sake! This is the second time within a day that I've experienced this type of pain... Agh..."

Beraham thought to himself as he clutched his chest. The elevator doors opened when he got to the ground floor, Breaham quickly looked around to see if there was anyone that would see him. But to his relief no one was around in the entrance. Breaham rushed to the entrance and exited the building to get to his motorcycle. As he approached his motorcycle Beraham could feel the pain in his chest slowly ebbed away.

"Weird didn't last as long or as intense as yesterday's one... Hopefully it doesn't happen for a while when it happens again."

Beraham whispered to himself as he took out his helmet from his carrier to put on. While Beraham was getting ready to leave for his home, up in Grace's office she was going through the building's security footage. Deleting all records that showed Breaham's time in the building. She stopped to watch the camera that recorded Beraham in the elevator clutching his chest and heavily breathing.

Grace took out her phone to call Heinkel, to give him a run down on Breaham's appointment.

After the third ring Heinkel answered the phone sounding quite groggy on the call.

"Hello? Whoever this is, I finished work early due to an unforeseen event, so please refer to my assistant if you wish to talk in person."

Heinkel said while in the background of the call Grace could hear someone groaning.

"Heinkel it's me Grace, I just finished your roommates assessment and so far with the data I have so far indicates that he seems overall quite healthy."

Grace explained to Heinkel, who by the sounds in the background was pouring himself a coffee.

"That's good to hear, but let's wait and see what the test results will say once they come back. Message me when you have been able to upload Beraham's records into the system."

Heinkel responded to Grace as she wondered if she should mention the incident that had happened in the elevator.

"Right... I noticed on the camera that Breaham had a mini cardiac episode. He looked like he was having chest pains, but as soon as he left the building he was all better. I already deleted all video footage of him as per your instructions."

Grace said as she knew that hiding that type of thing from Heinkel wasn't something she should as his V.P.

"Hmmm I see, thank you for telling me that, and also for deleting the security footage. I would've done it myself but after last night I have been feeling quite shitty today."

Heinkel said as he was going to hang up but Grace stopped him before he did.

"Heinkel there was something else I noticed while examining Beraham, there were a lot of scars across his chest and lower back and he seemed quite defensive whenever I tried to touch him."

Grace stated to Heinkel while staring at the video of Beraham in the elevator.

Heinkel was silent for a few seconds before he spoke to her.

"Grace... you're someone that I trust with my life and running a security firm, but I owe a great debt to Beraham for saving me when I was at my worst. So please don't look anymore into Beraham or look into his past."

Grace's curiosity wanted to push Heinkel for more information about her patients past injuries and secrets that involved Beraham. But she knew that if she pushed too much, Heinkel might actually get angry with her.

"Very well Heinkel, I will respect your friend's privacy but keep an eye on him… He might seem fine but you never know how good he is at hiding his pain."

Grace said as she hung up the phone call, and deleted the final video that had Beraham in it. But this only peeked Grace's curiosity into finding out more on Beraham.

--------·❖·--------

After he finished his appointment with Grace, Beraham drove straight home, just in case the mysterious pain in his chest happened again. When he arrived back home he noticed that Heinkel's car was parked in the driveway earlier, then Heinkel usually arrived from work. Beraham thought that perhaps Heinkel called in sick or finished work early.

Beraham opened the door to be greeted by Bianca who came bouncing forward to get cuddles and affection from him.

"Hello little one, why do you try to give me all this affection when I struggle to give it back to anyone?"

Beraham asked the small puppy as he set his bag and helmet on the ground, to then pick up Bianca.

"Perhaps it's because of that trait of yours, it makes her want to comfort you with affection, Beraham."

Heinkel said grougly as he came out of the living room wearing his pajamas.

"Well aren't you a sight for sore eyes, it's been quite a long time since you were this hungover."

Beraham said as he took his shoes off with one hand while balancing Bianca with his other arm.

"Boib mich... I heard from Grace that your appointment went well, and you should receive the results sometime next week."

Heinkel said as the two of them moved to the living room to continue their conversation.

"Hopefully it doesn't take too long, that way I can get William's mother off my back about that."

Beraham said, as Bianca tried to lick his face while he took his shoes off, making him chuckle at the little dog's attempts to show affection.

"Speaking of that incident at William's parents house... Grace told me that you had another mini episode of some kind in the elevator as you were leaving. And before you say anything, I already instructed Grace to delete any and all footage of you being there."

Heinkel said quickly as to answer Beraham's follow up questions.

"That's good to know, but that Vice president of yours, was quite curious about all my scars. And I doubt she believed that I got these on a bad hunting trip."

Beraham said as Joseph and Lee walked in from the kitchen to plop themselves on to the sofa with the others.

"Finally your back Besserdechnyy. I need you to tell Lee that I won our drinking challenge since the last thing I remember is you coming down to check on us before we passed out."

Heinkel asked as he switched on the television to watch the news. Lee gave Joseph a death stare at him claiming to be the victor, but he shrugged it off and looked towards Beraham to hear his answer.

"Well I came down to get a quick glass of water for myself, and when I checked on you two, Lee was singing some type of horrible chant all the while you were passed out on his shoulder."

Beraham explained to his roommates, as everyone else turned to Joseph who had a look of dread written across his face.

"Well Joseph looks like you are gonna have to bow down and tell me that I am the greatest when it comes to drinking games."

Lee said with the biggest grin across his face, that even Beraham had never seen before.

"Aghhh... I don't believe this... Fine you are the king of all drinking games and I can only hope to be as great as you one day..."

Joseph grumbled under his breath, while everyone else was bursting out with laughter at Joseph's resentment of having to say that to Lee.

"William said that he will be working late tonight, so we can eat dinner without him for today."

Heinkel said as he looked down at his phone to read the text message.

"So how about we do takeout for tonight? Since I'm kinda craving pizza and I don't think anyone is feeling up to cooking right now."

Heinkel suggested to the rest of his roommates, who all nodded in agreement for takeout as their dinner. While Heinkel went to grab the home landline and his wallet to put in an order for their pizza. The rest of them gathered together to discuss an important task that needed to be done.

"Alright so out of the four of us, who is able to go down to William's workplace and make sure that he gets home safely without his knowledge?"

Joseph asked as he looked between Lee and Beraham, to see if either wanted to volunteer for the job.

Beraham sighed knowing that he would probably need to do it since he didn't want to make his friends try and follow William and get caught.

"I'll do it since I know for a fact that neither of you want to do it, and I don't want to force Heinkel to do it since he was working all day unwell."

Breaham said as he got up from the couch, but was soon stopped by Lee and Joseph.

"Hey now Beraham, we ain't trying to leave all the bloody work to you!"

Lee said as he forced Beraham to have a seat back down on the sofa. So that they can talk with Beraham about their intentions.

"Both of us are pretty much over our hangover, so either of us cango since we are still unsure when you might have another dizzy spell."

Joseph said with a serious and concerned tone, leaving out his usual jokes and humorous self. Beraham looked between Lee and Joseph, he could see the looks of concern between the two of them.

"While it's nice to hear you both voicing your concerns, guys I've been told by Heinkel's colleague that there is nothing physically wrong with me."

Beraham said to them, but they still seemed unconvinced by his words.

"Keep this in mind, Lee doesn't have a driver's license, Joseph would probably get caught by William since he isn't very subtle when following someone. And since William already messaged Heinkel and knows that he took a sick day from work, so Heinkel can't do it either."

Beraham finished his explanation that seemed all too perfect and reasonable for Lee and Joseph to argue back.

"It might be the most logical and correct option, Beraham, but it isn't the most morally righteous option for everyone who cares about you."

Heinkel spokle up as he returned from the other room and got the attention of his roommates.

"You might be right on that Heinkel… But I want you all to remember that on your contracts, it says in these types of scenarios I have the final word. Understood?"

Beraham said with an assertive tone in his voice making everyone stay silent, while he stood up and took Bianca to the kitchen to feed her.

Beraham softly placed the dog down on the kitchen floor, took out the kibble and poured a small portion for the tiny dog.

After he finished serving the dog her dinner, Beraham noticed that his roommates all huddled into the kitchen.

"Will you at least stay for dinner? Let's at least eat dinner together before you go off."

Heinkel asked as Beraham stood up to face them with his arms crossed.

"Also I told the pizza place that the order is under your name and you will be paying for it…"

Heinkel finished saying and received a pissed off look from Beraham, but it quickly changed to grin.

"I can never leave angry in this household, you all always make sure that I won't be pissed when I leave."

Beraham said as he opened his arms to welcome his friends into a hug. They all quickly huddled into the hug, since everyone knew how rare it was for Beraham to offer hugs to anyone.

All Beraham could feel was a calming sense of mind when he could hear the sound of all of his friends' heartbeats in their hug. But as all good moments are just moments, it ended when one of the four friends passed gas loudly.

Once they heard it, and then smelled it they immediately scattered away from each other. Except for Lee who didn't even look the least bit ashamed at his fart.

"Bloody hell you guys! It's not like I was gonna announce that I was carrying a ticking time bomb that was gonna go off."

Lee said as he just left the kitchen to head back to watching his show.

<hr />

After eating pizza with his roommates, Beraham once again left the house for his motorcycle to head down to William's workplace. Beraham brought Bianca with him as an alibi to say he was just taking the dog on a walk. He snuggled Bianca into his jacket making sure that her head was able to stick out, as to make sure she could breath.

As he pulled out of the driveway, Beraham didn't want to spend too long in traffic, especially with a small dog in his jacket so he drove in and out between cars. He was able to reach the parking lot that was nearest to William's outdoor pool within fifteen minutes. He pulled into an empty spot between two large cars to make it harder for William to see his motorcycle.

He unzipped his jacket to let the little dog out, and as soon as Beraham placed her on the ground she bolted towards the beach.

Beraham locked his bike before he walked after William's dog. He whistled for Bianca to come back to him so that she wouldn't wander off on her own.

She ran back to him looking up at him with curiosity as to what he would do. Beraham took off his blundstones then his socks since it had been awhile since he last felt the waves between his toes.

As he listened to the waves and the lake crashing against his feet, a male voice whispered into Beraham's ear behind him.

"You'll never be able to save yourself from your curse. Even if you keep that boy safe, or teach him all you know... You know that it's a lost cause so why continue to complete this contract?"

The voice whispered, the coldness and sinister could be heard, making Beraham turn around in fear to punch whoever it was. But all he was hitting was air behind him.

"Fuck sake, I have to make sure that William is safe instead of mucking about... Come here Bianca."

Beraham said as he rubbed his eyes to clear the tiredness that he was feeling.

After he put his blundstones back on, he led Bianca down the pathway that would get him to William's pool he worked at. He positioned himself by the staff entrance far enough so that he would just look like another dog owner playing with his pet. Beraham at least would be able to see that William would leave safely from his workplace.

"Alright girl, will be waiting here just so then we make sure that your owner gets home safely… So while we wait, let's play around with this ball?"

Beraham asked as he started to pet Bianca while taking out a tennis ball for her to play fetch.

The little dog barked with excitement and joy when she saw the tennis ball appearing. She started to spin in circles as she waited in anticipation for the ball to be thrown.

"Go get it girl!"

Beraham shouted as he threw the ball a couple feet away so that he wouldn't tire out the small dog too quickly.

When Bianca brought back the ball to Beraham, she dropped the tennis ball in front of his feet as her tail continued to wag while waiting for him to toss it again.

Breaham continued to play fetch with Bianca over and over again, and would sometimes fake the throw to then just drop it in front of him to see if she would run after it. Which every time he threw it even if he faked the throw Bianca always ran after it.

Every so often a walker or a dog walker would walk up to chat with Beraham or ask to pet Bianca. They would always have questions like how old she was or what breed Bianca was. Berham would give only the bare minimum when he answered their questions the best he could. He wanted to keep the conversations short so as to not draw attention from the pool staff or form William when he left.

After saying goodbye to the fifth dog walker, Breaham laid down in the grass and let out a sigh of exhaustion. He hadn't had to talk to so many people in such a short amount of time, that he wished that William would just catch him outside his workplace then talk to another dog walker.

Bianca climbed up onto his chest and started to lick Beraham's face to make him feel better.

"Aghhh… If only I could let my true self free, then everyone would just leave me alone. Then I could focus on either making sure William is safe, or give you the proper attention, little dog."

Beraham said as he petted Bianca while looking up at the sky which was a mixture of orange, pink sunset.

"Why don't you stop trying to be the good person that you try to be? Why not lose that mask that you hide behind? Let out the fear you could show to those around you!"

The voice whispered into Beraham's ear making him shudder as he tried to ignore the tiny voice in his head.

"You won't be able to save William… Just like you couldn't do for everyone else before him… You can't even go by your real name, no matter how much you despise it."

The tiny voice continued to whisper into Beraham's ear but each time it speaks, it starts to get louder and louder in his head.

Bianca whimpered trying to stay as close as she could to Beraham, while trying to comfort him. Beraham sat back up when he heard the sound of someone approaching behind him. He balled up his fist in preparation just in case of the worst case scenario. He turned around to see who it was, and he wasn't expecting to see Margret standing over him.

"Hey stranger, good to see you again with little Bianca out and about."

Margret said as she knelt down to pet the little dog that was in Beraham's arms. Beraham relaxed his shoulders to look behind Margret towards the staff gate to see if William also left.

"If you were waiting for William, he had already left with some of our other co-workers at a different entrance. So you probably just missed him… It was in Beraham right?"

Margret explained to Beraham while also asking for his name just so that she wasn't mixing up him with one of his other roommates.

She stared at him with concern written across her face, and Beraham was trying to look away from her but she would just move in front of him.

"Is there grass in my hair or something? Because I'm not really one for eye contact with people…"

Beraham said as he continued to avoid eye contact with her.

"Are you alright Beraham? The reason that I am asking this is because before I approached you, it looked like you were having a nightmare..."

Margret asked as she sat down in front of Beraham, to show him that she wasn't leaving anytime soon. With a sigh of defeat coming out of Beraham's mouth, he decided to tell her the truth, since he didn't have the energy to try and make her leave.

"You are somewhat right... But I wasn't having a nightmare but more like I was reliving bad memories. I was trying to ignore them and shove them to the furthest part of my brain."

Beraham explained to Margaret while preparing himself for her to immediately change the subject, and leave the conversation. When he looked up expecting to see her with an uncomfortable expression across her face. But instead he was surprised to see that Margret looked more concerned.

"It's good that you were at least able to share this, if you ever need someone to talk to about your problems like this, I can be the one to listen."

Margret said as she made herself comfortable sitting in front of Beraham on the grass.

"Interesting... Why would you want to listen to a stranger's problems who you've only met twice? Why wouldn't I just tell William or one of my other roommates?"

Beraham asked with just a bit of skepticism towards Margarets intentions.

"Well from what I have been told by William, you are a rather private and emotionally reserved man, who keeps his problems to himself."

Margret said to Beraham who was mildly surprised by her answer to his question. But he kept his face from showing his surprise since he didn't want her to know that she was spot on with her guess. While he took a moment to recompose himself and come up with an answer, Bianca moved out of Beraham's lap and made her way over to Margaret to lick her hand.

"I honestly think that you would rather unload your problems on someone you barely know rather than someone you always stay strong in front of. You don't want to be a burden to them with your issues."

Margaret said as she picked up Bianca into her arms to give her some affection.

Beraham was truly speechless by all of Margaret's statements, that he felt something in his chest that he hadn't felt in a while. The warmth and concern from another person who didn't have ulterior motives to use him.

"So you're alright with me being completely honest with you? Because I am quite good at making people regret talking to me."

Beraham asked as he locked eye contact with her to make sure that she couldn't lie to his face.

Margaret leaned forward and without even batting an eye said her answer.

"Yes Beraham, I do want you to be completely honest with me and no matter what, I'll listen to you."

But before Beraham could be honest with her, Margaret's phone rang out, startling the both of them by the loud noise.

She looked at her phone and swore under her breath, by what she read on her phone.

"Shit, I have to go or else I will miss my bus home…"

Margret said as she placed Bianca on the ground to stand, Beraham followed suit but picked up Bianca into his arms.

"I can give you a ride on my motorcycle if you like."

Beraham offered to Margaret who was busy searching her bag for her wallet.

"No that's alright Beraham, I still have enough time to get to the bus stop. But not enough time for me to give you my full attention to listen to you."

Margaret said as she pulled out her wallet with triumph.

"Well then… Have a safe trip home Margret and thank you for listening to my venting."

Beraham said as he stuck out his hand to her for a handshake. Margaret looked down at the hand, she accepted the handshake but let out a sigh of disappointment.

"What is the sigh just now for?"

Beraham asked as the two of them walked down the pathway towards the bus stop, to drop Margaret off."

"Well... I don't usually greet or say goodbye to my friends with a handshake, it feels too formal and serious..."

Margaret explained to Beraham as they waited by the stop light, waiting for it to turn green.

"So do you want me to greet you with a high five when we say goodbye to each other?"

Beraham asked as he shifted Bianca in his arms so that he could raise his hand in the air. But Margaret let out another sigh of disappointment and annoyance as they crossed the street.

"I am too tired from work right now to try and teach you about socializing, Beraham. Next time we meet up I'm definitely making sure you know how to properly greet and say goodbye to friends."

Margaret said as she walked over to the bus stop, leaving Beraham hanging with his arm still up. When they stopped at the bus stop, Margaret noticed that Beraham was still keeping his arm raised.

She rolled her eyes but quickly changed her expression to a smile, she quickly gave him a high five just as the bus was pulling into the stop. Margaret quickly waved goodbye to him and hopped into the bus.

Beraham watched as the bus drove off, and he felt a twitch of sadness as it left down the street.

"Well girl, it seems like our job here is done since William headed home already. Then we shall head home as well."

Beraham said as he headed back to the parking lot which had his motorcycle.

After he made his way to the parking lot Beraham approached his motorcycle to leave.

"Well Our mission of watching over William was not successful... But it seems like we might have made a new friend today."

Beraham whispered to Bianca as he opened his jacket to secure the little dog safely, for their ride home.

"Man it's been quite a while since I've made a friend that wasn't involved with work..."

Beraham said to himself as he put his helmet back on, and double checked that the dog was properly secured in his jacket before he drove home.

Beraham started up his motorcycle and headed out onto the highway. As he drove past the cars in the lanes, he made sure to zig-zag through the cars since Beraham didn't want to get stuck in traffic when he had the dog with him.

As Beraham stopped at a traffic light, he couldn't help but feel that some of his burdens he carried for so long, was a little lighter after talking with Margaret.

"Maybe I could finally be honest with someone with my secrets... Or at least with some of them that I can't share with the rest of the guys..."

Beraham thought to himself as he waited for the light to change to green.

"Why trust someone you just met Beraham? Especially when it comes to sharing secrets? You've been down this road before, where you trusted someone and then they end up using you or betraying you."

The little voice in his head whispered to Beraham just as the traffic light turned green.

Beraham ignored the voice and continued to make his way home on his motorcycle. After driving for ten minutes, Beraham finally got home and parked his motorcycle in the driveway. He could feel Bianca inside his jacket trying to get out.

"Hold on little one, let me just get off my bike so I can get you out."

Beraham said as he turned off the engine and got off his bike. He unzipped his jacket to let Bianca out and placed her onto the ground. As soon as she was on the ground Bianca bolted towards the house barking happily. The front door opened and William came out to pick up Bianca and welcome Beraham home.

"Hello home, Beraham, but where did you go that got Bianca all dirty? Also why did you need to take your motorcycle?"

William asked as he noticed the dirt on her paws.

"I took her to high park to show her around the dog park area, since that would probably be a great place to take her on walks or meet other dogs."

Beraham said as he came up with this lie when he was at the lakeshore, just in case William would ask this exact question. Beraham hated lying to William, but he couldn't tell him where he was and why.

"Well I hope you didn't tire her out too much, because she still isn't used to meeting other dogs yet."

William said as he gushed over Bianca while giving her pats along her back.

Beraham watched the interaction that William was having with Bianca, he felt a twinge of happiness and nostalgia. He couldn't believe that the William in front of him was the same one he made a promise with many years ago.

Back then William couldn't even look someone in the eyes when talking to them, or even be able to give his own opinion to anyone.

"Beraham are you okay? You've been awfully quiet while staring at me for the past three minutes."

William asked as his face turned from happy to concerned when he noticed Beraham.

Beraham tilted his head to the side as he produced a grin for Beraham.

"I'm alright Will… Just been having a couple of reckless nights, so I'm feeling a bit tired after the day I had."

Beraham said as he walked up the steps and passed William to enter the house.

"Well I do hope you're not overdoing it at work, Because I doubt that you would want to have Lee take care of you if you get sick."

William replied back to Beraham as he followed him inside the house.

"Well then with that thought in my mind I think I'll head straight to bed and try to get some sleep."

Beraham replied quickly as he climbed up the stairs to head right to his room. But he wasn't going to sleep just yet, instead he was going to research how to properly greet friends or say goodbye to them.

"Hmmm… So you're supposed to have a secret hand shake with a friend that only the two of you know and have come up with?"

Beraham whispered to himself as he looked at different videos of people doing different handshakes with each other.

"Why are you still continuing to pretend that you can try and be friends with someone? They wouldn't only be a distraction."

The voice whispered to Beraham, but now he would just ignore what the voice in his head was telling him.

"So wait, people do these complicated handshakes every time they meet each other? People are really weird with how they greet each other these days."

Beraham said as he continued his research for hours. After a while Beraham could feel himself struggle to keep his eyes open, and couldn't stop himself from yawning.

"Perhaps some sleep is something I could use right now after such a long day."

Beraham thought to himself as he closed his laptop and got up from his desk to lay in bed. He didn't even change out of his street clothes when he fell face first into his pillow, since he didn't have the energy to do it.

As he waited to fall asleep in his bed, Beraham thought over the series of events that happened today. Having to go through all of those different tests with Heinkel's vice president of his company Grace. To spend his evening with Bianca down by the beaches at lakeshore to watch over William, but instead he spent it talking to so many people about Bianca and what type of dog she was.

And then there was Margaret, someone who was able to peek into Beraham's ironclad walls of emotionless personality and was able to make him talk about his emotions.

How could she make me feel so vulnerable and talkative? I haven't felt this way since... No never mind that I actually have work tomorrow so I need to sleep.

Beraham closed his eyes and as he drifted to sleep he could hear two familiar voices whisper to him from either side of his ears.

"Goodnight Beraham."

In Beraham's dream he opened his eyes to see that he was back at the park where he first met William. Beaham looked around to notice that no one else was in the park.

"Huh isn't this an interesting memory to dream about... Must be because I had been reminiscing about William today that now I'm dreaming about this memory."

Beaham said to himself as he knelt down to feel the imaginary grass flow between his fingers.

"Beraham?"

Two voices called out behind him in unison, giving chills along Beraham's back since he recognized the voices. He hadn't heard their voices in years nor seen them.

"Now what is our heart to none except us doing here in the past?"

One of them asked as she walked up behind Beraham and placed a hand on his shoulder.

"Yes, you should be still in the middle of the job that was given to you all those years ago. It started with this encounter with William right here... Right?"

The other female voice chimed in, as she also walked up and rested her hand on Beraham's other shoulder.

Beraham took a deep breath as he stood up slowly as he brushed the hands from his shoulder then the dirt off his jeans.

"This is only a dream of my own imagination, I am in control here not them,"

Beraham said out loud as he prepared to turn around to confront the two people he longed to see once again.

Beraham turned around to come face to face with his two older sisters, who both looked at him with confusion and concern.

"Little brother? Why do you look so sad to see us that you've started to cry?"

Beraham's older sister asked as she walked up to Beraham to wipe away his tears. That even Beraham hadn't noticed until she pointed it out to him.

His other sister stayed where she stood, watching the interaction between her twin and younger brother.

"You must be feeling quite happy to see us that you started to cry, Beraham... Especially since it would take a lot to make you cry when you tend to not show your emotions to anyone too often."

The sister that stood back from Beraham said as she let out a scowl.

"Come on sister, you know that he hasn't always been like that... Beraham had times where he needed us emotionally."

With the way this conversation was going, it was probably going to end up with the two of them arguing. And Beraham wasn't going to let his dream turn into a nightmare of his sister's arguing with each other about him.

"Enough with you too arguing about my emotions! Where the hell are you two? I've been searching everywhere around the world for so many years."

Beraham said while raising his voice and removing his sister's hands from his face, as he hid the emotions that were written across his face.

Both sisters looked at each other and just started to laugh at their younger brother. He was confused by their sudden laughter, like when he was younger and he asked a dumb question.

"Why ask such a silly question, Beraham? When you already know the answer to such a simple question?"

The sister with the fiery red hair stopped laughing to answer Beraham's question, with another question.

The other sister with the red hair that was more lighter and soft like the embers of a campfire. Also stopped laughing but looked guilty that she laughed at Beraham.

They both walked up to Beraham and each took one of his hands.

"Little brother... Don't forget the contract that you were given to be completed. This is the only way for you to rejoin us as a family again."

The sister on the left said as her expression had a look of sadness, as she looked into her brother's eyes.

"You were given allies who can help you and protect you... Even from yourself."

The sister on the right said to Beraham, but instead of looking sad she looked more upset.

"But how long do I stay by William's side? He is in such a better place in his life now, than when I first met him when I took this contract."

Beraham asked as he started to have trouble keeping his face from faltering in front of his sisters. And trying not to cry again in front of his sisters.

"Perhaps William isn't the only one you need to help 'Our Heart to None'... Maybe there is someone else that needs help more than William."

The sister on the right said as they both moved closer to Beraham's ears to whisper to him.

"Don't forget that not only will you never see us again if you fail, but the curse you bear will continue to haunt you and affect your life."

"It's time to wake up little brother, we hope to see you again Hea-"

Beraham's sisters were in the middle of saying, but was interrupted by Beraham being pulled away from them into the darkness once more.

The last thing Beraham saw before he was fully consumed by the darkness, was his sister's mouthing his original name. A name that he never wanted to be called ever again.

CHAPTER 9

Our Past will always be there as our Reminder

Joseph woke up to slowly get himself out of bed, he could feel the cool air of the morning wind wash over his body making him shiver.

"Hey doll, do you think you could warm me up…"

Joseph asked but soon realized that there wasn't anyone in his bed.

"Right, I forgot that I said that I wasn't gonna do anymore one night stands or dating for a while…"

He said to himself as Joseph let out a chuckle at the thought of waking up with no one else in his bed with him.

After Joseph got changed for work, he was passing by Berham's room when he felt something was off.

"Why do I have a bad feeling that Beraham might be in trouble again? Should I check on him?"

Joseph grumbled to himself as he seated on whatever or not he should check on Beraham.

"Nah I ain't about to enter Besserdechnyy's room by himself again… Did that once years ago and I almost got killed for it. He isn't the type of guy who likes people to approach him in his room while he's asleep."

Joseph said as he quickly walked away from Beraham's door to head downstairs to grab some breakfast. As he entered the kitchen Joseph noticed that no one was in here. He checked the living room if his friends were there, but to his surprise they weren't there either.

Joseph went back to the kitchen and noticed a note that was addressed to him on the refrigerator. He read through the note to see what it said, and noticed that it was from his roommates.

'Hey Joseph, we went to run some errands and take a walk with Bianca… Will be back home a little after lunch. William and Lee.'

"Well that explains where everyone is, but why hasn't Beraham gotten up yet? It's very unlike him to be sleeping in."

Joseph said to himself as he looked towards the staircase, wondering if he should check on him. He paced back and forth between the kitchen and staircase, going over the pros and cons of going into Beraham's room.

"Aghhh Screw it! I will just quickly stick my head in to see if he's awake, if not I'll just yell and wake him up from afar."

Joseph decided as he grabbed his coffee and downed it all in one gulp to prepare himself. Joseph slowly climbed up the stairs to check on Beraham. He could feel the dread creep up his throat as he grew closer to his friend's door. Joseph lifted his arm slowly to knock on the door, but before he could knock on the door he heard his friend screaming.

Joseph instantly bashed the door open when he heard Beraham scream inside his room. He ran in to see that Beraham had fallen out of his bed and his hand was bleeding.

"Besserdechnyy what happened? Why are you bleeding?"

Joseph asked quickly as he grabbed a towel and started to wrap Beraham's hand.

"Egh… Well I was sleeping recklessly so I must have knocked my glass of water off my table. So when I fell out of my bed my hand landed on the broken glass."

Beraham explained as he pulled himself onto the bed to check if he was cut anywhere else.

"Beraham is everything okay with you? Because recently it feels like you've been having trouble even before with these fainting spells."

Joseph asked as he sat down besides his friend as he finished tying the towel around Beraham's hand.

"If I am being honest I don't really know... It's like I've been this heartless and emotionless person for so many years, that now something has torn a crack in my mask and it's making my emotions spill out."

Beraham explained to Joseph as he held his head in his hands.

"Hey! You're gonna get blood in your hair like that, if you're not careful!"

Joseph said as he grabbed the back of Beraham's head and pulled it out of his hands.

"But that's besides the point right now... Beraham what were you dreaming about that would cause you to fall out of your bed like that? Because there was only one time that I saw you this messed up was when your family had abandoned you..."

Joseph said but soon regretted saying it, when suddenly Beraham punched him in the stomach and then put him into a headlock.

"Joseph, you are one of my closest friends that I've known the longest... But don't think that I won't hurt you if you bring up my family again."

Beraham said in his cold and emotionless tone of voice, at the mention of his family. Joseph could feel it in his bones that if he didn't come up with a plan soon, he might be in actual trouble.

"Aghhh... Beraham... Please understand that I wasn't thinking about what I was saying, when I was comparing what happened in the past to now..."

Joseph barely said between his gasps for air, as he could feel Beraham's grip tighten for a moment but then relaxed his grip and let Joseph go.

"When you put it like that… You might be onto something with this… Because that was the last time I actually felt like I hit utter rock bottom."

Beraham said tiredly as he examined his hand to make sure it wasn't bleeding through the towel.

"Well, cough cough… As long as you're not gonna try and kill me anymore… Why don't we head downstairs and treat that cut properly with Heinkel's first aid kit."

Joseph suggested as he lightly massaged his neck.

Beraham looked up at Joseph and nodded his head in agreement. Beraham stood up from his bed and offered Joseph his good hand to help him up. Joseph reluctantly accepted the hand and got pulled up to his feet, as the both of them moved around the broken glass and left Beraham's room to head downstairs to the living room to treat the cut with the first aid kit.

"Here, take a seat on the sofa while I go grab the first aid kit and dress it for ya."

Joseph suggested to Beraham as he went off to the laundry room to grab the kit. He noticed that Beraham just stayed silent and moved like a robot to take a seat on the sofa. He was acting like how he was the last time Joseph patched Beraham up.

"You know this reminds me of the time I had to patch you up six years ago when I had come back to Canada after accumulating a large bounty and debt back in Russia."

Joseph asked as he slowly unwrapped the towel to clean the cut that wasn't too deep. He started to clean the blood off Beraham's hand and proceeded to disinfect it.

"Gods you were in such deep shit… What did you do that made them send men after you all the way to Canada?"

Beraham asked as he let out a hissing sound in pain when Joseph dabbed the cut with disinfect and started rewrapping the hand.

"Well, when you lose a rather expensive sports car from a mafia boss, while also convincing the owner's wife to file for divorce and leave him? Then I wouldn't be surprised if he sent the whole red army on my ass."

Joseph answered as he made sure to tie up the bandage nice and tight around Beraham's hand. Beraham slowly examined his hand while making small movements to see how well he could move it.

"Well it's not like I was in a better situation when you found me... Because back then it wasn't my proudest moment."

Beraham said with a troubled smile across his face.

Six Years ago
Ontario, Canada

"Alright Joseph, you come back to Canada to find your friend and see if you can convince him to help you out of your shitty situation."

Joseph said to himself in russian as he made his way out of the airport to find himself a taxi.

After looking around his immediate area for a cab, he finally was able to flag one down for himself. Once he put his luggage in the back of the cab, he sat himself in the taxi and greeted the driver.

"Dobroye utro, could you take me to High Park?"

Joseph asked the cab driver who's only response was giving him a thumbs up, then started driving out of the airport.

As they drove down the highway, Joseph rolled the window down and watched the buildings and other cars pass by him. They were all probably heading to work in the heart of Toronto.

"Is this a return visit home sir? Or are you here for business?"

The cab driver asked Joseph to try and start up some conversation while driving.

"I used to live here years ago... Went to live in Russia for a while but decided to visit an old friend."

Joseph responded with as little detail or explaining required to answer. Since he didn't know who he could trust, nor tell this random cab driver what his plans were.

"Ahhh so you're meeting your friend all the way at the park? Does he live somewhere nearby? For you to stay with him?"

The cab driver said as they went down the waterfront by Lake Ontario, getting closer to the destination.

"Well more of I wanted to see this park again, this was the last place I saw all my friends before we went our separate ways… Wanted to feel the nostalgia of the memories that I had in this place."

Joseph explained as he started to get lost in his thoughts as he reminisced about the past.

"Well then sir, I hope you enjoy your time here in Canada and have a good day sir."

The cab driver said as he stopped the cab in front of one many entrances to High Park.

"Why thank you… Eddie, here keep the change since I don't really use cash too often."

Joseph said as he handed the cabbie his fare plus a little extra. Once he finished paying the driver and grabbing his luggage from the back of the vehicle. Joseph watched the taxi drive up the hill, making him realize that he would need to walk up the hill in this hot summer weather.

"Wow he leaves me at the bottom of the hill? After I gave him such a good tip and shared my life story???"

Joseph muttered under his breath as he slowly dragged his luggage up the hill.

Once he made it to the top of the hill, Joseph went over to the nearest bench and plopped himself down on it. To allow his lazy arse to rest since he wasn't too accustomed to the warm weather.

"Blyat… This Canadian weather is so much different then Russia's weather… I need some water if I try to find him."

Joseph murmured to himself as he checked his phone for the number that was given to him to use in dire emergencies.

Joseph quickly pressed the call button on the phone, so that he couldn't talk himself out of not calling his friend for help. He waited in anticipation for the caller to answer. While waiting Joseph looked around as it felt like someone was watching him. He could've sworn that someone was behind the tree that was off to his left.

Joseph tried not to look nervous so that he didn't alert the person behind the tree that he knew of their presence.

Joseph slowly stood up and pretended to do stretches to not arouse suspicion. He could hear the stranger slowly approaching behind him.

"If you even think about trying to fight me, we both know that I can take you down before you even make a fist."

A familiar voice said coldly behind Joseph's ear.

Joseph turned around to see that the voice belonged to Beraham who was wearing a short sleeve black hoodie, jeans and sunglasses to cover a annoyed look on his face.

"Besserdechnyy! It's so good to see you in modern looking clothes, instead of that black business suit you always wore like you're attending a job interview."

Joseph said as he opened his arms to grab his friend into a hug. But before he could even move in, Beraham pulled out a police baton and pointed it towards Joseph's chest to stop him.

"I know we haven't seen each other in a decade… But you should remember when we were younger I didn't like to be hugged."

Beraham said with a cold attitude towards Joseph as he jammed the police baton further into his friend's chest.

Joseph almost forgot how much Beraham was about physical contact with pretty much anyone. Joseph lowered his arms to show that he wasn't going for a hug anymore.

"I see that you try to be a cold hearted gentleman when it comes to hugs or any type of physical contact…"

Joseph said as he let out a sigh of disappointment as he turned around to grab his luggage off the bench.

"Why did you come here and use the number I gave you to use only in case of emergency?"

Beraham asked Joseph quickly, as it seemed like he wanted to get to the point of Joseph's visit.

"Well part of the reason is that I need somewhere to stay a low profile, since I got into some trouble with some mafia boss in Russia."

Joseph quietly explained, as he could feel the anger coming from behind him. Joseph slowly turned around while clutching his luggage expecting the worst, but was surprised to see that Beraham had a smirk across his face.

"Is this your new angry face Beraham? Because I never knew you to smile like that before."

Joseph asked as he suddenly felt a cold shiver up his spine when looking at that smile that was across Beraham's face.

"So Joseph, what do you need me to do then? Do you want me to get you out of a tough situation that even a man of persuasion can't get out of?"

Beraham asked in a way that seemed more like he wanted to confirm Joseph's request, and followed it up with his own question.

"Yes… I need you to either broker a deal with the mafia boss I'm in trouble with, or make me disappear from society for a while?"

Joseph reaffirmed his favor to Beraham, confused by Beraham's current behavior.

Beraham stared at his friend closely, the gears in his head whirling around as he was trying to figure out how he could profit.

"Well I guess this is a dire situation for you… So I'll help you out of this situation for a price though."

Beraham said with an even bigger grin across his face, like he just won the lottery.

"Okay… But as long as it's not another illegal contract again, like when we were younger and desperate for money."

Joseph said as he already felt like he was gonna regret asking for Beraham's help.

Beraham slowly put his police baton away into his pocket and urged Joseph to walk with him. He slowly walked behind Beraham to follow him wherever they were going.

"So where the hell are you taking me? And what am I gonna owe you for doing this?"

Joseph asked as the two of them walked along the pathway of the park, as a cool breeze blew through the trees causing them to rustle and leaves to fall off.

"You've known me for a long time as someone who loves to do favors in exchange for a favor from them. But sometimes if it's a dangerous or complicated one, I make a contract for them."

Beraham explained as the two of them passed by the cherry blossom trees, that High Park was known to blossom in the spring.

"Now for me to not only accept to help you, let alone get such a dangerous job to be completed. I'll need you to sign a contract of my own making, since you would owe me quite a debt after all is said and done."

Beraham said to Joseph as he stopped in his tracks to sit at a bench overlooking the lake. Joseph looked around his surroundings to see if there was anyone suspicious around. When he couldn't see anything out of the ordinary he sat down next to Beraham.

"It's good to see you still remember the scanning techniques I taught you before you left for Russia…"

Beraham pointed out as Joseph took out his pack of cigarettes, to take a smoke. He lit the cigarette then took a big puff before he spoke to Beraham.

"Stop trying to butter me up with these compliments, Beraham. Remember that I'm quite good with these types of situations, so stop with these tactics and give it to me straight."

Joseph said as he took another puff from his lit cigarette and blew out the smoke while tapping off some of the ashes.

Beraham let out a chuckle at what Joseph was insinuating to him.

"Well I don't need to explain the contract's initial contents just yet since it's still in the rough draft at the moment."

Beraham said as he wrinkled his nose in disgust at the smell of the cigarette.

"I see that while you were living in Russia you plucked up being a hhhh smoker..."

He said with disgust as he couldn't stop himself from coughing up a storm.

"Besserdechnyy, what are you going to make me do? Because you keep on avoiding what I will have to do in return."

Joseph yelled out loud as he started to get pissed off at Beraham, and decided to blow a cloud of smoke right into his face. Before Beraham could even move a muscle to dish out his punishment to Joseph, a loud thump caused the two of them to turn to see what made that noise.

They both saw a young man on the floor trying to pick up his books that fell out of his backpack. Joseph quickly rushed over to help pick up the books and handed it to the young man.

"Here let me help you with this, by the way are you okay?"

Joseph asked as he handed each book over to the young man to put back into his backpack.

"I'm alright... I just tripped myself over and happened to forget to zip my backpack up..."

The young man explained quietly and sounded quite nervous talking to Joseph.

"Ahhh don't worry about that man, we all make mistakes and usually when it happens we tend to learn something from them."

Joseph said as he handed the last book over to the young man, while offering his hand to help him up. The young man accepted Joseph's hand and stood up with his assistance. Once the young man was back on his feet, Joseph felt there was something familiar with this young man. Like he met him before, but couldn't remember from where.

"Well ummmm, thank you for helping me sir and I hope you have a nice day,"

The young man said as he quickly walked away to wherever he was heading off too.

Joseph quickly walked back to Beraham who was still just sitting on the bench waiting for his friend to return.

"Hey, did that kid look familiar to you? Because I could've sworn I've met him from somewhere before."

Joseph asked quickly while trying to recall from his memories.

Beraham just continued to study Joseph as if he was mulling over whatever or not he was going to say something.

"I'm quite surprised you don't recognize him after seeing his face so close up... But then again it has been quite a long time since you last saw William."

Beraham said as he looked past Joseph in the direction that the young man had gone.

"Podozhdi minutu! You're telling me that the kid I just helped was William?"

Joseph asked with a surprised look across his face. He couldn't get over the fact that he met William again after so many years had passed. But then Joseph thought something was weird with this encounter. It was too coincidental that he met William in High park like this.

"This is too much of a coincidence that William happened to cross paths with us here, as if someone had planned for this..."

Joseph said as he tried to figure out what was bugging him. But as he thought about it, Joseph realized something that Beraham was trying to do.

"Wait a second! Beraham, you aren't still trying to complete that contract that your family gave to you ten years ago?!?"

Joseph yelled out loud, causing him to receive a kick in the leg from Beraham who tried to silence him.

"God Joseph, please continue to tell the whole world our conversation. I insist, keep yelling it out for anyone to hear."

Beraham sarcastically said as his expression was telling Joseph to choose his next words carefully.

"Besserdechnyy… Please tell me you haven't been watching over William since we all left Canada back then?"

Joseph asked with concern for his friend's mental health, while Beraham stayed silent after he was asked that question. But to Joseph all the silence was enough to give him the answer he already knew.

"I need to do this Joseph, I haven't been able to see my sisters in almost fifteen years and they will never show themselves again until I have completed it!"

Beraham said as he started to sound like he was getting overwhelmed with emotions.

"Hey, hey listen to me and to my voice… Take a deep breath Besserdechnyy and try to stay calm like the lake in front of us."

Joseph suggested to Beraham as he slowly started to use his powers on Beraham so that he wouldn't lose control. Nor unconsciously use his powers because Joseph remembered that he should never let him lose control.

"So tell me this Besserdechnyy, why are you still watching over William? Does the contract indicate that you need to protect William till you're dead? Or is there a more meaningful reason you have to keep doing this to yourself?"

Joseph asked as he waited for his friend's answer while letting more of his power slip through his words.

"At— At first it was so that I could see my family again and ask them why I was forced to do this… But now I want to just help him not only to keep him safe, but not only protect him from the shadows but also by his side as his friend…"

Beraham tried to explain without holding anything back, due to Joseph's power of persuasion. But as Beraham finished his explanation for Joseph, he immediately snapped out of whatever trance he was in. And turned his attention to Joseph immediately with an angry look across his face.

"You better have a really good reason to do that to me Joseph, Because I will solve your problem by simply killing you myself!"

Beraham said with a cold tone of voice as he couldn't hide his anger from Joseph at this very moment.

"Hey you started to get overwhelmed with all this talk about your sisters that you would've gone out of control if I hadn't used them."

Joseph said as he noticed that someone was watching him and Beraham from afar.

"You probably haven't noticed this yet but there's a guy across from us that's just watching us. He also just pulled out a phone to call someone."

Joseph whispered to Beraham while watching the gentlemen walk closer to look at them.

"I can also see two more gentlemen approaching us from behind, and one of them pulled out their phone. This is too big of a coincidence... Let's have a change of scenery shall we?"

Beraham said as he got up and started walking in the opposite direction of where the three suspicious men were.

Joseph quickly followed after Beraham's lead, while leaving his larger luggage at the bench since it would just slow them down. And as they walked towards the forest that was off the pathway, the three men quickly walked after them.

"Besserdechnyy, shouldn't we head towards a more populated part of the park? Since then they can't do anything with the public watching?"

Joseph asked as he dodged out of the way to avoid a branch from hitting him, after Beraham flung it back at him. As they headed deeper into the thicker parts of High Parks forest.

"There is probably more than just the three we just saw... So trying to figure out who is a hitman and who is just a regular civilian would make this a lot harder for me."

Beraham started to explain but paused to make sure he wasn't going to trip over the ingrown tree root, before he continued to speak.

"So we bring them to a place that no one would go, like the middle of the forest so that it gives me a chance to solve one of your immediate issues…"

Joseph stayed silent as he didn't like what Beraham was insinuating. But they continued to walk deeper into the forest. After walking for another five minutes, Beraham stuck out his arm to stop Joseph in his tracks.

"Stay here Joseph and keep hidden in the bushes while I go and deal with the hitmen."

Beraham said as his expression darkened as he looked around like a tiger getting ready to hunt his prey.

"Are you gonna take them down with just a baton? Or do you have another weapon hidden somewhere else?"

Joseph asked with concern for Beraham that was going up against an unknown number of hitmen that could have anything from knives to guns.

"You don't need to worry about me Joseph, all I need to know is you are someplace safe and out of the crossfire."

Beraham said while pointing at some thick bushes for Joseph to hide in.

Reluctantly Joseph slowly inched himself into the bushes carefully. but as he was halfway into the bushes Joseph felt a leg shoved him into the bush. Joseph was gonna give Beraham a piece of his mind at what he just did, instead he kept quiet when he could hear the hitmen talking to each other.

Joseph peeked through the bush to see where Beraham was to try and warn him, but Beraham had already disappeared from sight like the wind. Joseph held his breath so that the hit men couldn't hear him breathing. All he could see through the bushes were the shoes of the hitmen.

There were at least five of them slowly walking by his hiding spot whispering between each other in russian. One of them knelt down to check for footprints, and the man slowly walked over to the bush that Joseph was hiding in. The man stopped in front of

Joseph's bush and stood in place as if waiting for Joseph to make a sound or run out of it.

Joseph wondered if he should try to fight the man in front of him and try to use him as a hostage, against the other hitmen. Though they probably would just shoot both of them since they would probably want to get the money for his death at the expense of their colleague.

Suddenly the sound of gurgling and choking broke Joseph's line of thought, and the sight of blood dripping down onto the ground in front of the man. Yelling rang out around Joseph as gunfire rang out with their silenced pistols, as they all shot randomly.

From where Joseph could see from the bush the first hitman that was killed had fallen to his knees with a sharp branch thrusted through his chest. Joseph put his hands over his mouth to make sure that he didn't let anyone hear his screams from what he saw in front of him.

After five minutes of gun fire, yelling and bodies hitting the ground, all the noise stopped and all that could be heard was the wind blowing through the trees.

Joseph decided to stay in the bushes and continued to stay still, because he didn't know if he wanted to see what happened.

The sound of a single pair of footsteps crunching through the dirt towards where Joseph was hiding was located.

"If you're done hiding— ughhh... I could use your help with something Joseph..."

Beraham said as he pushed the branches out of the way, for Joseph to crawl out of it. After letting out a sigh of relief that Beraham had taken care of all of the hitmen, he slowly crawled out from the bush and stood up.

Joseph's face went white when he stood up and looked at what happened to Beraham when he dealt with the hitmen. Beraham had blood stains all over his clothing, cuts were spread out along his arms, and from how Beraham was limping while holding his wounded waist.

"Fuckin hell Besserdechnyy… How the hell can you still be standing like this?"

Joseph asked as he quickly rushed to his friend's side to support him.

"Well it's not like any of those injuries could actually kill me Joseph, hehe…"

Beraham answered with a chuckle, but quickly turned into a groan of pain when Joseph grabbed his arm and waist.

"Why the hell are you trying to crack jokes now? Especially with these kinds of injuries and wounds?"

Joseph said with disapproval as they slowly walked away from the gruesome and bloody dead bodies that were all taken care of by Beraham.

After leaving the deeper parts of the forest and getting closer to the edge of High Park's forestry, which would lead them to the streets.

"Okay what's the plan now Besserdechnyy? Because I doubt you want to go to an actual hospital after what you just did and explain all these wounds."

Joseph asked as he helped lean Beraham against a tree to give them both a breather from all the walking.

"You're right that I don't wish to go to a hospital… All I need you to do is call this number…"

Beraham said as he fumbled to grab a piece of bloody paper from his torn up jeans. He handed it to Joseph who read the number then dialed the number to call this person. After the third ring the caller answered the call.

"Where would you like to be picked up sir? Have you finished your business with that Russian friend of yours?"

A male voice asked over the phone, then went silent as he waited for an answer.

"Tell him to wait on the road that would lead to the zoo and to make sure no else is around him when he picks us up."

Beraham said weakly as he struggled to keep himself from falling over.

"We need you to meet us by the road that leads down to the Zoo, and make sure there isn't anyone around since Besserdechnyy is seriously wounded."

Joseph said as he repeated what he was just told by Beraham while he ushered Beraham to lean on him.

"Understood sir, I will be there in five minutes so just look for an orange taxi when you get to the road."

The man said as he hung up the call, all the while Joseph put away the phone so that he could help Beraham walk through the forest.

"How far is the rendezvous point to meet this man from here?"

Joseph asked as the two of them slowly walked through the forest under Beraham's directions.

"It's not too far from here from the sound of cars we can hear, but make sure to wave him down so he makes sure to give us the all clear."

Beraham explained as he started to breath heavily and let out grunts of pains. As they neared the street that they would meet the driver, the sound of a car zoomed past them, but stopped then backed up to pick the two of them up.

"Well, our ride is here Joseph… let's get a move on so… We can get this over with."

Beraham said weakly as he started swaying back and forth, even with Joseph's assistance.

"Oi! Don't fall asleep or else I will be chased down by the Russian mob for the rest of my life without your help!"

Joseph shouted as he smacked Beraham in the face, as he rushed with his badly wounded friend to the taxi.

The taxi driver rushed to meet the two of them after opening the back door to let them in.

"Wait a second, aren't you my taxi driver that drove me here?"

Joseph asked as he recognized the driver as the one from the airport, while he put Beraham in the back seat.

"Sir just get yourself in for now so we can get my boss here patched up,"

The taxi driver said quickly as he rushed over to the driver seat, while Joseph got in without another word as to not waste anymore time. The driver took ten minutes to drive the both of them to a place where they could patch Beraham up.

They stopped outside an abandoned house on the outskirts of the city, where a lone house stood tall, with the other houses in shambles or burnt down.

"You could've chosen more I don't know... Less serial killer vibes in the neighborhood and more hidden secret base that has a security system..."

Joseph asked in a more worried tone since he tried to use humor to cover how nervous he was for his friend. He helped Beraham out of the car, to walk towards the abandoned house. Joseph brought Beraham into the house, then set him down on the stairs so that he could go searching for first aid kit

"The medical supplies are in the kitchen somewhere in the cupboards. Before you go find the first aid kit, lay me down on the table so that I can lay down..."

Beraham ordered as he started to become heavier for Joseph to carry him.

Joseph made sure that Beraham wasn't going to fall off the table, then rushed into the kitchen to check every cupboard till he found what he was looking for. While looking through the cabinets Joseph found packed food, cutlery and other miscellaneous objects. But not a first aid kit could be found in any of the cupboards.

Joseph could feel his heart sink with dread when he couldn't find the kit. Just as he was considering calling an ambulance to treat his friend before it would be too late. He noticed that there was a rather large cookie jar that was in perfect condition sitting in the sink.

"No way… there is no way in hell that Beraham would actually put medical supplies in a cookie jar of all places…"

Joseph muttered under his breath as he quickly ran to the cookie jar, lifted the lid to find all sorts of medical supplies inside it.

"Oh you gotta be kidding me right now!"

Beraham shouted as he grabbed the jar and ran it back to Beraham to give it to him.

"I found your stupid medical supplies! I don't know why you decided to store them in a cookie jar of all places!"

Joseph said with disbelief at his friend's sense of storing things.

"Well if someone tries to rob me they wouldn't steal from the cookie jar or suspect that I would put something valuable in it."

Beraham responded as he took the cookie jar and grabbed some surgical gloves and bandages to toss to Joseph.

"Put those on and grab some tweezers so you can pull the bullet that is in my upper arm."

Beraham said as he took out a bottle of disinfection out to dab it with a clean bandage so that the wounds wouldn't get infected.

Joseph looked down at the gloves in front of him, then at all of the multiple cuts across his body, and at the two gunshot wounds on his left arm.

"Can I say no to doing this?"

Joseph asked but immediately got the answer without Beraham needing to say a word. His expression was saying to Joseph, "You're gonna do it, or else I will kick your ass.'

"Well there's always a first time for everything… So might as well learn how to treat gunshot wounds right?"

Joseph said with a nervous laugh as he put the gloves on, and prepared himself to get this done quickly and efficiently patch his friend up.

CHAPTER 10

Don't Make a Deal that You'll regret Later on in Life

Under Beraham's guidance and detailed instructions, Joseph was able to remove the bullets from Beraham's arm. Then stitched up most of the deeper cuts and wounds that needed it. To get all of it finished, Joseph took over three hours to finish the more major and complicated injuries.

He bandaged everything to the point that Beraham was starting to look like a mummy with all the bandages and blood splotches seeping through.

"Not bad, could've done with less of you fake vomiting and gagging every ten seconds when putting in the stitches..."

Beraham said with a weak grin across his face as he examined Joseph's handiwork.

Joseph gave an annoyed and sickly expression to Beraham as he removed the bloody gloves off his hand and into a garbage can.

"I'm more of a lover of the body and fixing it with my company. Not fixing wounds like some combat medic on the battlefield."

Joseph said as he slowly started cleaning up all the used gauzes and Beraham's ripped up clothing.

"Joseph, is the cab driver still waiting outside?"

Beraham asked as he finished examining his stitches and bandages.

"Hmmm... Yea he's still waiting outside in his taxi at the moment, but why do you ask?"

Joseph responded then followed it up with a question, as he peered outside the window. When he turned to face Beraham, he noticed that his expression darkened with what he had to say.

"I need you to go out there and use your power to make him forget that he ever met you and me. And suggest to him that the reason he can't remember the last few hours is because he fell asleep a couple blocks away from here."

Beraham explained the favor to Joseph, who in turn was about to speak up about and ask Beraham why.

"And before you say anything, know that I give you my permission to use it on him. So go on and get it done before we continue our discussion about those hitmen."

Joseph was lost for words at Beraham's request. He didn't know how to respond, so like a robot Joseph walked out the room then out the house towards the taxi.

The driver saw Joseph coming out of the house and got out of his taxi to meet him halfway.

"Is everything alright with the boss? He looked seriously hurt, so perhaps we should go to a hospital to get properly treated."

The taxi driver asked as he turned around to grab his phone from the car. While he had his back turned away from Joseph, who grabbed the back of the cab driver's head.

"I apologize in advance but it looks like Besserdechnyy knew that you would ask too many questions... So listen to my voice very carefully."

Joseph whispered as he peered into the mind of the cab driver's memories and to experience them.

Joseph quickly told everything that Beraham wanted to happen to his memories, then altered the driver's memories to forget about

Beraham and Joseph. But before letting him leave, Joseph had one question for the driver to answer for him.

"Have you ever seen what your boss does throughout the day on a daily basis? Or seen him do something suspicious?"

The cab driver turned around and dreamily answered Joseph's question.

"He would usually spend most of his time watching over this one kid like he was some type of hidden bodyguard… And sometimes he would meet with all sorts of different information brokers to find two women."

"Interesting… he is still prioritizing finding those two even after they abandoned him… He says he is a cold hearted person, yet still won't let them go."

Joseph muttered to himself as he let go of the taxi drivers head.

"You are free to go once you leave this street, you will no longer remember meeting me nor Besserdechnyy now or ever in the past."

Joseph said as he watched the taxi driver slowly approach the taxi, reentered the vehicle then drove off.

Once Joseph could see that the taxi was no longer in sight at the end of the block, he headed back inside to check on Beraham.

"The taxi driver has been taken care of, he won't be able to remember anything involving you or me. So I think you now owe me—"

Joseph stopped mid sentence, when he saw that Beraham was removing all his bandages and stitches from his wounds. But he wasn't bleeding anymore and instead the fresh wounds now looked like they had healed over to leave only scars.

"Great timing that you got him to leave since it was quite uncomfortable keeping those stitches and bandages on."

Beraham said as he went into the kitchen, while Joseph quickly followed after him. His mind was blown by what he was seeing in front of him.

"You could've healed yourself this whole time??? Why did you force me to patch you up if you could've done this from the start?"

Joseph asked angrily as he shuddered at the thought of removing the bullet and stitching all of Beraham's injuries.

"Well one, I didn't want the driver to see that happening... Or at least until his memory was wiped and left the area. Second, I wanted you to remove the bullet since I can't heal with bullets in my body. And lastly doing this comes with a price Joseph and I were lucky to be able to pay it."

Beraham explained lazily as he grabbed an apple from one of the cupboards and took a bite out of it.

Joseph decided not to grill him for a more detailed explanation since there was a more pressing issue.

"So have you come up with a solution to dealing with my problem Besserdechnyy?"

Joseph asked as he leaned against the kitchen wall to await Beraham's answer.

"Before I tell you my plan to solve that problem of yours Joseph... Let us first discuss the terms and conditions of the contract that you will be signing as payment for me doing this."

Beraham said as he turned around to face Joseph with an evil grin across his face.

Up to a certain point Joseph didn't really care what he owed Beraham, as long as he was able to stop the russian mob from hunting him down until he was dead. But with how Beraham was acting about this contract that he had planned for Joseph, he was starting to think that he might soon regret it.

"So to start off, you'll be put into this contract for around ten or more years. Your main objective is to protect and assist William from any dangers, both physical and mental."

Beraham started to explain as he walked back to the living room towards the sofa, while Joseph followed after him and sat across from him on a lounge chair.

"There are some more mediocre rules that I believe are rather fair, but you can always look them over yourself to make sure that they are to your liking. You will also be provided with a job as part of your cover and of course if you have any request or conditions you wish to add before you sign… We can negotiate that as well"

Beraham pulled out many paper's and then a pen that he handed over the stack of papers over to Joseph. While looking over the contract with its many pages, and clauses. Joseph noticed that some of the requirements he would have to follow.

"Okay, so I already see three issues here. First it says here that I'm not allowed to interact with William and just treat myself like a shadow… This doesn't help us protect William from any emotional dangers. Two, were not allowed to date anyone while under this contract? Like hell I'll do this if I'm not allowed to meet and mingle with all sorts of beautiful women!"

Joseph said as he turned over one of the papers to start writing out his own terms and conditions.

"So what are you trying to suggest we do? What do you think we should do instead?"

Beraham asked without even batting an eye at all of Joseph's disagreements about his contract.

"That is something that I would need to think about, but for now let me tell you about my last issue… Why do you want me to never mention to anyone about your powers or the contract details that your family gave you?"

Joseph asked as he knew that no matter what circumstances, he wouldn't tell anyone about Beraham's past.

"Well let's just say that I am not willing to risk my secrets to be uttered out loud again, nor risk you guys interfering with my own contract."

Beraham answered as his expression turned to a more saddened face.

"Yeah I just read the punishments that would receive if I were to break or disobey anything listed on the contract… Must you really put these punishments in place?"

Joseph said with a nervous laugh as he had read that one of the punishments would be to receive a hundred punches to the rule breaker's body.

"Yes the punishments are required so that it gives you an incentive to not be careless during this contract. But you do bring up a good point with those two issues you mentioned before. Those we can definitely discuss and come to an understanding that we both will be to our liking."

Beraham said with another one of his evil grins as he pulled out new blank papers to be used to make new contracts.

Joseph's face went pale when he could've sworn that Beraham looked like the devil with his black pen and papers, and that smile was oozed with evil and malicious thoughts.

After many hours of discussing, arguing and compromises with Joseph's contract. It took them a total of three hours to come to a conclusion.

"Oh my god, I am never gonna be able to look at papers the same way after the amount of work we put into this... Why do you have to make a contract out of paper instead of digitally?"

Joseph complained as he stood up from his chair to stretch his legs.

"Well if everything is to your liking... Will you finally sign the contract Joseph?"

Beraham asked as he put the papers onto the table in front of him and Joseph with a pen. All that's left is for Joseph to sign it.

Joseph looked down at the papers, then back to Beraham, who for some reason reminded him of when they were younger and he was left all on his own with no one to count on.

"Yes I will sign it, but this feels like I'm signing my soul away to the devil or something..." Joseph said as he signed the contract and then handed it over to Beraham.

"I half was expecting the papers to burst into flames and disappear into ashes, that or I would sign it with blood."

Joseph said sarcastically as Beraham just shuffled the papers together then stored them into a folder.

"Well it's more of I trust you to follow these rules Joseph, because I don't like it when people break my contracts. It would be like you're breaking my trust in you."

Beraham said coldly as he wrote on the folder 'Joseph's contract' before he tucked the folder into his briefcase. Joseph looked at Beraham with concern written across his face. He was worried that Beraham might never be able to fully trust someone, or open his heart to anyone again. Beraham noticed Joseph staring at him, then spoke up.

"You don't need to worry about me Joseph, don't forget what my name represents. Because I was taught by my family to handle whatever life is thrown my way."

Joseph nodded his head to acknowledge what Beaham said to him, but he knew in his heart that Beraham's smile was forced and he was just trying to not have anyone worry about him.

"Anyways you've done your part of the deal, so now it's my turn to fulfill my end."

Beraham said as he got up from his seat on the sofa, to walk towards the stairs to the second floor.

"So what is your plan to get me out of this situation? Because they are already sending hitmen after me."

Joseph asked as he followed after Beraham to hear more about this plan of his.

"I'll just do what I always do, find this mob boss you got in trouble with and offer him a deal. And if he doesn't want to make a deal… there's always the stick method after the carrot approach."

Beraham said as he turned around to face Joseph before he headed up stairs. He had another smile across his face, but this time his smile looked more like he was secretly saying. 'I can't wait to get another deal done after all this.'

But Joseph didn't really care how evil he looked at that moment, since he could tell that this was one of the few times he truly saw Beraham look happy.

Back To the Present...

After they finished reminiscing about their past, the two friends couldn't stop laughing.

"Gods I still remember the way you dressed up to look like the godfather when you went to Russia!"

Joseph said as he coughed from laughing so hard with Beraham.

I think I still got that suit and hat somewhere in my closet!"

Beraham said as he got off the bed and shuffled over to his closet to find the clothing he was talking about. He tossed random clothing onto the bed to search for the suit or fedora hat. The sound of triumph came out of Beraham's mouth as he found the same black fedora he wore to Russia and put it on top of his head.

When he put the hat on top of his head, Joseph laughed even harder and louder than he was before. He fell off the bed still laughing at Beraham's appearance.

"This Besserdechnyy, is the person that you should always be. No worries or feeling like you have to keep a mask to hide your emotions all the time."

Joseph said as he calmed himself down from all the laughing he did. Beraham's face instantly went from happy and laughing to annoyed and distant within a second. He slowly took off the fedora and placed it on top of his drawer, then started walking out of his room. Joseph quickly followed after Beraham to confront him.

"Beraham you can't keep seeing this life of yours as just fulfilling another contract, I know that you're doing this so that you can reunite with your sisters... But even after more than a decade of searching you still haven't found a trace of them."

Joseph yelled after Beraham as he tried to keep up with him, as they both headed down the steps towards the kitchen.

"You are getting dangerously close to breaking one of the terms to the contract Joseph, choose your next words carefully."

Beraham warned Joseph while opening the fridge to examine the contents in there for something to eat.

"Beraham you can't stay in the past like this anymore, you've built yourself a stable life where you helped all of us out of bad situations. Hell, maybe one day you'll find love again!"

Joseph said as he placed his hand on Beraham's shoulder, who in turn shoved it off his shoulder quickly.

"Joseph… As I have told you before I will not give up on this contract… Especially since this one was given to me by my family and I have to complete it so that I can see them again!"

Beraham said as he left Joseph in the kitchen to eat his food someplace else away from him.

"Why don't you try and listen to your friend? Because he does raise a valid point."

A familiar female voice whispered into Beraham's ear, as he headed back upstairs to eat his food in his bedroom.

"True, we could be dead somewhere in the whole world without you even knowing."

Another familiar voice whispered into his other ear as Beraham sat himself on his bed with his fruits in a bowel. Beraham ignored the advice that the voices were trying to give to him.

"Honestly I might just need more sleep, or perhaps purchase some sleeping pills of the sorts. So that I don't need two voices telling me what to do like my guardian angels."

Beraham grumbled to himself as he grabbed his phone to check his messages. Most of the messages were from the usual people from his job as an information broker, William wishing him a good morning. Lee sent a cat GIF, Heinkel notifying Beraham that Grace had finished all the necessary paperwork to be placed into the clinic's system that she volunteered at.

"Hey Beraham, I know you probably want to be left alone after our conversation. But I don't like how we ended our talk… Can I tell you one last thing?"

Joseph asked through the door, sounding upset. Beraham got up from his bed, crossed his room and opened the door to face Joseph who was surprised that Beraham opened the door.

Before Joseph could even say anything, Beraham held up his phone in front of his face so that he could read it. He waited for a minute before he dropped the phone and invited Joseph in.

"Now that you're up to speed, I want you to go to the basement where I keep my safe and grab the contents inside of it."

His phone rang out once again, catching both of the young men's attention.

"The safe holds all of my physical copies of the contracts I've made since I was young. The password combination is each of our first initials."

Beraham said quickly so that he could focus on the new message. Before he could check the message, he noticed that Joseph had not moved from where he was while having an overly happy expression across his face.

"Okay I know that you are happy that I value you guys enough to use your names as one of my passwords… But I need you to hurry up and do what I said and get a move on!"

Beraham said as he quickly motioned for Joseph to hurry himself away.

Joseph still had a goofy smile across his face as he hurried to go and do the task he was given. Meanwhile Beraham read the text message that was sent to him.

'I don't care about the repercussions, because I know that you'll do it no matter what!'

Beraham felt confused and a sense of dread by what he was reading. But all he did was reply with a question mark as his response.

"Well at least now I can get William's mother off my back... I'll just have to see the results and Ms. Monroe's diagnosis."

Beraham thought to himself as he started to text a response back to Beraham. When he finished the message and sent it, Beraham noticed that there was another message from an unknown number. He was just going to ignore and delete what he thought was spam, but saw the preview of the message.

'Don't ignore me Beraham or else you'll regret it.'

Beraham opened the thread to a photo attached to the message underneath it. Before he looked at the photo another message popped up.

'I want you to null and void all contracts including your own, your terms and conditions are too much for me... so I want out of your hellish contract.'

'Who are you? Because if you want to null your contract then just tell me who you are and I'll cancel yours immediately.'

Beraham texted to the unknown number as he waited for their response. He decided it would probably be better to entertain this person just in case of the worst.

A minute passed and Beraham's phone rang out again, to let him know he got a message.

'That doesn't matter to me since like I said, I want you to destroy all of the contracts that you've made with everyone!'

The unknown messenger replied back, which made Beraham slightly annoyed by this person's absurd attempts to make him destroy his collection of contracts.

'You do realize that if I null and void all of these contracts then there would be major repercussions to some who are only held back by my contracts.'

Beraham responded back as he tried to keep calm and not let this unknown messenger get him to lose his cool.

A knock at Beraham's door broke his concentration from his phone.

'Look at the photograph, hopefully you will understand that I am serious about you destroying everything you love if you don't do what I say.'

Beraham scrolled back up to the first message to press on the photo that was linked to the first message that was sent. He could feel his heart drop from his chest, everything around him felt like it was going in slow motion as he looked at the photograph.

The unknown messenger sent one final message to Beraham, which broke the emotionless mask that Beraham had perfected over the years to show no weakness to anyone. One that he used to hide behind for many years in front of everyone.

'You made so many people try and find the most important thing in your life, yet here they are waiting for you to give in to my demands. Don't keep me waiting and head to this address for further instructions.'

"Do you really think that you'll be able to get out of this situation you're putting yourself through? Because I will punish you myself once I solve this!"

Beraham whispered to himself as he could feel his anger starting to boil over. He wanted to just use his powers to end this person's life and be done with this trivial matter. But he knew he couldn't so Beraham would follow the instructions given to him.

Beraham sent a message saying that he will meet at the place that was given to him with the suitcase filled with the contracts. He rushed down the stairs skipping two steps at a time to get down faster. As he reached the bottom of the steps he ran into Joseph who was waiting for him at the door with a large briefcase in his hand.

"Here's the briefcase Beraham, but are you okay? You look like you want to go and murder someone."

Joseph asked as Beraham hastefully put on his blundstone boots on, then snatched the briefcase from Joseph to walk out the door.

Hey! Now I'm getting worried, because you're good at hiding your emotions. But now you have the same look when you kill those hitmen at High Park for me."

Joseph called after Beraham as he stopped in front of Beraham and his motorcycle. Beraham stared down Joseph with his emotionless expression as he tried to get on his motorcycle.

"Don't you dare try and stop me Joseph! Whoever this is has not only threatened to end my livelihood but they are also holding someone I hold dear as leverage against me!"

Breaham said as he stepped forward to grab Joseph's shirt and shoved him out of the way.

"Beraham! Don't try to do this on your own... let's call Heinkel so that he can help us with this. He was literally hired to deal with these sorts of problems!"

Joseph argued as he started to trinckle some of his persuasive powers in his words to try and stop him.

Beraham stopped in his tracks standing still like a statue. At first Joseph thought that he actually stopped Beraham in his tracks, and he let out sigh of relief.

Suddenly Berham swung around and punched Joseph in the face without any warning.

"I thought I told you before that you can't use your powers like that, unless I gave you permission to use them!"

Beraham said with anger in his voice as he stood over Joseph after punching him.

"You said to not use them unless there were dire circumstances, or if I thought that someone was in danger!"

Joseph snapped back as he stood back up and took out his cellphone to call Heinkel and tell him what was going on.

"If you're trying to call Heinkel, I already gave him the location the blackmailer provided so I will have backup from his security firm with me... So don't worry, I have a clear mind going into this."

Beraham said turning to get on his motorcycle then started up the engine. Before he could drive off, Joseph jumped onto the back of the motorcycle without even warning Beraham.

"I can't stop you from going but I would be a fool to let you go alone before Heinkel's men arrive. Because who knows what we're getting ourselves into because of this."

Joseph said as he discreetly turned the tracker on his phone on, so that Heinkel was able to track their location as a precaution.

Beraham stayed silent as he mulled over whatever or not he should take Joseph with him.

"You better not make me regret bringing you along Joseph, because if you become a burden I will kick you off this motorcycle!"

Beraham said as he revved the engine and speeded off the driveway.

Millions of different scenarios ran through Beraham's as he worried about the many of the worst case scenarios that could go wrong.

"Beraham, who was it in the photo? It can't have been William since Lee is with him, Heinkel wouldn't make you react like this... who could the blackmailer have to make you almost lose your cool like that?"

Joseph shouted over the wind and cars they passed by, through their neighborhood.

"You would think after the many years we've known each other, you would've figured out who it is immediately."

Beraham yelled back without turning his head so that he could focus on the road ahead of them.

Then it dawned on Joseph of who it was that caused such anguish and stress to make Beraham react like this.

"It was my sister's Joseph... this fuckin dastard has my sister's who I haven't seen in years is holding them both hostage."

Beraham said as his voice faltered when he told Joseph. Joseph patted him on the shoulder to offer his support, and held onto the bike in anticipation. Beraham put the pedal to the metal as he sped up on his motorcycle to go and rescue his older sisters.

CHAPTER 11

I Will Not Lose You Again

Fifteen Years ago...
Toronto, Ontario

In front of an almost castle-like house, two young girls were playing on the swings with each other in the front yard. They swung from underneath a large oak tree, giggling could be heard between the two of them as they swung back and forth.

Just then the front door opened to reveal a tall sturdy looking man with black hair with a few lines of gray hair starting to grow, and had a lab coat draped across his shoulders. He called out to the girls to get their attention.

"Flora! Tara! Come here for a moment, I need you two to do me a favor!"

The man called out to the two young girls, who ran over to see what was needed of them.

"What is it father?"

Tara asked their father as the two of them looked up with curious looks across their faces.

"Your brother just finished with his doctor's appointment in his room, so he hasn't had a chance to play outside today... so I would like for the two of you to take him around the block."

The father suggested to them as he looked at his watch for the current time.

"But I want you two to remember that your brother shouldn't be out for too long in public with other people, and you can't leave him alone."

"Will make sure he isn't out for too long, but why is it that he is visited by so many different doctors?"

Flora asked as they followed their father into the house towards their brother's room.

"Your brother has had a lot of health issues since he was a baby so he can't leave the house for long periods of time. So I bring the doctors to him so that they can try and treat him."

The twins' father explained to them as they stopped in front of a sturdy oak door. He opened the door and the three of them walked into a dark room that had many stacks of books towering around the room, creating a mini maze throughout the room.

"Father really likes to get our younger brother so many books, it's kinda weird that all he ever asks for."

Flora whispered to her twin sister as they navigated through the book maze to where the young boy's bed was located.

Beraham, since you're done with all your appointments for today… how about you go play outside with your sisters or go on a walk around the neighborhood?"

Their father asked as he approached his son who was wearing a gray hoodie that was two sizes too big for him, and sunglasses.

"Okay… but can we maybe get a snack while we're out?"

Young Beraham asked as he looked past his father to see his two older siblings waving at him, with large smiles across their faces.

"I will leave that up to your sisters… But remember, the doctor said for you to keep the sunglasses on till he visits you again next week. So don't take them off for any reason, understand?"

Beraham's father asked with a stern tone in his voice and expression at his son.

Beraham slowly got out of his bed while nodding his head to his father. His father motioned to him to get a move on, and Beraham rushed over to Flora and Tara into their arms.

"Jeez Beraham, you're always so cute when you run to us for hugs. But don't worry, I will definitely get some snacks while we're out."

Tara whispered to Breaham as the three of them walked to the front door to go on their walk around the neighborhood.

"If only my son wasn't such a curse to this family… maybe then he could've lived a normal and happy life."

The father whispered to himself as he picked up a photograph that was on Beraham's bedside table. He wiped a tear from his eye as his expression went to hardened expression as he picked up a set of bloody bandages from behind Beraham's bed.

After the three siblings left the house, they headed in the direction of the playground that was near their home. They walked into the park and noticed that no one was on the playground.

"Huh I guess it will be just us on the playground today. So that means we will have more fun with just the three of us!"

Flora said with excitement as she pulled Beraham quickly towards the play structure. They climbed up the ladder then ran over to the slide, while Tara walked up behind them slowly so as to not tire herself too quickly.

After all of them made it to the top of the slide and sat down together to go down at the same time.

Beraham was in the front of their line, Flora was in the middle behind Beraham, and Tara in the back. They shimmied themselves forward until they slid down the slide, screaming out with glee and excitement. As they reached the bottom they all flew off the slide and landed into the wood chip ground.

"Woo! Let's go and do that again!"

Flora said as she stood back up to help her sister and brother to their feet.

"Yeah, no one just goes down the slide just once! We need to go down it a bunch more times!"

Tara agreed with Flora as they both ran back up to the top of the slide. Beraham slowly followed after his sister's at a slower pace up the play structure. Though out of the corner of Beraham's eye, he noticed a group of boys watching him and his sisters from afar.

Beraham brushed it off as just them being curious since he was finally able to spend more time with his sisters and getting to play outside.

After a while of going down the slide five more times, playing on the rest of the playground structures. The three of them finally took a break on the grass staring up at the clouds together.

"Wow it's been awhile since we all played together, especially since it was quite some time ago that Beraham got to visit the park. We should do this more often."

Tara said as she stood up with Flora to stand over their brother, who just seemed to be staring at nothing in particular.

"Now what is our little heart warmer thinking about?"

Tara asked as the two sisters reached out to their brother to lift him up onto his feet. Beraham didn't say anything but rather just let himself be lifted to his feet without answering their question.

"Well I think now after all that playing around, we all deserve a treat from the convenience store."

Tara suggested to Flora and Beraham who both had the biggest smiles across their faces at the mention of getting food.

"Then can we get some Villa Puffs? I really like to eat those ones."

Beraham asked as the three of them left the park to head to the nearest convenience store.

"Of course we can, don't you remember that Tara and I have quite the sweet tooth for chocolate and desserts."

Flora said to Beraham, while receiving an angry look from Tara. It didn't take very long for them to reach the store. Before they entered the store Beraham stopped at the door, looking quite nervous about entering the store.

"What's wrong, little heart warmer? Do you not want to enter the store?"

Tara asked as the two sister's kneeled down to face Beraham, who was trying to look away from his sister's gazes.

"Father said that as long as I keep my interactions with other people to a minimum, and not complain about today's doctor appointment, I could go play with you both."

Beraham explained as he held his head down in shame as he was worried that they would be disappointed in him. But instead he could feel his sister's warm arms wrap around him into a hug.

"Oh little brother of ours, don't worry about this. We're your sisters and we understand what you're worried about,:

Flora said as she held onto Beraham tightly.

"But little brother, why did you have to make such a deal with our father just to hangout with us?"

Tara asked as she lifted Beraham's head to look him in his covered eyes.

"Because my father said that if I were to go out after my last visit from the doctor's that my sickness might be infectious to those around me. So he said that if we make a deal, then I can play with you guys who are immune to my mysterious sickness."

Beraham said as he could feel his anxiety subside with both of his sister's presence being here.

The two sisters exchanged looks with each other, having a silent conversation between the two of them.

"Here, I'll go into the store and grab the Villa Puff, meanwhile Flora will stay out here with you."

Tara said as she left the hug to head into the convenience store to buy their snacks. After leaving Flora and Beraham outside the store, they walked over to a bench to sit and wait for Tara to come back. Beraham patted on the spot beside him to silently ask his sister to sit beside him, which Flora accepted and sat right beside him.

The two of them sat in silence as they waited for Tara to come back from the shop. Flora poked her brother in the stomach making him flinch since he didn't like it when people poked him. He looked to his sister to complain, what he wasn't expecting was her making a funny face at him. Beraham burst out laughing his head off so much so that he accidentally knocked off his sunglasses when he went to wipe the happy tears from his eyes.

"See, I know you look so much better when you laugh and smile little brother. You're too young to be trying to act all mature and worry about so many problems."

Flora said as she picked up Beraham's sunglasses then handed it back to him, who in turn quickly put them on.

"And remember that if you're in trouble, you have two awesome older sisters who will be there to help and save the day for you!"

Flora said with confidence as she pulled her little brother into another hug, while playing with his hair.

"And never forget that even though you wish to change your name, we will always love you no matter what."

Flora said to Beraham as Tara emerged from the store with their snacks.

Flora got up from the bench and rushed over to help carry some of the snacks. Beraham watched his two sisters interact with each other, hearing them laugh and smile with each other. Beraham felt that the promise that he made with his father was worth it after seeing his sister's expressions. All it took was for the doctor to perform some old type of medical practice on him and not to speak of it to anyone else. He still rubbed his arms and made sure to keep the sleeves down.

"Beraham let's go back home so that we can eat these Viva Puffs with some milk!"

Tara called out to Beraham to catch his attention as the two sisters snacked on some of them.

"You better have some for me or else I'll give the both of you the silent treatment for the rest of my life."

Beraham said jokingly as he ran over to grab one of the chocolate treats, and with that the three of them headed back home.

The sound of all three siblings talking and laughing amongst themselves, eating away the snacks they bought. For Beraham this would be one of the last happy memories of his sisters for a long time.

Back in the Present Day....

After driving downtown to the heart of Toronto, Beraham parked his motorcycle then walked over to where Joseph was waiting for him in the middle of the busy plaza.

"Have you received any more messages from this blackmailer?"

Joseph asked casually and nonchalantly as the two of them sat themselves at a bench. Beraham shook his head as he pulled out his phone just to double check his messages.

"No nothing yet... but they said to meet here in such a public place where there's so many unwanted eyes here. Something doesn't feel right."

Beraham said as he tapped his hand on top of the large briefcase, which held all the original copies of all his contracts he had made over the past ten years. This was his livelihood that was going to be given to some unknown person. But he knew that this would be a small price to pay if it meant that Beraham could see his sisters again. Just then Joseph's voice broke through Beraham's train of thought.

"Are you sure that I can't contact Heinkel and bring him up to speed with what's going on right now? Or at least ask for some backup?"

Joseph asked as he watched the crowd of people pass by them. He looked at each of them with suspicion written across his face.

"Even if you did try and explain this whole situation, Heinkel won't come himself since he is still watching over William at this very moment. So he can't leave William until he gets back home from their outing since that is what his contract dictates for him to follow."

Beraham explained to Joseph who was surprised to find out this small piece of information about one of his friends' contracts.

"And with Lee, if he isn't being a lazy sack of shit and ignoring his contract duties. He is tasked with handling any social interactions for William while also keeping an eye on all our expenses and investments, so he won't be able to help either."

Beraham explained further to quell any other questions that Joseph would try to ask him.

"Jeez man, those guys seem to have a lot more responsibilities and sub rules to follow then what mine does…"

Joseph said looking quite relieved by what his responsibilities entailed on his contract.

"The contract that I made for you was like a prototype for the three of you. I wanted to see how one of you would react to the terms and conditions of the original one contract and see what sort of changes or issues you would raise."

Beraham said to Joseph, but Joseph's attention was focused towards Beraham's phone when a ringing could be heard. But it wasn't coming from Beraham's phone, but underneath the bench they were sitting at.

"What the hell? What are we in some type of action movie or something?"

Joseph asked in disbelief while Beraham reached underneath the bench feeling around, till he felt a phone taped to the bench. He pulled it off and brought it out for him and Joseph to see.

Beraham studied the old flip phone, then when he turned it on and flipped it open he noticed an unread text message.

"They must be watching us from somewhere nearby if they were able to send this message in such a timely manner."

Joseph whispered to Beraham who was already checking the message on the flip phone, ignoring what his friend was telling him.

The text message on the phone was a photograph with a message underneath it. It read 'Go back to the place that it all started with your friends.' The photo itself was of a familiar abandoned house.

"Well Joseph, you can tell Heinkel that will be going back to the old house that you and I used to live in before we got Heinkel to join us."

Beraham said as he got up from the bench with a grim look across his face, as he tossed the phone to Joseph to see the photograph.

"Oh great… we get to see the serial killer house again, great… Just great…"

Joseph muttered to himself as he took out his phone to message Heinkel and update him on what was going on.

After another ride on Beraham's motorcycle through the city to the outskirts of the city, towards the abandoned street where destroyed houses littered along the street. All except for one house that was still standing tall at the end of the street but still was somewhat ruined.

"It's weird how this street has been able to stay the same after so many years. I wonder why the city or any realtor hasn't tried to tear this down and build something like a condo or a new set of houses?"

Joseph remarked as he got off Beraham's bike, then the two of them walked down the quiet and empty street.

"Easy, I paid off some city workers to not touch or let anyone try and use this land unless I give them permission."

Beraham answered as he stopped himself and Joseph when they were halfway down the street to park the Motorcycle from being seen behind a broken fence.

"Don't need to take such a heavy and loud vehicle with us, especially if I need my hands to not be holding this up."

Beraham said as he flexed his hand into a fist as a demonstration for his friend.

Joseph just nodded his head as the two of them continued to cautiously walk down the street of burnt down, and destroyed houses.

Beraham and Joseph slowly walked up the steps of the abandoned house towards the door. They stood outside the door scanning the area around them to see if there were any traps or signs of other people waiting to ambush them.

"Doesn't seem like this guy has anyone with him, nor any backup so maybe we could overpower him if he doesn't know what he's doing."

Beraham whispered as he checked the door for any wires or any type of triggers that could be put on a door.

"Has the blackmailer sent a follow up message since we were downtown? Or what do they want us to do once we get here?"

Beraham asked Joseph who had the phone in his pocket.

Joseph took out the phone to check it for any more text messages from this unknown blackmailer. And as he pulled out the phone, as if on cue a clunk sound could be heard from inside to indicate someone unlocked the door.

Both Joseph and Beraham felt uneasy when they heard footsteps retreating from the unlocked door.

Joseph... Stay back from the door when I open it. Just in case something bad happens when I open it alright?"

Beraham said as he moved himself beside the door with his hand on the doorknob. Without saying anything to him, Joseph walked down the porch to brace himself around the corner for whatever was going to happen.

Beraham took a deep breath then slowly opened the door. The sound of his own breathing was all that he could hear.

As he was able to open the door halfway without any issue, Beraham decided to open the door slightly faster but still was cautious as he did.

He was able to open the door fully without anything happening to him, and once he thought that there weren't any delayed traps he motioned for Joseph to come forward.

"Whoever unlocked the door must have been quite quick to run off and hide somewhere..."

Beraham said with a slight bit of anger in his voice as he tried to figure out where they would've hid his sisters.

"Let's check upstairs before we check the basement… But before we do that let's wait for Heinkel's security team."

Joseph suggested as he didn't like going into this house without any idea where this person could be, or if he was armed.

"No, I will not wait for them since at best this guy might be armed with a knife and I doubt this guy wants to face us or else he would've made his demands clear and told us to drop the bag somewhere for him to pick up."

Beraham said as he approached the old staircase that he'd hadn't climbed up in almost eight years to their old rooms. But as he put his foot down on the first step, Beraham heard the clicking sound of a gun from on top of the stairs.

Beraham raised his head to see a masked man holding a shotgun aimed at Joseph and Beraham.

"Well, well, well… Who would've guessed that you could get here so quickly? You dropped everything so fast to have a small chance to save your sisters you haven't seen in such a long time?"

The man said with a chuckle from up top the stairs, then motioned with his shotgun for Beraham and Joseph to walk up the stairs.

They both slowly walked up the steps slowly with their hands out and above their heads to not give a reason to be shot. The blackmailer moved backwards to let them onto the landing of the second floor, so he could put some distance between himself and Beraham and Joseph.

"You're pretty unlucky that you decided to search the second floor instead of the basement since that was where I'm keeping your sisters!"

The blackmailer said with a loud chuckle as he opened the door to one of the rooms, then motioned for the two men to walk into the bedroom.

"Now put these handcuffs on one of your wrists then loop it around the metal poles that are attached to the wall and raise your arms over your head as you attach your other wrist into the handcuff."

The blackmailer instructed them as he brandished his shotgun while tossing them each a handcuff for them. While they handcuff themselves against the metal poles against the walls, the blackmailer retrieves the metal briefcase which had all of Beraham's original contracts inside it.

"Before you go and pat yourself on the back for being such a clever man... there's a password required to lock on the briefcase if you want to open it."

Beraham informed the blackmailer who in turn froze in his tracks as he was about to leave them. The man turned back around dropping the briefcase and held his shotgun against Beraham's head.

"Do you really think you can make this harder for me? I am being quite charitable with the two of you up to this point. I could've just blast both of you and be on my way!"

The blackmailer shouted as he shoved the barrel harder against Beraham's head.

"Wasn't this going to be an exchange of my contracts for my sisters? Or did you forget what you planned for yourself?"

Beraham asked in a calm tone and cool expression across his face, even with a shotgun aimed at his head.

"Don't think that you can kill me and try to open it on your own, this briefcase can withstand a grenade exploding on it. And just so you know it requires a specific code that only I know, so let's be civilized gentlemen and broker ourselves a deal, shall we?"

Beraham suggested with an emotionless smile across his face as he stared down the masked blackmailer.

The blackmailer silently stared at Beraham, probably thinking on what his next move would be. After a minute passed the blackmailer lowered his shotgun from Beraham's head and placed the briefcase on the floor. He left the room and the sound of the door locking from the outside could be heard.

"Well, I think that went pretty smooth as could be… now all we gotta do is wait for an opportunity to present itself."

Beraham said as he lent himself against the wall without breaking a sweat or seeming like he was nervous.

"Really? Because all I see right now is us handcuffed against a wall in this abandoned house! With a man who is not only blackmailing you but is now holding us at gunpoint without even showing us where your sisters are!"

Joseph asked sarcastically as he tried to see if he could find a way to break out of the cuffs or see if they were loose.

"Why are you so angry about being in handcuffs Joseph? From what I could hear from your bedroom at night, you seem to be into wearing handcuffs."

Beraham said innocently, while Joseph's face turned red like a tomato in embarrassment.

"One it's what my date wanted to do that night, two I don't want to be handcuffed and wait for a man with a shotgun to come back and fuck us in a completely different way!"

Joseph said as he tried to lean back against the wall after having no success with his handcuffs.

"Don't worry, as long as we stay calm and collected, don't upset this man then will be fine… and Heinkel will come and rescue us."

Beraham said, just as the door opened and the blackmailer walked in with his shotgun pointed at Beraham.

"So I thought over what you suggested to me Mr. Beraham…"

The blackmailer said as he walked over to Joseph and Beraham to kneel in front of them.

"So let's make this easy… either give me the password combination and I'll let you both go. Or you don't and I'll make you pay for it with your friend here!"

The blackmailer said as he pointed his shotgun towards Joseph's head.

As soon as the shotgun was pointed in Joseph's direction, Beraham's facial expression darkened. He was seeping with anger at his friend's life being threatened.

"Huh not so chatty now that I'm threatening your friend's life instead of yours?"

The blackmailer taunted as he started to poke Joseph's head with the shotgun's barrel.

Joseph knew that if he didn't do something soon, Beraham might just get himself killed if he did anything rash.

"Now are you sure we can't just come to some sort of agreement? I'm certain that if we all calm down and you lower your gun we ca—"

Joseph started to ask as he slowly used his power to calm and persuade the blackmailer to put his gun down. But before the words could take effect, the blackmailer used the handle of his gun and slammed it into Joseph's face.

"Did you not hear what I was saying to your friend??? Keep your mouth shut and let me finish talking to him!"

The blackmailer yelled as he took out his phone to read something on it. He looked up and started to get back up.

"Now I have to go make an important business call now, so by the time I'm back you better tell me what the combination to the briefcase is, or else this room will be painted red!"

The blackmailer said as he left the room and slammed the door shut, then locked it back up again. Footsteps could be heard from the outside barreling down the stairs.

Joseph could feel the blood dripping down his face, from the pain coming from his right cheek.

"Well, it could've been a lot worse… right, Beraham?"

Joseph asked with a chuckle to try and lighten the mood. But as he tried to do it, he could feel the pain starting to become uncomfortable for him on his cheek.

He looked up from his slightly blurred vision, to see that Beraham for the first time in quite a while looked the angriest that

Joseph had ever seen him. And the room felt like the temperature was dropping with how silent it became.

Joseph hadn't seen his friend look this scary and terrifying since the time he took out all those hitmen from Russia for him. Even then he had a look of discomfort after he killed them, and that Joseph had to see that carnage.

"I apologize in advance Joseph, but I won't tolerate another second of this man's behavior anymore…"

Beraham said with a cold and heartless tone in his voice as he slowly stood up to examine his handcuffs, to plot his next move.

CHAPTER 12

I Apologize for showing this Dark side of Me

Beraham slowly got up from where he was locked against the wall and prepared himself to attempt to pull off his shackles. Joseph looked at him with a worried look across his face as he glanced down at his own shackled hands.

"Don't worry about me losing control over my powers Joseph… it's necessary for our own safety, plus I've run out of patience to deal with this man peacefully. So let's scare him into submission and get out of here!"

Beraham suggested as he started to fiddle around with his handcuffs, then tried to see how strong the handcuffs were.

"Or we can wait a little longer so that Heinkel's team get here and rescue us instead of trying to escape and get into a conflict with the man with a shotgun."

Joseph said as he tried his best to convince Beraham to not have to use his powers. But Beraham brushed it off, then focused on the wooden floorboards to see if any of them were loose enough to use as a weapon.

"Knowing Heinkel, even if he could mobilize a team as soon as he heard about our last location, it would take too long for them to travel here and save us. Especially since that guy does not seem like the type to wait for getting what he wants."

Beraham said as he found a floorboard that had rotted away but was still sturdy enough to use as a club. He pulled off the board and studied what it could be used for.

"Nice, the nail's in the board have rusted away, see if there are any around that you could use yourself. That or use a nail to lockpick your handcuffs."

Beraham instructed Joseph who was able to pull off a nail from a rotting floorboard and attempted to fit it into the handcuffs lock mechanisms to unlock it.

After many attempts at trying to unlock the cuffs, Joseph punched the wall in frustration as he couldn't have any success.

"These stupid nails are too thick to fit into the the locks!"

Joseph said in frustration as he continued to punch the wall, till his knuckle started to bleed. Beraham watched his friend punching the wall, when an idea popped into his head.

"Wait a second, these poles look like they were recently installed into the walls. So if we apply enough pressure to these old walls, it might break off for us and we can use these metal poles instead of the wooden floorboards."

Beraham suggested since he could already see some cracks on the wall where Joseph had been pucning before.

"That actually sounds like not a half bad idea, Beraham, but it probably won't work with the fact the man has a bloody shotgun that could easily kill us both with one shot!"

Joseph said as he was baffled by such a barbaric plan from Beraham.

"Well it's either we try and brute force our way to escape, or leave here in a body bag since that guy is probably not gonna let us go. Plus if we do give him the briefcase of all my contracts, he will have hundreds of contacts that he can use to blackmail more people."

Beraham said as he listed the three different scenarios to Joseph.

Silently Joseph walked as far as he could with his handcuffs to Beraham to raise his wooden floorboard.

"Well we better be quick and quiet before this man returns... so let's do some renovation to this house that I have been wanting to do for years!"

Joseph said as he smashed the wooden floorboard against the wall, making Beraham smile with this new found hope to get out of this and go find his sisters.

········▶·◆·◀········

After around ten minutes of stabbing and smacking the wall around the metal poles both of their shackles were getting looser and would soon fall from the wall.

"Alright, I'm gonna try and pull it out, can you try and help me with pulling it out as best as you can?"

Beraham asked as he was starting to wonder if the blackmailer had left the house, since he hadn't checked on them nor came back upstairs.

"Alright, on three... one, two, three!"

Beraham whispered as they both pulled on the bar as hard as they could. While they were pulling the metal pole from the wall, the sound of footsteps from the creaky old staircase could be heard climbing up.

"Shit! He is finally checking on us! We need to pull this out now or else he will definitely notice the damage around it!"

Joseph whispered quickly as they continued to pull and chip away at the wall to break off.

"Man you were right... This guy is gonna make us filthy rich, once we get our hands on all of his contracts!"

The blackmailer said outside the room, as if he was talking to someone.

"Double Shit! Looks like he did have an accomplice with him, we need to break this pole now or never!"

Beraham hissed under his breath, as they continued to pull at the pole that held Beraham against the wall. As the sound of the lock mechanism clicked unlocked, Beraham and Joseph were able to pull out the metal pole that he was handcuffed to and Beraham already had a plan attack in mind.

As the door opened, Beraham immediately ran over to the opened door to slam the metal pole against the blackmailer with the shotgun's chest. He gasped in pain at the sudden realization of one of his hostages being free.

He dropped his shotgun to the ground, clutching at his chest while trying to catch his breath. Beraham took that momentum to go after the blackmailer's accomplice who was frantically grabbing inside his jacket for his weapon.

Beraham swung the metal pole into the man's stomach, right underneath his ribs making him vomit up whatever his last meal was and a mixture of blood as well.

"Phew, it's been awhile since I allowed myself to be this violent with someone... And I will be especially harsh with you two, perhaps I'll use my 'Special powers' on the both of you."

Beraham said emotionlessly as his expression remained cold and stern, as he knelt down in front of the man who the blackmailer brought with him.

The sound of coughing, heaving and a slight bit of movement behind Beraham made him turn around to see what was going on.

"Umm Beraham... It seems like the blackmailer is trying to grab his shotgun."

Joseph said as he was still handcuffed to the wall, while kicking at the blackmailer from grabbing his shotgun.

The blackmailer struggled to grab his shotgun, then all of a sudden he clutched his chest as if he was in a heap of pain. Joseph felt his own heart skip a beat, when he realized what was going on.

"Beraham! Don't lose yourself again! Because you let go of your old self long ago! Leave your past self where it stays, in the past and remember you've changed since then!"

Joseph said as he started to get quite anxious and concerned by his friends actions and his mood.

Beraham stared and studied Joseph's expression for a moment, then the pressure that Joseph felt before was fading away. Beraham meanwhile leaned down to where the blackmailer laid across the floor to search his pockets. He found a set of keys, which he unlocked his handcuffs, then tossed them over to Joseph to uncuff himself.

Beraham then cuffed the blackmailer's arms behind his back so that he couldn't try to run or retaliate.

"Just wanted to return what is rightfully yours, though they look much better on you than me. Cuff his accomplice when you're out, then find out all you can from them about why they tried to blackmail me and how they kidnapped my sisters."

Beraham ordered as he picked up the shotgun to remove any threat just in case.

"Ok, I'll try to get everything out of them, but where are you going?"

Joseph asked as he cuffed the unconscious accomplice arms behind him.

"Where else? To the basement to free my sisters,"

Beraham said as he tossed the metal pole he was cuffed and gave it to Joseph. And with that final word, Beraham left the room. but before he did, he looked back at the blackmailer into his eyes and walked over to him and bent down to speak to him.

"You are very lucky that I was stopped by my friend since I was gonna give you a right proper punishment. I would've made your whole body scream in pain till you beg for mercy. But as I said before, you were lucky."

Beraham said with a disappointed tone in his voice, and whispered something else to the blackmailer who instantly sat completely still and tears could be seen falling down from under his mask.

"Well I feel a bit better now that I got everything off my chest… I'll be seeing you in a bit, Joseph."

Beraham said as he stood back up to actually leave the room and whispered under his breath.

"You can't escape from father time, whatever time you are given… you better use it to the fullest."

Beraham walked down the steps to the ground floor with the shotgun loosely in his hands. His mind was thinking about how he should act once he sees his sisters.

Before he could even reach the bottom of the stairs, Beraham could hear footsteps coming from the front door. Beraham sneaked up to the side of the front door and waited. Someone was slowly opening the door with caution. A barrel of a gun could be spotted entering the house.

"Whoever this is, if you're smart then you'll surrender right now, but if you're with Heinkel make it known and prove it."

Beraham called out to the person, who in turn stopped in place when they heard Beraham call out to him. Moments later and whispering, the door opened slowly to reveal Heinkel and several of his bodyguards walking in with body armor and guns out.

"Beraham you alright? You're not injured in any way, are you?"

Heinkel asked as he walked forward to talk and check Beraham for any injuries.

"I'm fine Heinkel, I'm just a bit roughed up is all… though Joseph had a nasty cut on his cheek from one of the assailants and maybe a slight concussion."

Beraham explained as he shooed away one of Heinkel's medics away from him and from taking the shotgun from his hands.

"Where is the playboy? I'm surprised that he isn't with you."

Heinkel said with a sarcastic tone but still sounded slightly worried when he couldn't see where Joseph was.

"He's upstairs watching over the two men that tried to blackmail me and kidnapped my sisters… I'm checking the rest of the house to find where they are."

Beraham said as he resumed his search for his sisters, but was stopped in his tracks by Heinkel grabbing his shoulder.

"My men can go help Joseph and take care of those idiotic blackmailers for you. But I will be accompanying you as back up just in case."

Heinkel insisted as he motioned to his men to start heading upstairs to assist Joseph.

"Very well, you can follow me if you must… But know that I won't promise how I will react when I find my sisters."

Beraham said as he flicked Heinkel's hand off his shoulder then walked to the back of the house where the basement door would be located. Heinkel followed after Beraham cautiously as he could tell that something was going on with him. But he wasn't too sure what it was, nor wanted to prod at him right now.

They arrived at the basement door to see that someone had put multiple locks on the door.

"Hmmm… I believe that my team brought a set of bolt cutters, if you give me a moment I'll go get it…"

Heinkel was saying as he grabbed his radio to tell someone to go grab a bolt cutter. But before he could even speak, Beraham cocked the shotgun and started to blast away at the locks.

After three shots from the shotgun all the locks were blasted to smithereens, Beraham handed the shotgun over to Heinkel as he opened the door to head downstairs.

Heinkel quickly told his men on the radio that the shots were coming from Beraham and not from another assailant. He then quickly followed after Beraham while saying under his breath.

"Fuck sake! The hell is up with you, Beraham? I haven't seen you this reckless in a long time!"

As they reached the bottom of the steps, Heinkel tapped Beraham on the shoulder to get his attention.

"Hey, I know this is rather late to ask you but are you okay after all that's happened to you?"

Heinkel asked his oldest friend who stayed silent until he spoke up after a moment had passed.

"At first I was anxious, afraid that my sister's were in trouble and endangered after so many years of searching for them only for them to die if I didn't follow the instructions of that man who had them... But after dealing with those two upstairs and seeing how Joseph was put in harm's way... I am hoping this will be worth all the stress and fear we went through."

Beraham responded as he turned on the basement lights to see an empty and abandoned room, except for a door at the very back of the room.

"Henzol... are you ready to see them again? Or if anything worse is behind there?"

Heinkel asked using Beraham's nickname that he only ever used when they were alone or if he was concerned about him.

"We will see Heinkel... Either way all I want is to see my sisters again, even if it's for a single moment."

Beraham said as he started to lower his barriers and emotionless mask to a more sincere and worried.

THe two of them approached the door that only had a simple bolted lock on it. Unlike the numerous locks that were on the basement door at the top of the stairs. Beraham unbolted the door, slowly reaching out for the doorknob to open it and be reunited with his two older sisters again.

He opened the door and could feel his heart drop from what he saw in the room.

······················◆·◆·◆·····················

Meanwhile upstairs in the room where Beraham and Joseph were held, Joseph was trying his best to stop Heinkel's men from roughing up the blackmailers and further than what Beraham had done before.

"Oi! Don't just grab them like they're a bunch of furniture! They already got hurt from Beraham and we still need to question them!"

Joseph yelled as the bodyguards were trying to bonk the two blackmailers on every door frame or wall as they carried them between them.

"Sir please have a seat and sit still so that I can assess if your injuries require you to go to a hospital."

One of the medical bodyguards said as he tried to to clean the blood from Joseph's cut on his face.

"It will be fine, I've been through worse injuries, but for now my friend asked me to talk with those two so that I can get more information about why they tried to blackmail him."

Joseph said as he brushed aside the medics hands from him, as he followed after the bodyguards who were escorting them outside to the cars.

"Okay I don't really care what happens to those two, but for now I need to get the information from them now!"

Joseph said as he was still being ignored by all of the bodyguards.

"Just so you know, our boss Heinkel told us that if we ever met a man named Joseph, then we are to ignore him but still take care of him if injured."

The medical bodyguard informed Joseph of the reason why all the bodyguards were giving him the cold shoulder.

"Man, I knew that Heinkel disliked me, but who would've known that he would make even his staff hate me?"

Joseph said as he decided to lean on the van while he waited for Beraham and Heinkel to return from the house.

While he was waiting for his friends, Joseph still was worried about Beraham almost using his powers on the blackmailers.

Joseph never really knew for certain how Beraham's powers really worked or what they were.

All of a sudden one of Heinkel's men fell to the ground clutching his chest, as if he was having a heart attack or couldn't breath.

The other bodyguards started rushing over to their collapsed co-worker to help him. But before they could even take another step, they all collapsed to the ground just like the first one. Joseph looked towards the blackmailers who were in the truck, but even Joseph could feel something cold and dark wrapping itself around his heart like an invisible hand.

"Where are they?!? Where are those two low lifes???"

Beraham shouted with fury and anger as he stormed out of the house, looking around frantically to where they were.

Joseph couldn't stand as he fell to his knees, nor could barely form a sentence with his mouth as he tried to call out to Beraham.

"H-hey Beraham..."

Beraham ignored his friend calling out to him, immediately rushing towards where the blackmailers were being held in the truck. Joseph watches as the once calm and level headed Beraham, smash his way through the truck's window to open the door and drag the man out of the vehicle.

"I guess that I was being too easy with only telling you the year and place of where you would die, how about I tell you when exactly you die and how it happens!"

Beraham shouted as he forced the man to kneel down in front of him, while he clenched his fist.

"Please sir, I was only doing what I was hired to do! Please have mercy on me!"

The man begged as tears streamed down his face. But the expression that was across Beraham's face was unchanged, both of being emotionless and seeping with anger.

"Henzol! Stop whatever you're doing to everyone! It's hurting my employee's, Joseph and I!"

Heinkel called out from the front steps of the house, as he desperately struggled to walk towards Beraham. Beraham looked towards Heinkel, then looked around and noticed what was going on in his surroundings. He took in the sight of all the bodyguards laying on the ground clutching their chest gasping for air, and both Joseph and Heinkel barely were able to keep standing up.

Beraham let the man go and just like that the invisible hand that had a death grip around Joseph's heart suddenly disappeared. Heinkel immediately rushed to check on his employees, while Joseph grabbed the blackmailer that was kneeling in front of Beraham and tossed him back into the truck.

"I'm— I'm sorry... I– I'm going to go somewhere to clear my head before I go home. I'm sorry about your co-workers Heinkel, send me their medical bills if they require a doctor."

Beraham said as he rubbed his temple while slowly walking away towards his motorcycle.

Heinkel walked over to Joseph after making sure that he checked on all his employees.

"I'm gonna need your help to alter my men's memories so that they don't remember what just happened, but this is the first time I've witnessed Beraham use his powers..."

Heinkel whispered to Joseph as he checked the time on his watch.

"That's only half of what Beraham can do... But what was it that triggered him to lose control like that?"

Joseph asked as he watched Beraham slowly put his helmet on, then started to climb onto his motorcycle.

Heinkel looked back at his employee's to see how close they were. When he thought that no one was trying to listen in on their conversations, he turned back to Joseph with a worried expression on his face.

"When Beraham and I searched through the house to see if where the blackmailers were keeping his sisters, and as we searched through the basement we found this room in the back that was locked with a single lock."

"Make sense... don't know why we tried to look upstairs first, since it's common sense for kidnappers to store their hostages in creepy looking basements."

Joseph said as he remembered the multiple nights he would watch the shows with his dates. But received a punch to the shoulder from Heinkel as he knew what Joseph was thinking about from the dreamy look across his face.

Heinkel brushed it off and continued telling Joseph the rest of the situation that happened in the basement.

"Anyways, when we unlocked the door, there was only a single lock on it, unlike the first door which had many locks on it that Beraham shot them off with the shotgun—"

"Jeez never expected Beraham to be so reckless, I honestly thought that was you firing the shotgun. Since whenever there's a firearm involved you would be handling them."

Joseph said as he interrupted Heinkel again with another remark of his, that wasn't necessary.

"I swear to christ! It's like it's your god damn purpose in life to annoy the ever living shit out of me!"

Heinkel muttered angrily under his breath as he started to ball his fist. Joseph noticed the gesture and silently apologized by bowing down to Heinkel.

"So when we headed over to the door to open it, the room was completely empty… It was the room in the photograph that you sent me. But it didn't look like anyone was living there nor being held against their will…"

"Beraham immediately left the room as soon as he saw that it was empty, I could feel his power leaking as he ran away and well you know the rest…"

Heinkel finished his explanation as he looked at Beraham with a look of sadness and worry, but then turned his attention to the time on his watch and made a clicking sound with his tongue.

"I hate to make Beraham leave on his own, but I need you to help me… so tell Beraham to message me when he gets home."

Heinkel asked with a disgusted look across his face as he asked for Joseph's help.

"Of course I can tell him, so that he won't forget since he seems a bit absent minded at the moment. Then I'll help you with your employees."

Joseph replied as he walked over to Beraham, while Heinkel went to get his men in line to wait for Joseph to come back.

"Hey Beraham! I'm gonna be helping Heinkel with his employee's 'well being,' so make sure to message one of us when you get home alright?"

Joseph said to Beraham who just looked tired and sad. Joseph hated that he had to leave Beraham on his own after all that they had been through, but he knew that Heinkel couldn't explain what happened to them. So the best solution was for Joseph to use his powers to alter and erase the memory of Beraham's power inflicted on them.

"Okay, I think I'll just drive around on my motorcycle for a while before I head home. Need some time to myself and think things through."

Beraham said as he flipped the front cover of his visor down to cover his eyes. He then drove off down the street that held many memories for the four friends except William. Some memories they wished would stay in the past to be forgotten.

Joseph watched his emotionally complicated friend drive off, he hoped that he could quickly get through with helping Heinkel. So that he could be there for his friend.

"Hey, are you ready to do this? Because I want to finish this quickly, so that you and I can interrogate the two blackmailers to find out more for Beraham."

Heinkel said anxiously as they watched Beraham disappear around the corner.

"Yeah, let's get this over with…"

Joseph said as he recalled the last time he had to alter someone's memories. And ironically enough he had to alter a lot more people than this, when Beraham's powers went out of control after the disappearance of his family.

Joseph could remember how he was ordered to alter over fifteen different people's memories. And how the final order he received was

Chapter 13

Can Someone Learn to be Emotionally Stable Again?

After leaving Heinkel and Joseph to deal with the aftermath of Berham not only losing control of his powers, but also revealing it in front of so many people. The good news was that it was in front of Heinkel's men and the blackmailers, so it wouldn't be too hard for them to deal with the aftermath.

Whenever Beraham overexerted himself at work, or was overwhelmed with emotions and was emotionally drained, he found riding on his motorcycle gave him a sense of peace.

But after what happened today he felt like he went through a rollercoaster of emotions, and Beraham knew that driving around wasn't gonna be enough to make him feel better.

Beraham dropped by his favorite burger restaurant to pick up some food for himself, when he left the restaurant he noticed a LCBO one building over.

"Why don't you buy a bottle or two? You know from what other people say how alcohol numbs the senses and emotions for some people…"

The same little voice whispered into Beraham's ear.

"Perhaps I should visit my quiet place today, it's been awhile since I last visited it."

Beraham said to himself as he walked back to his motorcycle to store the food in his carry on. Just as he was about to drive off to his destination, Beraham's phone rang out, he saw that it was William calling him.

Beraham silently looked at his phone, mulling over whatever or not to answer the call. But he knew if he didn't answer the call, then William would worry about why he wasn't answering. Reluctantly Beraham answered the call.

"Hello, Beraham speaking, how can I help you?"

Beraham asked as he tried to sound as normal as he could.

"Hey Beraham! Just calling to hear how you're doing today! Since I pretty much haven't seen you all day."

William yelled over the phone, while Beraham decided to sit back on his motorcycle and snack on a couple of french fries as he talked with William.

"Yeah it's been a long and draining day for me, so I'll just eat a burger at my quiet place before I go home."

Beraham said as he could hear in the background of the call, people cheering on William's end of the call.

"Are you at a party William? Because if you are, then you surprised me in a good way."

Beraham asked as he felt a slight bit better that William was enjoying himself.

"Yeah, Lee and Heinkel took me out for some clothes shopping, then afterwards we met up with some of my co-workers from the pool to go to a dinner and bar afterwards."

William explained to his friend as he sounded quite excited over the phone about his day.

"But then Heinkel had to leave due to some type of work emergency back at the office, so he left before we could get to the drinks... I hope he isn't doing anything too dangerous at work."

William said as he started to mumbling to himself and going off topic. Which meant that William had been doing a lot of drinking already.

"Well, I won't keep you much longer Will. Since it seems like your friends are calling for you to come back to the party."

Beraham said to William since he didn't want to keep his friend from enjoying his night of fun, nor letting his burger go cold.

"Okay, but before I let you go, Lee said he wanted to talk to you about something if I got you on the phone."

William said as he said his goodbye and passed the phone over to Lee, so that he could talk to Beraham.

"Thanks Will! I'm gonna take the call outside so I can get some fresh air and hear Beraham."

Beraham could hear Lee say as he was given the phone. There was a moment of silence while Lee made his way outside before he spoke to Beraham.

"Alright I think I'm far enough away that William won't be able to hear me… Are you okay Gan Chori? How are you after all that shit that happened?"

Lee asked with concern towards Beraham.

"I'm fine, so is Joseph for your information, gods both you and Heinkel seem to have quite a seeping dislike for Joseph."

Beraham said as he decided to switch the call to his earbuds as he decided to continue this conversation while he drove to his quiet place.

"There's just something about him that makes me want to smack the back of his head, maybe it's that stupid smile of his."

Lee said in a ticked off tone, like just talking about Joseph was putting him in a sour mood.

"So did you just want to ask me how I am Lee? Because I'm heading to my quiet place to enjoy my burger I just got."

Beraham asked as he was slowly feeling more tired and annoyed with this meaningless conversation. Lee stayed silent as he could tell that Beraham was starting to get annoyed.

"Alright I just wanted to check on you… don't worry about what happened today, we will make sure that no one, not even William will know what happened. But promise me you won't try to deal with your emotions by yourself, since you've never really been good with dealing with them."

Lee asked his friend before quickly hanging up the call, before he could reply back to Lee.

After his talk with both William and Lee, Beraham drove through downtown Toronto towards the Humber river which was over by Jane and Lambton bridge.

He drove through numerous neighborhoods until he stopped to park his motorcycle in front of the entrance, to follow the pathway that would lead underneath the Lambton Bridge and next to the Humber river.

"It's been a long time since I have been here, and it is still as quiet and peaceful in the evenings."

Beraham whispered to himself as he walked down to sit under one of the pillars to the bridge that was nearest to the river.

"Hmmm, I kinda want to feel the river water rush between my feet... I'll finish eating my food first then do that."

Beraham decided as he situated himself near the river while taking his boots and socks off to quickly dip them into the water.

"Ahh! Cold!"

Beraham yelled out as he quickly took his feet out of the river, but then back in once he got used to the temperature. Beraham took out his burger and started to chomp down on it, anticipating how delicious it would be. He found that the burger was missing something, like it tasted the same, but still was lacking.

Beraham continued to eat the rest of his burger, half-heartedly and just sat in silence once he was done. He listened to the wind rustling the tree branches, the sound of the river rushing past his feet, as it splashed against the rocks. The sound of nature at its most basic form, it always gave a tranquil and peaceful atmosphere for Beraham's hectic and complicated mind.

"Just because you feel better after a little nature view doesn't mean that you are all fixed up."

The same little voice whispered into Beraham's ear, the sound of laughter echoed in his head. Beraham shook his head to ignore that voice and started to do some breathing exercises to calm his mind.

"You still are the same broken little boy I abandoned, to weak and stupid with his emotions that all you ever knew how to do was follow my every order, like an obedient puppy or puppet."

The voice whispered louder into Beraham's ear, who in turn finally recognized whose voice was always whispering these bad thoughts.

"Congratulations Son, it only took you how many years for your subconscious to realize that the little voice of doubt has been your own father?"

Beraham's father's voice echoed sarcastically in his son's head.

Beraham closed his eyes and wrapped his arms around his legs, tilting his head down to form himself into a ball. He continued to practice the breathing exercises to keep himself calm and to not lose his composure.

"Hey Beraham, is that you?"

A female voice asked, sounding nervous and worried for him.

Beraham looked up to see Margaret of all people standing beside him, looking down at him.

"Are you alright? Because at first I thought that you were asleep so I didn't want to disturb you, but also make sure you didn't fall into the river."

Margaret explained quickly to Beraham, while kneeling down to take a seat beside him.

"Well, today was a rather shitty day for me... so I just decided to come to this spot to eat dinner and just listen to the atmosphere of the river and nature."

Beraham replied to Margaret as he lowered his feet back into the river. While Margaret studied Beraham, as if she was trying to decide something for herself.

"If you're having a shitty day, then we will just have to figure out how we can salvage your day!"

Margaret said as she quickly took off her shoes and socks, so that she could dip her feet into the river. She instantly yelled out in fright at how cold the water was to the touch.

"Aren't you supposed to be used to the cold water? Since you know, you're a lifeguard? And you need to be prepared to save someone no matter the weather conditions?"

Beraham asked with a sarcastic tone but couldn't hide the small grin across his face.

"Hey! I rescue people in a pool in which most of the time it's been pre-warmed, so don't judge me for reacting to cold water, Beraham."

Margaret said as she lightly punched Beraham's shoulder.

Beraham remembered the research on how to greet a friend from the night before, and he thought now would be good to show Margaret all he had learned.

"I almost forgot to tell you that I have looked into different ways to greet friends or say goodbye."

Beraham said to bring up a new topic to talk about with her.

Margaret had a confused look across her face, as she looked like she wanted to say something. But decided to hold back what she wanted to say and let Beraham explain himself.

"So from what I learned from the internet, is that friends come up with their own special and complex handshake to show how great of a friendship they have."

Beraham explained as he lifted his hands in the air to demonstrate a high five routine he saw on one of the videos to her. Margaret raised her hand to clap his hand, when she held Beraham's hand she pulled his hand down to bonk him on the head.

"Oww! Why did you do that?"

Beraham asked as he rubbed his head in confusion, as he wasn't too sure why Margaret bonked him on the head.

"Didn't you say that those who have their own special handshake have a strong friendship?"

Margaret asked innocently to Beraham who nodded his head to answer her question.

"So why can't I add that I get to hit you in the head? So that you aren't sad and our handshake is only special to us?"

Margaret asked as she poked Beraham's forehead with her finger.

"Are you being sarcastic with me about the handshake? Because in the video's they weren't this violent with their friend nor with their handshake routine."

Beraham asked while preparing to defend himself from any more of Margaret's attacks. But instead of another smack, all he felt was her shoulder tapping into his.

"Man, here I thought when I first met you at the lakeshore with your roommates... you were this tall, scary guy with a cold personality that would scare away anyone who approached him."

Margaret started to say to Beraham, who in turn looked semi annoyed and concerned by what he was hearing.

"Buuut... With us meeting up more often, I'm starting to see someone who truly cares for his friends, but who also has invisible scars that he hides from his closest friends."

Margaret finished saying as she picked up a flat stone and tossed it into the river.

"You wasted a perfectly good skipping rock just now..."

Beraham said bluntly as he stood up from where he was sitting and wandered over to the shore.

Margaret also stood up and rushed after him, to figure out what Beraham was doing. She peered over his shoulder to see that he was collecting flat stones from the ground.

"You started a rock collection to cheer yourself up, Beraham?"

Margaret asked as he stood up, grabbed her hands to give her some of the stones he had collected.

"I liked to skip rocks when I was younger, I would make my sisters take me out to any river or lake to skip stones with them. We would see who could make the rock skip the furthest."

Beraham explained as he moved to the edge of the river to show her how to skip the stone across the river.

The two of them took turns skipping the rocks as far as they could. So far Beraham was winning by making his stone skip seven times. Meanwhile Margaret could barely make it past four skips.

"How long ago did you say you stopped skipping rocks? Because it feels like you definitely practice skipping rocks in your spare time, Beraham!"

Margaret asked out of frustration as she only was able to get her rock to skip three times again.

"I might've fibbed a bit about not doing it in years... but I only meant I never did it with anyone else, besides my older sister's since we were quite competitive."

Beraham said as he threw his last rock, then looked back towards Margaret to see how many more stones she had left.

But instead Beraham saw that she had picked up a huge rock and chucked it into the river beside him. Making the water splash all over him, when it landed beside him. Beraham was soaked from head to toe with water, and could hear Margaret laughing at him.

"Oh no, my bad... I couldn't tell if that rock was flat enough for me to try and skip it... So it's bad that you got wet there, because of me."

Margaret said in a sarcastic and unapologetic voice.

Beraham stood silently staring at her, trying to figure out how he should retaliate. And the way he could was throwing Margaret into the river, or do the same thing and throw a giant stone when she was near the edge.

Instead Beraham slowly walked up to Margaret without saying a word, looked her in the eyes and said.

"You know since I'm feeling so miserable and wet, I could really go for a hug to warm up!"

He lunged forward and embraced Margaret with his wet clothes to exact his revenge.

"Oh you asshole! Can't you just have let this slide? I have gone the whole day without getting wet at work! Now I'm all damp because of your pettiness…"

Margaret shouted as she tried to sound angry but couldn't stop herself from smiling.

"Well you poked the bear, so you better be ready for the claws!"

Beraham said as he let go of Margaret, then heard the sound of a phone ringing. Margaret quickly checked her bag and pulled out her phone to see who it was.

"That's me… Give me a minute to answer this, Beraham."

Beraham nodded his head as he sat back down where he was eating his burger, so that he gave Margaret some space to take her call. As he sat there waiting for her, a thought crossed his mind as he turned his head to her.

'When was the last time I had this much fun with someone other than my roommates?'

This thought actually made Beraham realize that the last time he had this much fun was with his two older sisters.

"Sorry about that, it was just my boss asking if I could come in early tomorrow, but I said no of course. Not really much for waking up early for my shifts."

Margaret said as she put her phone back into her bag, to then sit back down beside him.

"Hey Margaret, I have a rather deep and serious question to ask. But I wanted to know if I can ask you this and if you're comfortable with it."

Beraham asked as he looked into Margaret's hazel colored eyes.

"I would say no after your wet bear hug, but since I am such a forgiving person, I'll hear you out."

Margaret replied with a sly smile across her face, that meant she would've listened either way.

"I've always had trouble expressing my emotions to people… especially when it comes to first impressions, because as you described me as a scary and somewhat distant person with a cold personality."

Beraham started to explain as he looked down at his own reflection in the water.

"I've grown up to be a person that wouldn't show his emotions on his sleeves, nor allow even those close to me to see how I am at my most vulnerable. And half the time I feel like I put a barrier or a wall between myself and those around me."

"So in your own opinion Margaret, do you think someone who is emotionally challenged like me... Could I ever learn to be emotionally stable? Like a normal person?"

Beraham asked as he locked eyes with Margaret, so that he could see if she was telling the truth or not. He was desperate to know what her answer would be.

"Honestly I think you can learn to be more open and show others your negative emotions, starting off with those close to you, Kinda like what you're doing with me right now."

Margaret answered as she lifted her hand to wipe off some water droplets from underneath Beraham's cheek.

"Just so that we both know, you're wiping away the water that splashed on my face and dripped from my hair."

Beraham said quietly as he cleared his throat, as he leaned back so that Margaret couldn't see his expression.

Margaret smiled warmly at Beraham with how cute he was being. They sat there in silence as they both listened to the different sounds of nature around them.

After a while of silence and listening, Margaret stood up from beside Beraham to grab her bag.

"This has been a rather interesting evening for me, Beraham. But I have to get going for dinner with my family. So I'll see you another time."

Margaret said while Beraham stood up as well to say goodbye to her.

"Understable, it might not feel like it, but a considerable amount of time has passed since you joined me."

Beraham said as he started to collect his garbage and his helmet. He wanted to head home since he felt a lot better and was feeling quite tired.

"Thank you for spending time with me and cheering me up, I'll also be heading home since I am feeling quite tired after today's events. But it was nice to be able to skip rocks with someone again."

Beraham said as he put out his hand to say goodbye to Margaret.

"Oh for crying out loud Beraham, bring it in you dumbass."

Margaret said as she pulled him into a hug. Beraham wasn't expecting this, so at first he stood still unsure of what to do, but accepted the hug by wrapping his own arms around Margaret who was just a head shorter then he was.

A moment passed and the two of them separated from each other and walked up the pathway that split off in different directions. They waved each other goodbye and set off in different directions to their homes.

Beraham made his way back to his parked motorcycle, he sat himself on the motorcycle and put on his helmet.

He couldn't help but notice that his chest felt warm, despite being damp from the river.

"So this is what it feels like to have friends?"

Beraham said to himself under his breath as he revved his motorcycle and sped off down the road.

While Beraham was mulling over how happy he was about getting to know Margaret as a friend.

Margaret had been waiting for Beraham to leave, before she doubled back to the Lambton Bridge. As she stopped near the back of the bridge, she waited for a few moments then let out a sigh of impatience.

"If you're that worried about Beraham seeing you, then you're fine since I could hear his motorcycle driving off. I really don't know what you did to him, but next time you're worried about your little brother... Check on him yourselves instead of asking someone on the street!"

Margaret shouted out loud as she tapped her foot impatiently on the ground.

At first all that Margaret got was silence except for the river. But then two young women appeared behind trees and shrubbery.

"Honestly you two were lucky that you asked someone that actually met your brother before, because I doubt he would talk about himself to anyone else."

Margaret said to the two young women, while sounding more irritated by what she heard from Beraham about his sisters.

"She does have a point Tara, how long are we going to hide from our little brother?"

Flora asked her twin sister, a worried expression formed on her face after watching the interaction between Beraham and Margaret.

"Nothing… there's nothing I want more than to rush over to him and give our little heart a hug…"

Tara said in frustration as she bawled her fist up and then released her grip as she recomposed herself.

"You know that we can't go against our father's wishes, not until our little heart finishes the contract he was given to by father."

Tara said as she tried to stay strong for her sister, but Flora was looking down at the ground. Margaret could tell that the two sisters hated that they couldn't console their own brother even though they were so close to him.

"You don't have to tell us everything you and our brother said… But could you at least tell us if you think he will be okay?"

Flora asked as she walked up to Margaret, grabbing her hands with a pleading look across her face.

Margaret shifted her gaze between the two sisters and could tell that they truly wanted to know how their younger brother was doing.

"Well Beraham said he was having a pretty shitty day, he seemed to be someone who is troubled by his own emotions and showing it to others."

Margaret started to explain the basics of her meet up with Beraham, with each negative word she said it seemed like a stab to the gut for his two older sisters.

"But as soon as we changed the topic to something else he changed the tune quite fast. We had some fun skipping rocks, talked some more, and by the time we both left he was a lot happier than when I first saw him."

Margaret said as she finished her explanation, while leaving out the parts where Beraham was being emotionally honest with her.

"Hmmm... well then I guess that will be good for now, let's go Flora, there's still work to be done."

Tara said as she walked past Margaret, with Flora following right behind her sister.

Before Margaret could leave for her house, she felt someone tap her shoulder quickly. She turned around to see that it was Flora that was tapping her shoulder.

"I wanted to thank you for being there for our little brother... It has been a really long time since we have seen our brother due to certain circumstances. I think when he sees me and Tara, he will just hate us for leaving him all those years ago."

Flora said as she looked quite sad with a tear falling from her face.

"I wouldn't be so sure about that, when we were talking together, Beraham missed you guys whenever he talked about you and your twin sister. And would talk about all the good memories he had with you both."

Margaret said as she decided to tell this to Flora, since she wanted Beraham to be able to see his sisters again. After saying this to Flora, Margaret turned around and walked off to finally head home.

She did turn back once to see if Flora was still there, but Beraham's sister disappeared from where she was before like the wind.

213

"Man, here I thought Beraham couldn't be any more mysterious and interesting... this just makes me more curious to learn more about him and his past."

Margaret whispered under her breath with a smile across her face, until her phone rang out and she looked down to see that her brother was calling.

"Shit! I am really late for dinner now... Damn me and my curiosity!"

CHAPTER 14

I Have More Questions then Answers to My Problem

Beraham slowly pulled his motorcycle into his driveway, after driving from the bridge. Due to his damp clothes and the wind from when he was driving home on his motorcycle. Beraham was freezing even though it was still a warm summer evening, he still felt quite cold.

"Achoo! Damn I might have caught a cold."

Beraham whispered to himself, as he slowly made his way up the steps to the front door to let himself into the warm house. As soon as Beraham opened and closed the front door, the sound of barking could be heard on the other side of the house. Bianca came scampering from the living room, to stop in front of Beraham whilst turning onto her back to get belly scratches from Beraham.

"Hey there little dog, aren't you just the thing I need to make me happy!"

Beraham whispered to the dog, as he picked her up and hold her close.

Beraham held Bianca close to him, as he walked up the stairs to take his damp clothes off and change into his pajamas. Beraham quickly made his way into his room, placed Bianca on his bed and changed out his damp clothes. As he took off his clothes, Beraham studied all the scars over his left side of his chest all around where his heart was and the rest of his back recalling how he got them. He brushed over the many scars and could feel the negative emotions and memories resurfacing from the back of his mind.

The sound of gun fire echoed in his ears, men screaming out in pain only to go silent moments later. And the sound of his father laughing at him was the strongest memory of negativity that haunted Beraham the most.

Only the sound of Bianca's barking and whimpering, brought Beraham back to his senses and hushed out the bad memories. Beraham kneeled down to the dog, to soothe her with some ear scratches and words of encouragement, before he continued to put the rest of his clothes on.

After he finished putting his pajamas on, Beraham layed down on his back to allow the little Teacup Yorkie onto his chest to receive affection.

After a while of laying on the bed and petting Bianca, Beraham could feel the fatigue hitting him. It finally was catching up to him at how long and emotionally draining today was for him.

Beraham with his remaining strength quickly moved Bianca to his right side above his arm, so that he wouldn't accidentally roll on top of the little dog. Bianca whined in protest at the sudden move, but Beraham was already closing his eyes.

And for once he didn't have a nightmare, nor a dream when he fell asleep. All he felt was a peace of mind and nothing else.

While Beraham was sound asleep at home. Across town in Heinkel's security office basement, Heinkel and Joseph were finishing up their interrogation of the two blackmailers.

"Sigh… whatever Beraham said to this guy really broke his mind. Nothing we are doing is making them give up who hired them… unless they were two idiots who thought they could make a quick buck from blackmailing Beraham."

Heinkel said as he cleaned his hands of the blackmailer's blood from his hands in the sink.

"No, if they were working alone then how would they find out about Beraham's sisters? Or that Beraham even kept paper copies of all his contracts at home and not in a bank for the extra security. And they had a photo of his sister's tied up in that room you guys found in the basement."

Joseph said to Heinkel to counter his thought.

"Well either they never met the person that hired them, or the person in question used them as pawns to get something out of Beraham."

Heinkel said as his phone rang from across the room, to indicate he had a text message.

"Could you grab that for me Joseph? I rather not grab my phone while I have someone else's blood on my hands."

Heinkel asked as he continued to scrub his hands to get the blood off. Joseph nodded and then headed over to check the message on Heinkel's phone.

Joseph turned over the phone and saw that there were two text messages, one from Beraham and one from Lee.

"So Beraham messaged you saying he is gonna eat dinner at his 'quiet place' then he'll go home once he's done, while Lee messaged you to ask if you could drive him and William home since they are quite drunk."

Joseph said as he read the text messages out loud so that Heinkel could hear it.

"Do you want me to answer the text messages for you?"

"Hell no! I am not gonna let you know what my password is to my phone! You would probably try and prank me or try to make me look like an idiot!"

Heinkel shouted as he searched around for a towel to dry his hands.

Joseph let out a soft chuckle, because he knew that's exactly what he would've done. And Joseph placed his friend's phone back down on the table, then another phone notification rang out. Joseph checked Heinkel's phone for more messages but saw that there weren't any new messages.

He quickly pulled out his own phone and saw that there was a message from his unknown phone number, he read the message and could feel his blood boiling over in anger.

"Hey Heinkel, I need to smooth things over with my job so I'll see you back at home."

Joseph said as he put his phone away, to make his way back to the elevator.

"Alright you do that, I'll hand these two blackmailers over to the police then pick up Lee and William from the pub they are at."

Heinkel shouted to Joseph, who made his way into the elevator and waited for it to take him to the parking lot. Once Joseph got to the parking lot he got out of the elevator and made his way through the parking lot.

Until he noticed that a couple men in suits were following behind him at a safe distance. Joseph stopped where he was, to address the four of them.

"Unless I am mistaken, but what are Heinkel's security men following me? Because if you are, I would love for you guys to pick up my dry cleaning since I'm already late."

The four bodyguards flinched at what Joseph said, but they still stood at attention as they waited for him to move.

Joseph sighed with disbelief and frustration as he didn't have time to try and lose these men. Must be that Heinkel wanted to make sure that Joseph was safe in his own weird way.

"Okay let's do this then, for the next hour or so you will stay in this parking lot and make sure everyone but me can make it to their cars safely."

Joseph said to them as he used his power quickly to rid himself of the security detail. Joseph made sure that the dazed bodyguards were positioned in front of the elevator so that they weren't in anyone's way. Once he felt like they weren't in harm's way, Joseph quickly left the parking lot and made his way to an open street so that he could flag down a taxi.

Joseph gave his driver the address that he needed to quickly get to, and said he would pay extra if he could get there within an hour or less. After driving for a while, they arrived in front of his house he owned with his friends.

Once paid for the cab fare, Joseph made sure to wipe the driver's memory of ever driving Joseph to his home as a precaution.

Making sure that the driver was far enough away down the street, Joseph quickly made his way into the house, without even taking the time to remove his shoes. He made his way up the stairs two at a time, rushing over to Beraham's room and getting ready to bash open the door to confront the person who messaged him.

Before Joseph could kick the door in, a man opened the door and it was the same man who sent him the text message while at Heinkel's office.

"Goodness Joseph for someone who always preaches about being a lover not a fighter… never in the years I've known you when you were a child did you ever raise your fist to someone."

The man said with a chuckle as he ignored Joseph's fist raised and the hatred that was written across his face, as he slowly entered Beraham's room.

"Why the fuck are you here? Especially when he could wake up at any moment when he is right there on the bed?"

Joseph asked the man as he gestured with his hand to where Beraham stayed asleep in his bed with Bianca resting beside his head. The man didn't immediately answer Joseph's question, instead he walked over to the bed to sit beside Beraham.

"Why on earth little Joseph would I need a reason to see my own son?"

Beraham's father asked as he brushed a hand across his son's face.

Joseph took a step forward to stop him from touching Beraham like that. But then Beraham's father pulled out a pistol to aim towards Joseph.

"Sadly I thought you might've brought Heinkel with you, so I had to bring such a disgusting weapon into this house just in case you tried to fight me."

Beraham's father said in frustration as he let out a sigh.

"I thought I told you that I wanted some alone time with my son, and to make sure the other two didn't show up. Instead you come barreling up the stairs like an elephant making so much noise that could wake my son up!"

"That is something I wish to know right now… Why are you seeing your son like this after so many years? You told him that unless he completes that almost impossible contract, only then will he be able to see his family again!"

Joseph asked as he stood still to not provoke him into shooting his gun.

Beraham's father looked at Joseph with a confused expression on his face, by the question he was asked.

"That was put in place for Beraham and his sisters to follow since they would try to meet and ruin what Beraham needed to experience first hand. And anyways, this is put in place for them, not me since I would need to check on his health every now and again."

Beraham's father explained as if he was simply explaining why the sky was blue to a child.

Joseph wished that he was better trained in close combat like Heinkel was. He would probably have been able to disarm and then turn the tables in this type of situation.

"You know it has been such a long time since I asked to keep me up to date on my son's well being… How about for old times sake, can you tell me how my son has been doing these days?"

Beraham's father asked as he turned his full attention to Joseph, with the gun pointed at him.

"Like I would ever do anything for you again! Only reason I told you what you wanted to hear was because I was young, naive, and worried for Beraham's safety!"

Joseph said angrily as he couldn't figure out how Beraham or the dog wasn't awakened by all that was going on.

Beraham's father looked angry for a moment, but then noticed how Joseph was just staring at his son.

"Ahhh you're probably wondering why my son isn't waking up and going on a rampage when he sees me? Well let's just say I am a man of science so I put some knock out gas through your vents so that neither he or the dog would wake up."

Beraham's father said with a grin as he tapped his son's face with his free hand. His expression stayed the same, showing neither affection or any other emotion across his face.

He still kept the gun trained on Joseph without even lowering it once.

"Now then... tell me how my little research subject is doing? And I am only gonna ask this once, so do the right thing little Joseph."

Beraham's father said with a cold attitude as he shifted the gun in his hand over the trigger.

"Well sir, Beraham did have to deal with a recent blackmailer who we thought had his older sisters, and wanted Beraham to destroy or hand over his contracts."

Joseph started to explain, as he felt awful about spilling what happened to Beraham, since Joseph knew that he wouldn't want anyone to know what happened today.

"So how did he react to that situation when they weren't there? Angry? Betrayed?"

Beraham's father asked as he sounded excited and intrigued to know his son's reaction to the situation.

"Yes he was quite angry to the point that he started to use his powers on everyone around him... Even Heinkel and I were affected by it and we don't even know exactly how they work."

Joseph answered as he shivered when he could feel the memory of what happened. Even though he only witnessed a fraction of what it was.

"Oh gods, if only I had been smarter with the setup. Maybe put up some cameras or at the very least hidden ones… Then I could've seen it for better research purposes."

Beraham's father said to himself, unaware that Joseph was slowly inching closer to him.

"Well, it's good to hear that my son isn't able to hide his powers all the time, plus this outburst of anger shows good results… It took years for me to get him this worked up, Did he kill anyone by chance during his outburst?"

Beraham's father muttered to himself as he lowered the gun to the ground, as he was lost in thought.

Joseph saw his opportunity to turn the tables on this situation. He lunged forward to grab the gun from Beraham's father, but as soon as he moved Joseph could sense someone was behind him.

The person behind Joseph grabbed his arm, twisting it behind him, then kicked the back of his leg to make Joseph stay on the ground and from moving.

"Sorry about that little Joseph, I forgot to introduce my personal bodyguard, I tend to lose focus when it involves my work or family. So I hired someone to always watch my back."

Beraham's father said with a chuckle as he snapped his fingers, for the bodyguard to let Joseph go. Joseph slowly stood back up to see an almost seven foot tall man towering over him to make sure he didn't try anything else.

"Well it's been fun catching up with you, but I have many things to do. Oh and keep my son from looking or finding his sisters… And remember little Joseph, no one can ever love my heartless like his family does… I made sure of that."

Beraham's father said with a cold attitude as he left the room with his very tall bodyguard right behind him.

Joseph slowly walked to the bedroom window to make sure that Beraham's father had left the house. Once he confirmed that he saw the two men leave the house and into their car, Joseph let out a deep sigh of relief when Beraham's father drove away.

"Fuck sake! That man really knows how to push my buttons… He still isn't using the name Beraham, still tries to use the name Beraham hates."

Joseph said as he went over to check on Beraham and the dog.

"Your father says that you can't be loved by anyone, that's probably why you love to make contracts with people… So that you can feel like you have a connection with them."

Joseph said as he slowly grabbed the little dog from on top of Beraham's head.

"But that man couldn't be any more wrong, because you have started to open up to us, your roommates. Even to that strange girl we met outside of William's workplace… You are slowly learning to rely on others and continue to open your heart to them."

Joseph whispered as he rearranged Beraham's blanket to cover his full body to keep warm. Once he made sure Beraham was nice and snug in bed, Joseph quietly exited out of his room.

As Joseph made his way to the stairs with Bianca, he could hear the front door open and muffled voices could be heard downstairs.

"Hey Joseph! Get your ass down here and help me with these two drunkards!"

Heinkel shouted from the front door as the sound of Lee and William could be heard singing a song. Joseph quickly placed the dog down on the ground and rushed quietly down the steps towards his three roommates to quiet them down.

"The three of you quiet down! Beraham came down with a cold I think, so he's resting right now. Can you guys just quiet down?"

Joseph explained as everyone nodded their heads to show they understood what was going on.

They all headed towards their own rooms that were either on the second or third floor.

"So we will see each other tomorrow morning for Heinkel's special morning breakfast, alright?"

Lee shouted with a smug grin across his face.

Everyone stayed silent for a moment as Joseph covered Lee's mouth from yelling. They all looked towards Beraham's room to listen if he woke up from all the noise. But from the lack of noises and the sound of light snoring, Beraham thankfully didn't wake up.

"What the fuck did I just tell you not to do?"

Joseph hissed angrily at Lee who just just shrugged his shoulders in response with a dumb grin across his face.

"Let's not argue or fight right now... Because half of us are drunk, or have had a long day at work. So let's all head to bed and sleep it off."

Heinkel suggested to the four of them as he sounded too drained from today, to be dealing with all these shenanigans that were going on.

"Okay... but this is really weird to see the two of you agreeing on, well anything."

Lee said as he started to lean against William for support.

"Here William, let me take care of this drunkard and take him to his room. That way you can clean up and go get some sleep."

Joseph offered as he went around to pull Lee onto his shoulder to let William go to bed.

"Thank you, he was starting to get a little too heavy for me to keep holding him up."

William said as he let go of Lee so that he could head to bed. The four of them each went their separate ways. William and Heinkel left for their rooms on the third floor, while Joseph, with a lot of effort on his end, was able to get Lee into his room and into the bed.

Lee let out a loud burp after he flopped onto the bed, as Joseph retreated away from to avoid the smell of the burp.

"Why did you have to yell out like that? You already should know what Beraham had gone through today... So it's better if we let him rest."

Joseph asked as Lee attempted to take his shirt off, but with little success.

"Well I wanted to talk with you in private, but then you would want to talk either downstairs or your room. So I thought why not act really drunk and obnoxious so that I can talk with you and stay in bed."

Lee explained to Joseph while wrapping himself in his blanket with his stupid grin across his face.

Joseph was speechless by the lengths that Lee would go so that he could be as lazy as could be.

"Now then, can you tell me who was here at our home? Because making Heinkel forget which turns to take to go home, is very tiring and hard to do while drunk."

Lee said as he waited in his wrapped up blanket for Joseph to answer his question.

"Did I not say the reason in the text message I sent you?"

Joseph asked as he could've sworn that he texted an easy excuse to Lee, so that he wouldn't grow suspicious of the reason.

"Can you stop Heinkel and William from arriving back home for as long as you could? Pleading emoji, winking emoji and love eye emoji…"

Lee read out loud the text message that Joseph sent him. They both cringed at the text message, as Lee put his phone on his bedside table.

"Shit… I ummmm had a woman over and I didn't want you guys catching me in the act of passion with them."

Joseph explained quickly as he tried to not sound nervous in front of Lee.

"Let's just cut the bullshit, because I am too tired and drunk to stay reasonable right now."

Lee said as he stood up on his bed to tower over Joseph with a serious expression across his face.

"It was Beraham's father who was here, I knew how much Heinkel hates him… so I wanted to avoid a dangerous conflict between the two of them."

Joseph said as he waited for Lee to yell or walk off to tell Heinkel about this. But instead he sat back down on the bed and silently stared at Joseph.

"I see… that makes sense, thanks for telling me and you won't have to worry about me blabbering this to Heinkel. But how did Beraham react to seeing his father?"

Lee said allowing Joseph to breath easy but could tell that Lee was more worried about Beraham's reaction.

'Beraham wasn't awake when he was here nor woke up the entire time during the visit because his father gassed our house to make sure Beraham wouldn't wake up."

Joseph informed Lee as he was slowly nodding off on the bed.

"This can be something we can deal with in the morning, when we're both not tired or one of us reeks of alcohol."

Joseph remarked as he turned to exit out of Lee's slightly messy room.

"Goodnight Joseph, see you tomorrow."

Lee said as he laid down in his bed to sleep off his hangover.

"Goodnight Lee… Let's hope this doesn't turn into something worse, we can't let the past happen again."

Joseph whispered as he went to his room to sleep.

CHAPTER 15

The Promise We Made
The Vow I Took

Ten Years ago
Toronto, Canada

Beraham remembered the day which was the start of many hardships to come in his future. It was a cold Fall evening and Beraham had just finished the assignment that his father gave him.

He was already quite used to his life of isolation to the outside world, being homeschooled by his father and many visits from tutors each week.

He didn't really care about studying, it was just a way to kill time for the day. Beraham felt most happy when either his friends came over to play, or when his sisters came back from their high school.

Sadly they had extratesticular activities or club meetings, so they would be home late tonight.

Beraham's room door opened to reveal his father, who was dressed up for an evening walk.

"Good, you've completed your assignments for today. Come with me for an evening walk, won't you?"

Beraham's father said as he walked through the ever growing maze of books that littered in Beraham's room. His father walked up to his son and handed young Beraham's jacket.

"What about Tara and Flora? They still are not back from school."

Young Beraham said nervously as he put his jacket on quickly as he ran after his father, who was heading towards the front door.

"They are both in their final years of high school, so I trust them to come home safely on their own."

Beraham's father answered as he slipped on his shoes and wrapped his scarf around his neck, before he turned to look at his son.

"Make sure you have everything before we leave, you never know what could happen."

Beraham nodded his head to let his father know he understood. Beraham quickly grabbed his wallet and gloves, plus his hat as well to show how prepared he was for any situation on this walk.

Beraham's father let out a chuckle at his son's actions, which was rare for him to laugh very often.

"Such a reliable and mature son I have raised into a proper man."

"Father I'm already twelve years old, where are we going anyways?"

Beraham asked as they left their neighborhood, in which Beraham was told never to leave this area without his sisters accompanying him.

"I wanted to show you something very important, and also do me a favor that is top secret."

Beraham's father said as he pulled his son close to him as they passed by a group of joggers.

The two of them continued to walk in silence while the sun was starting to set. Eventually they arrived in front of High Park gates that led to the giant park inside.

"Why did we come all the way to High Park? Is this where the really important favor is?"

Beraham asked as they wandered into the park without any specific direction.

"Don't worry about that right now, instead how about you tell me how it went with the doctor today?"

Beraham's father asked as he reflected his son's question, with one of his own. His expression changed from happy to dread when his father brought up the appointment with the doctor.

"It was fine… he took a couple blood samples from me then made me do some stress exercises, or psycho evaluations as he called them."

Beraham answered quietly as he rubbed his arms at the thought of the needles he had to go through today.

"Hmmm… I'll have to ask him for the results… Did he happen to do the 'Nirvana Test' with you?"

He asked his son as they found themselves in the middle of the pathway which led to the park's own cherry blossom trees. Though they were bare since they were out of season. Since they would usually bloom in March or April.

"Yeah, but even though he says each time the test was successful, I'm still having those nightmares."

Beraham explained that just talking about the nightmares made him feel tired and wince like there was an invisible pain in his chest.

They continued to follow the pathway, as the sound of the Gardiner Pond could be heard as they continued their walk.

"We will wait here for now, let's sit on the bench and rest for a bit."

Beraham's father said as he put his arm out to stop his son from walking. They went over and sat on the bench together looking out at the pound as it slowly got darker in the park.

"Father… are we waiting to meet someone here?"

Beraham asked his father who just remained silent as they sat on the bench, avoiding to answer his son's question.

"Do you remember that time when I let you play with your friends at that park three years ago?"

Beraham's father asked out of nowhere, to indicate that he wasn't gonna answer young Beraham's question about the favor.

"Yes, it was the first time I got to play with other kids my age at a park, and I also got to help someone out of a bad situation."

Beraham replied as he felt the happiness of those memories resurfacing of that day.

"Why did you help that child? You already had Heinkel, Lee, and Joseph to play with you... So why go through the trouble to help someone else?"

Beraham noticed that when his father asked this question, it sounded like he was slightly angry and annoyed with him.

"At first I just wanted to see what was happening to that boy, because at the time it looked like he was being bullied into going somewhere out of the adults supervision. But when we followed them, I saw that the boy was getting beaten up by the bullies so I told Lee and Joseph to go get the child's father."

Beraham explained while his father pulled out his phone and started typing a message on the phone. He stopped typing when he noticed his son staring at him, Beraham was waiting for him to finish his texting before he continued his story. He gestured with his free hand for Beraham to continue with his story.

"Afterwards when the issue was taken care of, I briefly spoke with the boy who was bullied. His name was William and he was quite thankful to us, and that he wished for us to be friends."

Beraham finished explaining as he hoped that with this story, his father would allow him to hangout with William after.

"Such an interesting variable that we have run into... I guess the time has come for me to go into the next phase."

Beraham's father muttered to himself as he finished typing on his phone and sending the message.

He turned to his son and produced a hundred dollar bill, which he handed over to Beraham.

"If you only had a hundred dollars to your name, how would you spend it son?"

Beraham's father asked as he studied his son to see how he would answer. But Young Beraham was in awe at seeing such an expensive bill being given to him.

"I think I would go and buy a cake for all of us to eat together, save the rest for more snacks and buy a new book to read."

Beraham answered as he continued to examine the bill with curiosity.

"Not bad of an answer my son, but forget about the books and cake, you would need every single dollar for either shelter, food or other supplies. You need to make sure you have the basic supplies while you go and try to find a job for yourself and have a stable income."

Beraham's father explained to his son as the sound of his phone rang out again.

"One second son, I need to take this call real quick. Just stay here and keep your phone on just in case."

Beraham's father said as he got up from the bench and walked away from Beraham to answer his phone call. Young Beraham sat in silence as he patiently waited for his father to finish his phone call.

He studied the bill even though it was getting even darker and harder to see what was in front of him. After about ten minutes Beraham took out his phone to check the time, While also wondering what was taking his father so long. Just then Beraham's phone rang out and it showed that it was his father calling him.

"Father? Where are you? Did you get lost in the dark or the pathway on your way back?"

Beraham asked nervously as he tried to stay calm and collected while he was alone in this large park.

"I have already left High Park, you will have to make your own way home. Good Luck my son."

Beraham's father said over the phone and then hung up the phone without another word.

Beraham stood absolutely still, petrified as he realized that his father was serious about leaving him alone in this huge and dark park. He quickly tried to call his sisters to ask them for help, but neither of them answered his call.

"Why aren't they answering? It's way past when they would've finished with their school activities… They wouldn't ignore me like our father had."

Beraham whispered to himself as he heard the sound of a branch break behind him. Beraham broke into a sprint as soon as he heard the sound, he ran down the pathway he took with his father but was having trouble remembering the exact path back to the gate.

It was a lot harder to retrace his steps, since there weren't a lot of street lamps around the whole park, so Beraham kept second guessing himself on which way to go.

Young Beraham could feel the fear in his chest, something he thought he had gotten over the feeling of being alone or in isolation all on his own again.

When his emotions were starting to overwhelm him, Beraham practiced the breathing exercises that his father taught him. He took a deep breath in and pretended to force those emotions into a box that would stay hidden for another time.

"This is getting me nowhere, when I'm feeling like this… First things first, use your map app on your phone to figure out where you are, and how to get out of here."

Young Beraham calmly said to himself as he pulled out his phone and opened the map app to figure out how to get out of High Park. Beraham followed the directions on his phone. After ten minutes of walking around carefully around the park, Beraham found the large gates of High Park's main entrance.

As Beraham passed through the large gates, he let out a sigh of relief that he was able to get out of the dark park on his own.

"Beraham!"

A voice called out to him, Beraham turned to see Joseph running towards him while breathing heavily.

"Your… Father… called us to say that you were lost in the park. So we came here as soon as possible to find you."

Joseph explained while panting as he tried to catch his breath.

"But from the looks of it, you were able to get out of the park all on your own, so why did you run from your father? Did you guys get into another argument?"

Joseph asked as he texted Lee and Heinkel that he found Beraham.

But Beraham was confused by Joseph's question, since it seems like his father told his friends that he had run away from home.

"So my father said that I had run away from home? And that you guys could probably find me at High Park?"

Beraham asked as he tried to call his sister's again, but it still went to voicemail from both of them.

"Yeah about twenty minutes ago he called me to help him search for you with Lee and Heinkel's help."

Joseph explained as he waved to Heinkel and Lee who were about a block away from them, inside of the park with flashlights out.

"Beraham are you okay?!? You didn't get hurt anywhere did you?"

Heinkel asked as he quickly checked over Beraham from head to toe to make sure he wasn't injured.

"I'm fine Heinkel, don't worry about me for now. Though I am surprised to see Lee here and not in bed."

Beraham said as he brushed Heinkel's hands off of him since he needed to go home and talk with his father.

"I gotta go guys, I need to go quickly since I can't contact my sister's nor is my father picking up their phones, so they are probably worried sick."

Beraham said as he started to head off down the street, and noticed that his three friends were following after him.

Heinkel walked up beside Beraham to speak to his friend.

"We want to make sure that you get home safely, and make sure you don't get lost on your way back again."

"Thank you, all of you for coming to find me. I don't know what I would've done without all of you guys."

Beraham said to his friends as the four of them continued to make their way back to Beraham's home.

On the way back, the four boys were just talking amongst themselves, making jokes and fooling around. The more they talked the less stressed out and anxious Beraham felt, about his father leaving him alone at the park and none of his family answering his phone.

"Hey did you get to tell your father that you'll be changing your name?"

Heinkel asked young Beraham as Lee and Joseph moved closer to them so that they could listen to the conversation.

"No not yet, I haven't had a chance to tell him… but I think he already knows that I will, since he only addresses me as his son."

Beraham answered as he made a mental note to talk to his father about that since he already put in the paperwork with his sister's help.

"Hey do you guys smell that in the air?"

Lee asked as they were close to where Beraham's house was located. Every one of them noticed the smell of smoke, and then noticed the black clouds erupting into the air a street away from them.

"Oh no, Flora! Tara! Father!"

Beraham cried out as he bursted into a sprint down the street, his friends calling after him to wait for them.

But the young boy didn't hear them, nor decided to listen to them, for he was focused on what was ahead of him. He rounded the corner and Beraham saw that multiple houses were on fire, and at the end of the street in the heart of it all was his own home. There were many firefighters rushing back and forth fighting the many fires around them.

First responders were also all over the place, guiding residents of the houses to a safe area, to help the injured or to keep a head count of all the residences.

Beraham ran up to the area that all the residents were staying at, to look around to see where his family was. Unfortunately he didn't see them anywhere in the crowd.

Beraham was about to run his way through everyone towards the house, but stopped when he heard his phone ring in his pocket.

Beraham took out his phone with both hands as they were trembling after everything that was going on. He looked at who was calling him, and was surprised to see that it was his father.

Beraham quickly answered the call, hoping that his father and sisters were safe.

That and to find out what was going on with his father leaving him alone in High Park.

"Father? Where are you? I'm in front of our house and it's on fire with all the rest of the houses in our street! And is Flora and Tara with you?"

Beraham asked quickly with his questions as his friends caught up to him, and were equally shocked by all the fires that blazed around the street.

"My son, it's time for you to begin the favor that I wanted you to do, I did mention there would be requirements for you to be allowed to do it."

Beraham's father said over the phone without even asking if his own son was okay.

"Wait... what do you mean by that father? Where are you and my sisters?"

Beraham asked as he couldn't make sense of what his father was telling him.

"You seem very protective of this William, that you wish to protect him. So I order you to protect your friend from all physical threats and from those within his mind, but you must do this in the shadows. Never reveal yourself to him."

Beraham's father started to explain making sure that his son couldn't interrupt him, so he continued to speak to Beraham.

"You will stay stone cold and emotionless during this contract, never show any weakness to anyone, you will not form any type of relationships. No lovers, no friends or anything of the sort!"

"You will guard William for ten years, which also includes any penalties that might be added throughout this contract to your time of guarding. You will not have any access to any of my money nor any that was listed under your name, and Finally you will not be allowed to see your sisters until you've finished the contract."

Beraham's father finished explaining this favor that turned into a contract, over to his son over the phone.

"But Father, how am I supposed to do that? Our house is burning as we speak! And I only have my wallet and the small amount of money that's in there."

Beraham asked frantically as he felt sick to his stomach, as he realized now why his father gave him the hundred dollar bill.

"So you finally realized why I gave you the bill, then have you realized as well why I took you to High Park? Don't worry those three friends of yours can help you back onto your feet."

Beraham's father said as the sound of female voices could be heard in the background of the phone call.

"Is that Flora and Tara? Can't I at least talk with them to know if they are safe?"

Beraham asked quickly as he wanted to hear his older sister's voices. To confirm that they were okay with never seeing him again, for the next ten years, or to help him get out of this contract.

"Sadly your contract started the moment I left you in High Park, and the girls have agreed to not see you until you've completed the contract."

Beraham's father said as he talked to someone near him on the other end of the call. There was talking and arguing going on in the background, but his father turned his attention back to his call with his son.

"You now know what needs to be done my son. If you don't finish this contract I've given you, then you'll never see us again and be alone for the rest of your life without your family… good luck my son, and make me proud."

And with that final remark, Beraham's father hung up the phone, without even giving his son a chance to talk.

Minutes passed as Beraham silently looked at his phone, then at his house burning away all his memories. The people and noises around him, couldn't be heard as he was too focused on digesting what had happened to him.

He could feel his heart beating slower and slower as he couldn't understand what was going on.

First responders tried to approach Beraham to ask him questions, but were turned away, or his friends would have intercepted them from speaking to Beraham.

"Hey, is your family alright, Beraham?"

Lee asked while Heinkel and Joseph were continuing to talk with the police and paramedics.

"I– I can't see my two sisters for the next ten years… my father says that they agreed to not see me or talk with me until I finish…"

Beraham tried to whisper to Lee as he clenched his chest, he could hear everyone else's heartbeats around him and all he wanted to do was silence them all. He could hear everyone's heart beats starting to rapidly beating and some starting to beat slower, Beraham held back the tears he could feel welling up inside of him.

But then Beraham felt Lee pulling Beraham into his arms, to give him a hug to comfort him.

Beraham also felt Heinkel and Joseph joining in on the hug, making it into a group hug. Beraham knew that they were surrounding him, so that no one could see him. A moment passed and young Beraham silently cried as he couldn't keep his brave face on any longer.

As the tears flowed down his face, he couldn't help but feel his own head and clothes becoming damp from his friends crying as well.

The sound of everyone's heartbeat was slowly fading away inside his head and all he could hear was his friends' heartbeats around him.

Beraham made a vow to himself, he would do whatever it takes to complete his father's contract. And once he did, he would force his father to tell him the reason why he would put his son through these hardmenship and tragedies.

But to also reunite with his sisters who were the only people he knew that truly loved him.

As the four of them stood huddled together, the sound of rain started to pour down on everyone. The sound of cheers could be heard from everyone around them that the rain would help with dowsing out the remaining flames.

But for young Beraham all he could think was his next move to protect William with all his heart.

THE END

Epilogue

Toronto, Ontario
Downtown

"Come on Flora! We were gone for too long, so father's security team will be suspicious that it took us this long to eat at a restaurant!"

Tara whispered to her twin sister, as they got out of the elevator to their hotel.

"Don't worry about it, the restaurant we booked to eat at is known for taking a long time to get their food and I already talked with the owner to lie about us being there just in case."

Flora said with confidence as they rounded the corner to greet their bodyguards, but were surprised to see that their father was standing outside their hotel room.

"Shit."

Both sisters whispered in unison as their father's head bodyguard noticed the two sisters only now arriving from their supposed dinner.

The head bodyguard leaned down to their father and whispered into his ear. Flora and Tara quickly rushed over to greet their father.

"Father, you're back early from work. Did the business meeting for your research finish earlier than what you expected?"

Tara asked as she greeted her father with a hug, then let her sister greet their father the same way.

"Oh that was merely a formal introduction to my benefactores who have invested into my research. I would've actually been here a lot sooner, but I had to make a quick visit to a key part of my research."

He replied as their father had a suspicious look across his face, as he looked between his two daughters.

"Shall we continue our conversation inside your room? My knees are starting to act up from all the standing I've been doing today."

He suggested as he waved his hand, to indicate to the bodyguards to open the door for him and let them through.

As they all made their way into Flora and Tara's room, the twin sisters looked at each other with the same thought going through their heads.

'Father doesn't have any knee problems.'

Once they all were in the room only Father's head bodyguard stayed inside as he positioned himself in front of the door. Tower over everyone else with is hands remaining by his sides with a blank expression across his face.

"Now that we don't have any unwanted listeners... let's talk about your encounter with your little brother shall we?"

Their father said in a calm and yet slightly irritated and angry tone towards his daughters.

The two sisters stood frozen, like deers caught in a car's headlights. They knew that there wasn't a way for them to lie their way out this.

"Don't worry girls, I am not that angry with either of you. As long as you didn't talk with him nor let him see either of you, then all is well right?"

Their father said as he gestured for his head bodyguard to come forward. The man brought a briefcase that he was holding for his boss, handed it over to him, and then walked back to his original position in front of the door.

"After your so-called little experiment that you asked us to be a part of at that house, of course we would want to check on how he was doing."

Flora said as she stepped forward with an angry and pissed off look across her face. And it was fully directed towards their father.

"And as you said before, we didn't break any of the rules of the contract, so there is nothing left to discuss, father!"

Tara said as she went to open the door to let their father leave their room. But the bodyguard stopped her at the door and motioned to her to head back to their father.

"Just because I say that I'm not angry doesn't mean I'll tolerate how close the two of you were to your brother seeing either of you!"

He said as he kept a calm expression across his face.

But his daughters knew after being raised by him, that even though he looked calm and nice right now. Behind that face was a pissed off man who didn't like that someone almost messed up his research.

"Father, we have always followed whatever you've asked of us. Even making us do horrible things that affect our little brother, or invertably hurting him with all your different tests."

Tara started to say as she glanced behind her, to keep an eye on the bodyguard.

"My daughters, keep in mind the research that I've done with your brother for almost his entire life. With this research it will be life changing. I am almost done with my research, so be patient my daughters, and know this will be over soon."

Their father said with a big grin across his face, as he opened the briefcase to reveal many folders with names on them and hundreds of different papers.

Both sister's let out a gasp as they recognized what those files were and knew where their father procured this from.

He looked up from the briefcase to notice his daughter's expressions, for some reason he looked excited and smug.

"From the look on both of your faces, you know where I got this from? Sadly he was smart enough to keep his friend's contract and his own someplace else from his collection."

Their father said as he grabbed a random file and flipped through the contents inside.

Tara was the first to recover from the initial shock, and spoke up immediately with an annoyed tone.

"You visited Beraham? You who have always told us over and over again never to interfere nor make contact with him, but you up and steal his contracts he has made over the past ten years?"

"Tara my dear, unlike you and your sister I made absolutely sure that my son wouldn't even know I was there… and what have I told you about using that fake name that your brother came up with?"

Their father yelled with anger as just hearing Beraham's name was making him pissed off and made him lose his composure.

"That boy really thinks that he can hide from the birth name I gave him? And instead come up with all these different names he gives to himself."

He muttered under his breath as he let a fraction of his true colors out in front of his two daughters.

The twins exchanged a look between each other. They both knew that one of the few things that angered him the most, was when Beraham changed his birth name to the one he has currently. Or when Beraham didn't react the way he was supposed to react by his father's calculations.

"But what are you gonna do with all his contract Father? Because he will notice them missing sooner or later."

Flora asked as she was nervous, how Beraham would react to his years of work suddenly disappearing from his home.

"You won't have to worry about that young miss, we switched the briefcase with another one, and put some of the contracts into the fake one so that if he does check it will seem like they are all there. There will be no issue for your father to simply borrow them and get all of them copied and put back in place."

The head bodyguard spoke up, for the first time since entering Tara and Flora's room.

"But that's not the point I'm trying to make here, the end of my research is on the horizon. With these contracts as a part of my research study and proof we can move on to the final testing for the test subject."

Their father said as he closed the briefcase and stood up from the armchair to exit from his daughter's hotel room.

"Here are the notes of what the final test that your brother will undergo... Be ready my two daughters, because I won't be going easy on him from now on."

Their father said as he handed over a file to Tara, then headed out of the room with his bodyguard.

After they both left, Tara walked over to the bed to sit down to read the file.

"He really hasn't changed his view of Beraham, he still treats him like a test subject for his research, instead of his own son!"

Flora complained as she sat beside her sister as she tried to look at the notes their father left them.

"Flora... Our brother is in serious trouble with what our father has planned for him,"

Tara said as her face went pale and her hands started to shake as she handed the papers to Flora as her eyes started to fill with tears.

Flora looked down at the file's, the first thing she noticed was the names that were lined in red.

"Tara, we need to break out of our father's contract, or else Beraham will be forced to do something unforgivable to his friends."

Flora whispered as she felt sick to her stomach. She continued to read through multiple documents that described the different tests and scenarios that could happen during this experiment or Beraham's decisions.

"But what about the consequences that our father put for us, in case we broke the contract?"

Tara asked, but already knew what her sister was thinking before she even needed to say it.

"We have been silently following what our father has told us to do for so many years... afraid that Beraham would be punished if we didn't comply with what was planned for him. But if we don't do anything soon, Beraham will live up to father's original expectations for him."

Flora said as she grabbed her twin sister's hand to comfort her.

"For now let's follow along and interfere with this experiment wherever we can, and if worse comes to worse... we meet with Beraham and hide from our father."

Flora said as she got up from the bed and started to put together a go bag just in case.

Meanwhile Tara was still staring at the folder, as she remembered the final words she said to her younger brother ten years ago...

"Remember little brother, even though you think you're always alone. You won't be without your two big sisters here to fill in that lonely heart of yours."

A younger Tara said to her little brother before she headed off to school with Flora and leaving Beraham for the last time in a long time.

Now that she thought about it, what her father had planned for Beraham would do the opposite of what she promised to him all that time ago.

But for now, Tara pushed those thoughts to the back of her mind. As she got up from the bed to help her sister with creating a go bag in case things go south in the future.

Meanwhile down the hall of his daughter's hotel room. Beraham's father sat down in his room's armchair and let out a loud sigh of annoyance.

"Those two may not understand why I am doing all this to my son... And yet they still try to check on him despite my orders not to..."

He complained to his head bodyguard, while the very tall security guard walked over with a glass of whisky in his hand.

"Please do not worry yourself about your daughters sir, that is what you hired me and my agency for."

The security guard replied as he handed his boss the cup of whisky.

"You're right... After so many years of studying my son's actions, I can finally achieve my research final goal. And then sell it to the biggest companies or to the whole world!"

Beraham's father said with glee as he was excited for what was to come.

"May I ask why you named this experiment after your son, sir?"

The head bodyguard asked as he read through the security briefing that Beraham's father provided to him, which was slightly different then the researchers directives.

"Because this will make that son of mine finally realize that he can't escape his name sake that I gave him. I gave him that name after he was born and soon realized that it made sense for him."

Beraham's father said as he swirled his whisky around before he took a sip.

"Well then sir, I shall go now to get some of these preparations in order. Goodnight sir, I will see you tomorrow."

The head bodyguard said as he exited the room, leaving his client to drink his whisky.

Once his bodyguard left him alone, Beraham's father got up from his chair and walked to his dresser. He rummaged through his dresser until he pulled out a photograph of his wife and daughters.

"Soon my love, the person who took you away from us will pay and my research will provide our daughter's the life you wanted for them."

The father said as he kissed the photograph, then stored it into his jacket pocket that was located over his heart.

"Beraham, Herzlos, Besserdechnyy, Gan Chori... all these names and yet they all mean the same as his birth name... Just wait a little longer son. For the personal hell I created for you will be over soon."

Beraham's father whispered as he looked at his master file he made only for him to see. And had a grin across his face.

The experiment in question was one that would either break Beraham emotionally and make him lose all his friends. Or make him go through even worse trauma to complete his research.

THE END

Printed in the United States
by Baker & Taylor Publisher Services